Shenanigans

Heather Norman Smith

Every Season Books

.

Published by Every Season Books.

Dedication

To my mama, *Nana* to my children.
I love you.

Therefore the redeemed of the LORD shall return, and come with singing unto Zion; and everlasting joy shall be upon their head: they shall obtain gladness and joy; and sorrow and mourning shall flee away.

Isaiah 51:11 (KJV)

Chapter One

Friday afternoon, October 12

Lavinia Lewis's oversized leather bag was a hodgepodge of geriatric necessities and schoolboy gags. Next to the Rolaids was a box of snap pop fireworks. Underneath the black eye kaleidoscope was the medical alert necklace she refused to wear, much to the dismay of her daughter. But Amy Lynn worried too much.

The bag sat in the passenger side floorboard of her Buick, cradled between the sneakered feet of her grandson, Dylan, whom she gave full reign of the radio on the way to the dentist's office. The nine-year-old pushed a different preset button every minute, bouncing from Talk to Oldies to Gospel to Reggae. She stopped him only once, to listen to the end of a Ray Stevens song. Dylan giggled as she belted out the chorus with the passion of a debuting artist at Carnegie Hall. That was the only way to do things—all in, or not at all.

Lavinia sang about a crazed squirrel in a Mississippi church and waved one hand about wildly like a conductor. She stopped as a faint ice cream truck melody came from the depths of her bag, the vibration of it dulled by the cushion of the rubber chicken. She turned the radio down with her conducting hand and leaned far to the right to dig out the phone, searching blindly. But as the car hit the shoulder, the bump and rumble of gravel under tires served as a reminder—Bluetooth could answer instead. Wonder of wonders, this modern technology. She righted the wheel and studied it, searching for the button. Another ring later, she'd found it.

"Hey, baby," Lavinia said. The glowing blue numbers on the dash display told her it was Amy Lynn, but she already knew.

"Hey, mom!" Dylan said.

"Mama, are you letting him ride up front?" Amy Lynn's voice was fierce through the car speakers.

"Did you call *just* to ask me that?" Lavinia said.

"Of course not. He just sounds really close to the microphone."

Lavinia glanced around the car. Was the microphone somewhere in the dash or in the door like the radio speakers?

"*Is he* in the front seat, Mama?"

Grandmother and grandson shared a mischievous glance. "No, dear. I know you prefer for him to ride in the back." She hoped her tell—a slightly higher pitched voice—was covered up by road noise and the air conditioner at full blast.

"Okay, well…thank you for picking him up from school for his appointment." Amy Lynn's tone was softer. "I thought I would be able to meet you at the dentist, but now I've got a parent conference and the principal wants me to meet with the new student teacher for second grade. Do you mind taking him home? Lucas is there, and I should be home by four thirty."

"Of course, I don't mind!" Lavinia said in her normal, non-lying timbre. She held onto the privilege of driving like a winning lottery ticket.

Amy Lynn acknowledged her son, saying goodbye to both of them quickly, and the car beeped to signal the call had disconnected.

A gnawing sensation then worked its way from the middle of Lavinia's throat down to the top of her stomach. It sat there and churned until she coughed it up as an admonition to Dylan.

"Baby, promise me you won't ever lie to your mother like I just did."

Remorse always made Lavinia's southern drawl sugary like cotton candy. She dropped the last half of the ending r's and made the long i's say their name twice.

Dylan pointed his face toward the ceiling then brought his chin to his chest with two big nods.

"I'm afraid I'm not a very good influence," Lavinia said.

"You're cooler than Mama, though."

Lavinia's heart swelled. She tried the compliment on proudly, but it wouldn't be right to keep it.

"Why do you say that, baby?" she said.

"'Cause she says I'm not big enough to ride up front. But I'm taller than Jackson in my class, and he always rides in the front seat. He made sure to tell me so." He rolled his eyes, chestnut brown and nearly covered by a swoop of wavy brown hair with the kind of sun streaks women pay good money for.

"*Not big enough?* Why, you're practically grown!" Lavinia gave an indignant, lip-rippling horse snort. "But your Mama is pretty cool, too, baby doll. She just worries about you. Because she loves you. She's a mama. That's what mamas do." She reached over and patted Dylan on the knee, and the car veered again, this time only slightly.

"I know." He paused. "And she worries about you, too, Nana." He fiddled with the straps of Lavinia's bag in her peripheral. "I hear her and Dad talk about stuff. They don't think I can hear 'em, but I do."

"About me?" she said, feigning surprise. "Why would she possibly worry about me?"

Lavinia steered the car onto a side street, a little too fast, and Dylan fell into the car door.

"She says you're gonna get yourself in trouble playing

pranks on people," he said as he righted himself. "She says you've made some people mad."

It was a rhetorical question.

Lavinia let out a quiet huff. She caught a glimpse of her annoyed expression in the rearview mirror and forced herself to get rid of it, replacing it with a smile. A smile was a woman's most important accessory, after all, though the chunky strand of pearls that only left her neck at bedtime was a very close second.

"Oh, it's just harmless gags," she said. "I like to have fun. They don't hurt anybody, and I make plenty of old people laugh. It's good for them. For all of us."

Lavinia balked at the idea of getting into trouble. She wasn't a child, for Pete's sake. Sure, the director of Cypress Shores had threatened to kick her out if she didn't quit playing pranks. But he hadn't meant it like that. Marvin was talking about the big stuff. Like when she threw all those Tootsie Rolls in the swimming pool and when she switched the signs on the doors of the men's and women's restrooms. And when she toilet papered his office.

A grin crept across her face at the memories. But she kept it much simpler now.

They're all innocent, little jokes. Who gets mad about a little joke?

"You can tell your mama not to worry about me, baby," Lavinia said. "And never you mind about it either."

"Okay, Nana. I'll tell her...but it won't do any good. You know how she is." Dylan shrugged his shoulders.

Lavinia did know. She thought often about Amy Lynn's tendency to worry, and she tried to analyze its source. It had to go as far back as when Amy Lynn lost her real daddy, Lavinia's son. That's when Lavinia and Edgar had gone from being her grandparents to being her parents. Amy Lynn was only three, but losing her twenty-two-year-old-father had left a mark. It stamped her with a seal of insecurity she still bore thirty-three years later.

Lavinia thought more about her precious Samuel—how up until the accident he was so determined to take care of Amy Lynn, even working two jobs while taking classes at the community college. Lavinia and Edgar could have paid for everything Amy Lynn needed, and much of what she wanted, but Samuel was hard-headed and hard-working, just like his daddy. He had insisted she was his responsibility.

Lavinia shook off the memory of her handsome, gone-too-soon son and put the car in park. She held Dylan's hand to cross the busy parking lot. She'd been careless enough already with the fib she told Amy Lynn.

"I don't think this summer's ever gonna let go!" Lavinia said. The knowledge that a North Carolina summer could last until Thanksgiving wouldn't stop her from complaining. "Middle of October and still pushing eighty." *Pushing eighty. Just like me.*

Cool air welcomed them as they entered the glass double doors of the office building, and Lavinia let out a sigh of relief. Dylan led the way toward his dentist. As they passed a large, gilded-framed mirror in the hallway, Lavinia stopped briefly to inspect the humidity's effect on her foundation. She raised her glasses and patted at the perspiration that had accumulated beneath them with the tip of her pointer finger, then took a moment to fluff her short, wavy hair. The hair was housecat gray with champagne undertones and just the slightest hint of lavender; and she liked it the same way she liked her Ray Stevens music—with some volume. Sufficiently fluffed, she adjusted the pearls so that the clasp was perfectly centered at the back of her neck.

Lavinia gave herself a satisfied wink. For a woman of seventy-nine and three quarters, she looked pretty good. She dared to think, attractive. Not in an unnatural way, like some of the artificially plumped up, pulled back, and sucked in women at

Cypress Shores whose decades-old midlife crises procedures were pushing their expiration dates. Lavinia looked every day her age, but she wouldn't have it any other way.

Inside the office, Lavinia and Dylan checked in at the desk. The fifty-something receptionist peeked out from a sliding, frosted glass partition. She confirmed Dylan's information in the computer and slid the partition shut quickly, dispensing with the formality of pretending she liked her job.

Before they could sit, a pretty, young hygienist came out smiling and called, "Dylan Davenport."

Dylan gave Lavinia a mischievous playboy wink. "Nana, you can stay here. I think I'm fine to go by myself."

She smiled and rolled her eyes then held her hand near her face and gave a wiggly-fingered wave goodbye. "I know, I know. You're practically grown."

Lavinia hoisted her bag into her lap and dug out the smartphone. She passed the first few minutes of the wait by playing her word game—a favorite pastime. When the phone sounded a loud, triumphant chime for a high-scoring word, everyone in the crowded waiting room looked at her, sending her long fingers fumbling to find the silent switch.

After Lavinia beat her opponent—whom she'd learned weeks ago through chatting was a Swedish shoe salesman named Wilmer— she sent him a message congratulating him on a good game then put the phone back into her bag. From the table beside her, she picked up an issue of *Southern Living* with Reese Witherspoon on the cover then put it back when she recognized Reese's pretty blue dress. She'd already read that one.

A Bible underneath the stack of magazines caught her eye. It was a lighter shade of blue than Reese's dress, and for lack of anything interesting to read, Lavinia picked it up. She ran her fingers across the Gideon's International symbol on the cover—a double-handled pitcher with a flame coming from the top. When she opened the book, its thin pages picked sides, some falling to the left and some to the right, so that she found herself in the book of Proverbs and immediately drawn to a single verse.

A merry heart does good, like medicine,
But a broken spirit dries the bones.[1].

She read it again, then again, unable to move on. Hunched over and squinting at the small print, she rubbed the translucent paper between pointer finger and thumb. Lavinia gave a half-hearted look upward. "I'm trying," she said under her breath. "I'm trying."

She set the Bible on top of the magazines, took the phone back out of her bag, and started a new game with Wilmer. Her first word happened to be *floss*, though she hated to use two *s's* right off the bat instead of saving them for an easy plural.

When Dylan came back with a shinier smile, he was still googly-eyed from his time with the hygienist. He talked a mile a minute about how nice she was and that she smelled so good, like bubblegum. Lavinia told lover boy that it was only the flavored mouthwash he smelled.

Dylan finally dropped the subject when they got to the car, but only because Nana jumped into the driver seat and distracted him by slipping a whoopie cushion under his bottom just before he sat down. The crude noise rang through the car, evoking a hardy laugh, as body noises always did, and he forgot all about Haley the Hygienist.

"I can't believe you got me again, Nana!" He held his stomach and doubled over.

Lavinia threw her head back and laughed with him. Laughter—the kind that tightened stomach muscles until they ached and left the lungs momentarily devoid of air—was a treasure. Each

---

[1] Proverbs 17:22 (NKJV)

episode, each exuberant fit of hilarity, pushed the needle of her vitality meter forward. It was a moment of triumph, as audible joy prevailed over the temptation to cry or complain over any number of situations about which one could be unhappy.

"Hey, Nana, guess what." Dylan recovered from his laughter.

"What, baby?"

"I've got a special word for your jokes, you know."

"Oh, yeah? What is it?"

"I call them shenanigans. Get it? She-*nana*-gans? 'Cause you're my nana, and you play pranks on people!"

"Well, aren't you clever?" Lavinia said proudly. She turned to him as she cranked the car. "Anybody who knows big words like that must be grown up enough to ride in the front seat."

***

Lavinia didn't take Dylan straight home. Instead, they took a detour through downtown Southport, onto Bay Street, and stopped the car at Waterfront Park where she let him throw crushed up crackers out the window to watch seagulls swarm the car. His mother wouldn't let him feed the birds from her car, due to the inherent risk of bird droppings on the hood.

No matter how many visitors were at the park doing the same thing, the birds always acted as if they hadn't eaten in days and were willing to fight to the death over a tiny piece of ToastChee. He'd seen it a hundred times, but it never seemed to get old.

"Hey, look at that!" Dylan pointed to a bird on the hood of the Buick with orange cracker in his beak. "The little one got the biggest piece!"

Lavinia commented on the spunky gull then looked out over the rippling water. A few sailboats and two fishing boats dotted the wide expanse. A big barge appeared motionless, silhouetted against the horizon. The scene was like the painting that had hung in her master bathroom, in the house where Amy Lynn grew up—the picture she had studied every day while imagining what it would be like to live there. Gratitude swelled within Lavinia's heart. She and Edgar *did* get to share their retirement dream, for at least a little while.

The Home of Salubrious Breezes lived up to its name. Lavinia was in the best health she'd been in for years, invigorated by the salt air and soothed by a peacefulness that seemed to hang over the city like a fluffy shade cloud. The two-hundred-twenty-five-year-old port town was alive with art and history and attractions, yet, as she saw it, maintained a downhome charm simply unmatched in all of Brunswick County. It had captured her heart before she knew it and become *home* in no time.

Part of what made Southport home was family. Amy Lynn had moved there years before her parents, when her new husband was offered a job with the police department. Lavinia and Edgar had planned to join them as soon as Edgar retired from his career as a bank executive in Wilson, two and a half hours away. But, as they told their daughter so often, things don't always work out as planned. Edgar and Lavinia had just sold their house when the stroke happened; then Lavinia spent six months in rehab relearning how to be Lavinia while Edgar stayed in an apartment near the hospital.

Lavinia handed Dylan a second pack of crackers, not in any hurry to leave her favorite spot. While Dylan made the birds fatter, Lavinia spoke to Edgar in her mind.

That delay only made the dream more special, didn't it, honey? After my recovery, it came true every day. For two years. And we spent hours on these wooden benches, content to do nothing but be together and watch the Cape Fear flow out to the Atlantic. Oh, and the picnics with the grandsons! And afternoons spent fishing on the pier. Those years were the best.

Too soon, the crackers ran out and the birds flew away, then Lavinia drove Dylan home to his quiet neighborhood of oak tree-lined streets near the school. She pulled into the short paved drive and rolled down the window, calling out to Lucas who stood at the door. She had texted him from the park to let him know she was on the way.

Dylan leaned over and kissed her on the cheek, making the corners of Lavinia's mouth stretch outward. He sprang from the car as Lucas ran from the house, leaned his head in through the open window, and kissed her on the other cheek. Then Lucas turned back so fast she barely saw him.

"Bye, Nana!" they called in unison as they raced inside, no doubt to be the first to grab the remote.

"Bye, boys!" she said. "I love you!"

She let out a contented sigh and put the car in reverse. Before she backed into the street, Lavinia did a double take at her reflection in the rearview mirror. There was a faint black smudge on her left cheek.

"Lucas! That booger! He got me."

She dug a linty tissue from her bag and touched it to her tongue, then rubbed at her cheek with it, still smiling.

Gotta be eyeshadow, she thought. *Pretty clever. I never woulda thought of a black eyeshadow kiss. Not bad.*

She hoped Lucas wouldn't be in trouble for messing with his mama's makeup. They didn't *both* need to be on her bad side.

Lavinia backed out of the driveway, and at the stop sign, she looked in the mirror again. There were no cars behind her, so she fished the phone out of her bag and texted Lucas an emoji with a stuck-out tongue. Funny things, those little cartoon faces; there was one for almost any occasion. The phone dinged at her before she could put it down, and a purple, devil-horned emoji appeared on the screen. She smiled. Next it was her turn in the text message battle.

Anything to make those boys happy.

Chapter Two

A haven of leisure. A place to live out your best years in style and comfort. We offer scenic waterfront views and all the amenities of a resort hotel. Choose one of our modern, private villas or a lovely suite in our state-of-the-art assisted living facility. At Cypress Shores, we know you can't put a price tag on peace of mind. Let us give you the quality of life you deserve.

Everything the brochure had promised was true. Cypress Shores Retirement Community was positioned in a breathtaking spot, right on the bank of Dutchman Creek—a wide peaceful stream that connected two larger sections of the Intracoastal Waterway, where egrets camped among the marsh grasses and inconspicuous armies of tiny gray crabs ran amok along the bank.

The villa she called home was in a magnificent location, close to the boardwalk that led to a little white gazebo and a short walk from the cafeteria and Senior Central, the activity hub of Cypress Shores. The villa itself wasn't all that different from her first home in Southport—the grand Victorian on the waterfront that she had shared with Edgar—just much more compact. And the amenities were simply unmatched. For two years, Lavinia hadn't had to clean, or change light bulbs, or stoop down to pull the stubborn little weeds that sprouted up next to the driveway. Not to mention the facilities. A haven of leisure, indeed.

Lavinia steered the Buick through the ornate metal gates of

her much sought-after neighborhood. She passed the *Welcome to Cypress Shores Retirement Community* sign and smiled at the last word. She wasn't there for luxury or location. She'd made it her home for the *community*, like her Tuesday night bridge club, the Wednesday morning book club, and her dear friends Henry and Sylvia who lived three doors down.

To Lavinia's dismay, the only person who lessened her love of community living was standing in her driveway when she arrived. Her brow furrowed at the sight of Gordon Proctor, her curmudgeon next-door neighbor. He stood with hands on hips, scowling, daring her to run him over. Lavinia inched the burgundy Buick forward, but still he stood in front of the garage, refusing to move.

The sun reflected blindingly off of Gordon's mostly bald head. *I hope that's not some sort of beacon,* she thought. *It could be a signal for all the crochety old men of the world to rise up and unite. Then we'll be in trouble.* Lavinia laughed out loud at her private joke.

She had no choice but to leave the car parked in the driveway, though she did briefly imagine running Gordon over. Not the car-on-body impact part, just the aftermath of him carried away on a stretcher, the toes of his shoes sticking out from underneath a white sheet.

"Well, hello, Gordy!" Lavinia said from her car seat, with an especially syrupy tone. She reached up and grabbed the top of her open door, using it to pull her creaking bones out of the car. She hoisted the pocketbook onto her shoulder and adjusted the jacket of her lavender pantsuit.

"I've told you not to call me that, Mrs. Lewis," he said. He made her name sound like a curse word. He folded his arms across his chest and rocked back and forth on the heels of his orthopedic tennis shoes, the ones Lavinia had pictured sticking out of the sheet in her daydream.

"Oh, that's right. I'm so sorry. You did tell me that, didn't you?" She drew out each word like pulling salt taffy, modulating up and down as she stretched them thin. "Well, to what do I owe this...um...pleasure, Mr. Proctor?" She approached him as if they were old friends, instead of what they really were.

"Did you leave your television on, with the volume turned up loud enough to wake the dead?"

"*Nooo,* Gordy...I mean, Mr. Proctor. That's just Sylvia. She's borrowin' my television for the afternoon, and, well...she's just a little hard of hearin'." There was an unspoken darlin' at the end of Lavinia's sentence—the purposefully condescending one, not the sweet one—punctuated by her hand placed on Mr. Proctor's arm.

"Your set, your responsibility." He shook her hand away. "It's been blaring most of the afternoon! I couldn't even take my nap!"

"You mean you can actually hear my television from *inside* your house?"

"Well, no. But I tried to sit outside for a while, and it assaulted my ears! Then I got so worked up over it, that when I went back in, I couldn't sleep."

Lavinia imagined again. This time it was Proctor in a bonnet and bib with a rattle in hand, wailing about his blankie. She stifled a giggle and, mustering a hint of sincerity, offered an apology for the inconvenience. He didn't accept.

"You better be glad I didn't call Marvin," Mr. Proctor said. "I almost did, you know." He raised his eyebrows and leaned his face forward, as if he expected Lavinia to thank him for not reporting her to the Director of Cypress Shores.

"And what's he gonna do? Marvin and I are good friends," Lavinia lied.

"Yeah, right. He's got you on his list, and you know it. Exactly where troublemakers like you belong."

Gordon's statement pushed Lavinia to the edge, and she abandoned the gentility with which she was raised. "Oh, lighten up, Gordy," she said, then she clicked the lock button on her key fob, letting the *beep beep* from the car signal the end of their conversation. Without further apology, she brushed past him and made her way up the brick walkway to the front door.

"I'm warning you, Mrs. Lewis!" he yelled after her. "Next time, I won't be so patient with your antics!"

She pretended not to hear the threat. Lavinia passed between two purple dahlias still in bloom, opened the unlocked door, and ambled inside. Her curved-backed friend Sylvia stood at the living room window, eyes wide and remote in hand. The television was off, and all was quiet.

"What a welcome home, huh?" Sylvia said.

Lavinia closed the door and pushed her back against it. "Heavens to Betsy! That man!" She let out one giant sigh, pushing out the negative energy along with the air. Her load was lighter by the next inhale.

"I'm sorry you're havin' to deal with him again, Lavinia," Sylvia said. The twang in her gravelly voice gave her away as a high-country transplant, though she had lived at the coast for fifteen years.

"Oh, never mind him. What can Gordon Proctor do to me?" Lavinia shrugged. "Never, never, never you mind." Her hand spun in the air with each *never*.

"I was watchin'," Sylvia said, "and I'da been out there faster'n you can say *Bob's-your-uncle* if'n he tried anything."

Lavinia smiled and nodded. Sylvia's protectiveness was sweet, but she'd never seen her friend move anywhere quickly. Sylvia was healthy as a horse and strong as an ox, but also as wide as one.

"Gordon reminds me of that dummy I saw on television,"

Lavinia said, matter-of-factly. She dropped her bag with a thud onto the little mahogany table by the door.

"Lavinia, I know he's a bully, but there's no use for name-calling."

"No! I mean a real dummy, like a puppet. What's his name?" She stood with one arm folded over her stomach and the pointer finger of the other hand over her lip. Her eyes narrowed in concentration.

"He was on a morning talk show just last week." She paused until it came to her. "Walter! That's it. The grumpy old man puppet. He looks exactly like him! Doesn't he? They have the same face." What a relief it was to have placed Gordon's doppelganger.

"Oh, yeah. He does. And I think I did see that on television." Sylvia made her way across the room slowly to join Lavinia at the breakfast nook table. "The pretty little blond anchor interviewed him, and he acted all grumpy because she wouldn't agree to go out with him," she said. Sylvia used a new hand gesture for each different thought. "I know it was just a skit, Lavinia, but I think it was in poor taste to have an old puppet ask out a young married woman. Especially one who's seven months pregnant. Don't you?"

Lavinia hadn't thought of it before, but she agreed with Sylvia. Though her jokes were sophomoric, and of questionable taste, when it came to most matters of decency, especially between men and women, Lavinia stayed on high ground.

"Hey! Maybe that's why Gordon gives you such a hard time!" Sylvia said. Her time-worn voice sounded harsher when she was excited. She straightened up for a moment in her chair then relaxed back into her natural c-shape.

"What's why?"

"Because he wants to go out on a date with you. It makes sense. He doesn't think you'd go out with him, and he's trying to get your attention. Just like little boys picking on little girls in school.

Don't you remember that?" Sylvia's forearms dug into the edge of the table and she leaned forward, silently coaxing Lavinia to remember.

Lavinia thought back to the pigtail-haired girl she used to be and the boy who sat behind her and tugged on those pigtails when the teacher wasn't looking. Edgar had done it until Lavinia started wearing her hair down around the seventh grade and he finally told her how he felt.

"Well, if he thinks I wouldn't go out with him, he'd be right!" Lavinia said. She shook her head from side-to-side and swiped her palms together briskly, as if brushing off a squished bug. *"Imagine!"*

"He must really like you. He banged on the door every half hour from the time you left. But I just turned my hearin' aid down and turned the television up louder when he started. All that bangin' made it hard to hear my shows."

"Oh, Sylvia..." Lavinia chuckled. She reached over and patted her friend on the hand. "I guess we should cut him a little bit of slack. After all, he is a Yankee. He can't much help it, now can he?"

The two friends at the table were as different as the lights and shadows that splotched the linen tablecloth between them, made by a low-in-the-sky sun flooding through the manicured boxwoods in the side yard. Lavinia was on the tall side and had a medium build—not skinny by any means, but neither was she plump—while Sylvia was decidedly short and wide. Lavinia had a strong nose and jaw, inherited from her father who was of Jewish descent, and high cheekbones from her mother who claimed, though it was unproven, that her great-great-great-grandmother was full-blooded Cherokee. Sylvia was younger than Lavinia by almost ten years. Her face was round and her eyes narrow. But beyond appearance, they had much in common, including quick wit, slow speech, and an abiding love for all things southern.

Sylvia got up and made her way to the door, nodding in agreement. She grabbed the handle of her walking stick propped up in the corner.

"Thank you for letting me come over to watch my programs," she said. "Henry's been watching ESPN all day. And if I have to hear about sacks and snaps and tight ends anymore, I'm gonna lose it." Lavinia chuckled and said *oh, Sylvia* with only a forward wave of her hand.

"Well, you let him watch all those silly sports games he wants," she chided. "And you rub his feet. And bring him breakfast in bed every once in a while. And don't complain when you think he's not listening. One day he might be gone, and you'll be wishing he was still here ignoring you." She looked at Edgar's picture on the mantle.

"I know, honey. You're right." Sylvia sighed. "He's been drivin' me crazy for goin' on fifty years now. I reckon I wouldn't know what to do without him."

Lavinia stood up and walked with Sylvia out into the sunshine.

"No, you'd figure it out," Lavinia said. "But you wouldn't want to."

Sylvia started toward her home up the street, and Lavinia watched her, wishing Sylvia had driven. It was nice to see her getting some exercise, but she'd been waiting for a chance to slap a sign on the back of her golf cart. There were two ready in the entryway table drawer, made from construction paper and markers the boys had left. One said, *Follow me to AA*, and the other said, *I brake for old people*. Lavinia wasn't sure which one to prank Sylvia with first, but just thinking about it made her giggle.

"What are you taking to the potluck, Lavinia?" Sylvia asked over her shoulder.

"Oh, shoot! I forgot today is the second Friday. I guess I'll just have to get some Oreos from the cupboard and throw them on a platter. That's good enough, I guess. What are you taking?"

"Henry put on a pot roast this morning."

"*Ummm*, pot roast. See there, darlin'? You got yourself a good man!"

"I know, Lavinia. I know. He's a good'n."

Sylvia had almost made it to the driveway of the next villa when Lavinia called out in a shrill voice. "Sy-yl! Watch out for that snake!"

Sylvia defied gravity with her jump. She stooped over, moving her head and torso in sweeping motions as she inspected the pavement all around. The fist that held the walking stick was pressed against her heart, and the other hand was wedged between her clenched thighs. Her breaths came in short, strong bursts.

"Did you almost wet your pants?" Lavinia called, laughing.

It only took Sylvia a moment to catch on, and she joined in the laughter. The pair carried on loudly—Lavinia with a high, chirping chuckle and Sylvia with a breathy baritone guffaw.

"Okay. Now…I've…wet my…pants." Sylvia could barely speak; and the laughing spell made the corners of her eyes leak, too.

Lavinia and Sylvia laughed until Lavinia's neighbor to the left opened the door and poked her head out. Lavinia waved to her.

"Go back in, Marge," she said. "Everything's okay."

The pencil thin, white-haired woman looked at both as if they'd lost their minds, nodded *okay*, and closed the door.

"Oh, Lavinia," Sylvia said. "There's never a dull moment with you."

"I'm glad you can take a joke."

"I'm just glad there wasn't really a snake!"

Sylvia was right. There were no slithery creatures in sight, except for Mr. Proctor, who stood by his mailbox with his jaw clenched, glaring at Lavinia.

Chapter Three

It was a fitful night for Neville McGrath. He dreamed of being awake in a coffin with his eyes glued shut. Through his closed eyelids, he could see everyone that came by and looked in the coffin. One by one, heads appeared above him, most with blank expressions. They came like an assembly line, each peering in for two seconds then turning robotically and moving on. Every other face he saw belonged to his nephew, Donald. Between the Donalds, the visitors were clients Neville had defended over the years—men, women, young, old. He saw those accused of minor traffic violations and those charged with serious offenses, the kinds Neville tried to forget. Still, he remembered each defendant, each case, as if reading straight from the files he kept in his office.

The only faces that broke the emotionless stare belonged to the guilty ones. The guilty whom the court had found innocent, each leaned over and smiled in an admiring way, with their hands clasped, heads tilted, and a dreamy look in their eyes. The guilty ones looked at him like he was a puppy or a couple getting married instead of a dead body in a coffin. Donald's face was always the same—pained, but without tears—until the last time he peeked in. The last time, he wore a maniacal, teeth-bared grin that distorted his entire face.

Neville woke up and swung his feet off the side of the bed, ready to run, until he realized he was in his bedroom alone, in the one-bedroom apartment where he had lived for the past twenty years.

***

Neville felt much better after a shower. He shuffled to the kitchen in his socks and boxer shorts and fed his Persian cat, Alibi; then he put on a suit and tie like he did every morning of the work week. He stood in front of the mirror in his tiny bathroom and shaved his face, maneuvering the blade carefully over minute hills and valleys. The gorges in his forehead were made deeper as he raised his brow in concentration.

The morning show hosts sounded off from the front room. Two female news anchors wished the male anchor a happy birthday. He held the razor in midair and peeked out of the bathroom.

How old did they say he is? My truck is older than that!

He finished shaving, rinsed the razor, and laid it in the slimy soap dish on the back of the sink. He picked up a comb and ran it through his silver hair a handful of times, then used a nice-smelling pomade to tame the wiry, gray eyebrows. Before he glued them into place, the brows, still a few shades darker than his head, reminded him of Alibi's whiskers, sticking out in all directions.

"And now, back to the latest news," the more serious female anchor announced.

Nothing new about those headlines. Always the same biased drivel! His thoughts found a voice. "I only keep you on for a little noise, Mrs. News Lady!"

Alibi came around the corner from the kitchen and rubbed against his pant leg, purring. "No, I wasn't yelling for you, kitty," he said. "I was talking to that sound machine over there." Neville held onto the sink to steady himself as he bent down to pick up the cat, scooping her underneath the belly and letting her four legs dangle.

He stroked her back one time then placed her on the floor again.

Neville looked at his watch. Time to go, and without his coffee. He would get it at the office. Even if he'd wanted some before work, all three mugs were dirty anyway, and he didn't feel like washing one.

He started out the door then turned back for his cane propped in the corner. A touch of arthritis and a sciatica flare-up at the same time meant a third leg was smart prevention from unexpectedly meeting the ground. He grabbed the cherry wood stick with the clear glass knob handle, locked the front door, and walked three steps to his truck. The vehicle's door creaked as he opened it and clanked when he closed it. He brought the engine to a roar with a turn of the key.

You've got plenty of life left, don't you, truck?

Neville rolled down the window to enjoy the salty air, and because the air conditioner no longer worked.

Ten minutes into the drive, halfway to his office from the apartment, Neville began to think about the dream again. He replayed the images, the people, the coffin. Perspiration formed beneath his collar.

What does it mean?

Neville absent-mindedly reached into the center console for a pack of Camels, then drew back an empty hand. He'd been mostly smoke-free for two years, but that last pack had been his security blanket. For months he'd shown restraint, only reaching for one sweet-smelling stick during times of heavy caseloads. A familiar friend to ease the stress. But he'd burned through the remainder of the *just-in-case* pack within the last month, trying to decide about the move.

The cell phone in Neville's shirt pocket rang, and he slammed the disappointingly empty console shut. It would either be his secretary or Donald. He never gave clients his personal number.

Neville flipped open the phone, hoping it was Shirley.

"Hello, Uncle!" Donald said.

"Hey, buddy. How's things?" Neville answered. The courtesy wasn't manufactured. He loved his nephew, and he generally enjoyed talking to him. But he wasn't in the mood.

"It's fine, doing fine," Donald answered. "As a matter of fact, I'm in my happy place, up at the cabin. Just kicked back and taking in the view of the lake."

He didn't call to gloat. Neville knew he was calling for the same reason he'd been calling since the beginning of summer—to encourage him to move to Liberty, Maine to live with him. The only son of his dearly departed sister, Donald had recently retired from a career in vinyl siding, sold the business, and bought a cabin on the edge of Lake St. George.

"How's the fishing been lately?" Neville said.

"Amazing, Uncle! You wouldn't believe the walleye I caught last week. It was a real beauty. Of course, I could text you a picture if you'd invest in a more high-tech phone."

"I'm smart enough without needing a smartphone. I've told you that." Neville chuckled. "All those devices are more trouble than they're worth."

"I hear you, Neville." Donald didn't push. "But I bet if you saw all the pictures I post on Facebook, you'd have an easier time deciding to move on up here. And not just the fish. The colors of the leaves are spectacular right now."

"I bet they are, Donald. I bet they are."

When the conversation was finished, Neville flipped the phone shut and put it back in his shirt pocket. He turned on the radio to feed his brain some new thoughts, spinning the little round dial in search of talk radio politics. A smooth, powerful male voice sounded from the speaker. After only a few seconds, Neville punched the knob to turn the radio off. Silence was better than some preacher.

Neville soon pulled into the short driveway of his office, a brick 1940s A-frame house he'd purchased three years ago, when it was rezoned for commercial use. He knew buying property so late in the game seemed odd to some, but it was a sound investment.

The sign out front was a little white square staked into the sandy grass. It read *Neville K. McGrath, Attorney* in plain black letters. No need for a large sign. His reputation was advertisement enough.

Neville slid out of the pickup and took his time getting to the door, careful not to slip on the acorns that littered the paved walkway.

"Boss, you don't look so good," his secretary said as he entered the office.

"Shirley, I'm eighty years old. I haven't looked good in thirty years."

Shirley laughed, a high-pitched staccato cackle, and her high, full ponytail of tight red curls bounced.

"Oh, stop it. You know you're still a catch." She rose from her seat behind the desk, took Neville's suit jacket from him, and hung it up on the coat rack in the corner. "All those ladies at Moose Lodge Bingo nearly swoon every time you walk in!"

"Don't be silly." Neville grinned. "Look at this spare tire." He patted his belly with both hands.

"Those ladies don't care about a little spare tire, Neville," Shirley said. "They go on and on about your handsome face!"

"Yeah, and I'm sure my bank account has nothing to do with it either."

He shuffled to his office thinking about the clacking hens with rows of cards lined up in front of them and markers in hand waiting for *B11* or *O72*, and how they dotted their cards like chickens pecking at scratch. The women weren't shy about their admiration for him, but he avoided their advances, subtly when it worked and downright rudely if necessary. His sense of self-preservation was stronger than the need for niceties. The only reason Neville went anyway was because Shirley asked him.

If I've made it as a bachelor this long, I'm not about to get attached now.

Neville had been running from old women for a long time. When he was a young man, he ran from young women. He'd spent his life running, mainly because he didn't know what to do if he got caught. The only woman in his life, now that mother and sister were gone, was Shirley Whitaker. As close to family as he could claim, Shirley and her husband Chuck were also part of a very small group that Neville called *friends*.

A picture of efficiency, Shirley stepped to the next room and came back quickly with a cup of coffee and a note. She'd certainly come a long way since Neville hired her, right after he first opened the practice. He'd watched her go from a new high school graduate with more ambition than common sense, to an indispensable member of the practice, having earned an Associate Degree then her paralegal certificate in the evenings after he took a chance on her.

"Didn't sleep well again last night, huh?" she asked, still stirring the powdered creamer into the warm beverage.

"It wasn't too bad."

"Uh-huh," she said. "How long have I known you?"

He didn't answer.

After weeks of Shirley asking what was wrong, Neville had finally told her about the dreams a month ago. Now she could read any disturbance to the previous night's REM cycle on his face the moment he stepped into the office.

"Don't you think those crazy dreams have something to do with a certain *big decision* you're trying to make?"

Neville ignored the question and her gaze as he shuffled through folders on his desk, pretending to look for a case file.

Shirley kept the whole office pristine except Neville's desk. She wasn't allowed to straighten that.

She sat down in the chair across from his desk, crossed her legs, and leaned forward, as she kept on stirring.

Shirley wasn't the most professional-looking secretary and legal assistant. She wore flowy culottes every day of the year, up until the first frost when she switched to long denim skirts with tights underneath. Her face always looked freshly scrubbed, and her hair was always pulled into the same bouncy ponytail. But he couldn't have found a friendlier face to greet his clients, or a more dependable employee, anywhere.

"You know I support you either way, right?" Shirley said, upbeat. She gripped the edge of his desk, then went back to stirring.

He finally looked up and gave her a nod.

"Don't let me be a factor in your decision, Neville. I'll be all right. I just want what's best for you."

Neville put his elbows on his desk and rested his forehead momentarily on his fists. Before the gold signet ring on his left hand could leave an impression in his skin, Neville looked up at his assistant. "I know you do, Shirley. I know you do." He let out a heavy sigh. "I'm just not sure I'm ready to be put out to pasture."

"But you could still practice law in Maine," she said gently. "Or you could do it part-time here. You could sell this place and work out of your apartment. Just when you feel like it."

The love in Shirley's words was obvious. Nobody would practically talk themselves out of a job for any other reason.

"I guess you're right. There are lots of options," Neville said. Shirley's optimism was like a virus.

"You'll know when it's time to slow down." She looked down at the tornado of café au lait and stopped stirring. "Until then, keep being *The Great Neville McGrath* and don't worry about it." She paused. "And, well…for what it's worth, you know I'm praying for you. And Chuck is, too. We both pray for you, every night."

"Um-hmm."

He didn't have to ask her to change the subject.

"Hey, your buddy down at the police station called. Officer Davenport." Shirley looked down at the note she'd taken from her pocket, then stood. She handed Neville the lukewarm coffee then the piece of paper with the handwritten message.

Neville looked at the number written neatly in blue ink on the yellow post-it. Not the police department number. Maybe a cell.

"He says he really needs your help, boss. Says it's personal. But"—Shirley cocked her head to one side and grimaced— "I'm not sure you'll want this one, boss. It sure sounds like a doozy."

Chapter Four

Sunday morning, October 14

"Vinny, I need to talk to you. Are you sitting down?"

The early-morning sun filtered through the blinds on Lavinia's bedroom window in shades of pink and orange. Even in her sleepy stupor, she recognized the voice of her son-in-law on the other end of the line.

"Lee, what are you up to, darlin'? Are you workin'?" She sat up slowly and reached for her glasses on the nightstand, then stood and reached for the cotton house coat draped across the straight-backed chair in the corner. Holding the phone between her ear and shoulder, she put the garment on over her silky pink nightgown.

"Listen, I need to tell you something. I wanted to be there," Lee said. His voice was panicked. "But the chief wouldn't let me. Said it was a conflict of interest. But I couldn't let them—"

"Slow down. What are you talking about, dear?"

"Amy Lynn doesn't even know yet, but I needed to call you before they show up."

"*Who* shows up?"

"The officers. They're on their way."

Lavinia laughed loudly into the handset. "Oh, silly. You can't get me. I know you're trying to get back at me for calling you and pretending to be from the IRS. I told you, sweetheart, I wouldn't dared to have done it if I'd known you really *were* being audited."

"No, Lavinia. This isn't a—"

"Oh, hold on one sec, sweetie. Somebody's at the door."

"Vinny, wait! That's what I'm trying to—"

Lavinia dropped the cordless handset onto the bed and left the room to answer the door.

She didn't bother looking through the peephole. It was a gated community with a guard stationed at the entrance, and it was probably Sylvia anyway. Or maybe Gordon had complained about the plastic flamingos she stuck in his yard while he was away on Saturday and it was Marvin with another warning.

When she opened the door, it wasn't Sylvia, or Marvin, or even Gordon.

"Lavinia Louise Lebowitz Lewis?" said a young, uniformed police officer. The officer was shorter than Lavinia, and he stared down at the notebook in his hand while he spoke.

Throughout her childhood, whenever her mother or father called *Lavinia Louise*, she knew she was in trouble. Twice as many names felt like twice as much trouble, but she held onto to a tiny glimmer of hope that the officer was part of Lee's very elaborate revenge prank.

"Yes, I'm Lavinia Lewis. Is everything okay?"

"Ma'am, I'm afraid not. There's been an incident, and we have some questions to ask you."

"Incident? *Why*..." Lavinia felt confused. "It was just two plastic flamingos! Some people love them!" She looked over at Gordon's yard where her gag gift remained.

The early morning air held the first feel of fall. Lavinia pulled the housecoat around herself tightly and tucked her hands under her arms.

"Mrs. Lewis, I'd like for you to come with us, please. We need to ask you a few questions."

"Questions about what? Is it trespassing to put a flamingo in a yard?" Lavinia was politely indignant. "It was a gift! And I think they look real nice in Gordy's yard."

"Ma'am, we'd like to talk to you about what appears to be a poisoning here at the retirement community. It's a bit more serious than plastic flamingos."

Lavinia's mouth dropped to a gape. Another officer stood at the bottom of the driveway, next to the car, with hands on hips. She looked from one officer to the other, back and forth, waiting for one of them to crack a smile. They didn't.

She was given time to dress while they waited outside. Lavinia stumbled back to the phone where she'd left it on the flowered bedspread. Lee was still there, anxious, apologetic. She assured him she'd be fine. She'd done nothing wrong. But after she hung up the phone, her fingers trembled as she buttoned a powder blue blouse and slipped on a pair of navy, elastic-waist slacks. She picked up her pocketbook from the table beside the door and stepped outside.

As Lavinia walked with the officer to his car, she scanned the rows of square, brick houses on each side of the street. Her eyes darted from yard to look-alike yard, feeling a small relief that no one was outside to witness what was happening to her.

Poisoning? They think I poisoned someone?

With each step, the *Cops* theme song got louder and louder in her brain.

Bad boys, bad boys...

The officer helped Lavinia into the back of the squad car, then it closed with a daunting, echoey thud.

A metal screen separated her from the officers in the front seat like a cage. Lavinia's still-trembling hand reached to her upper chest, just beneath her collar, and slid up to her neck before she let out a gasp. She'd forgotten her pearls.

***

The interrogation room wasn't like on television. It was pleasant, like an office breakroom. Not that Lavinia had ever worked in an office. But she'd visited Edgar's work plenty and had seen them on television shows, too.

She sat on a little couch while the two officers sat at a table facing her. They each held a cup of coffee. They even offered her a cup, and Lavinia started to relax. She declined politely, as the only beverages to cross her lips were sweet tea at every meal and water in between. Occasionally orange juice, if her acid reflux was in check.

"Mrs. Lewis, we want you to try very hard to remember everything about Friday night. *Okay?*" said the tall officer. He spoke slowly and loudly.

She nodded. *Do they think I'm senile?*

"Mrs., Lewis, when you left your house, did you go straight to the retirement community dinner?" Officer Shorty said. His smiling baby face gave her comfort.

"No. I had a stop to make first. I had to go pick up Rosie, like I promised."

***

Friday, October 12

Lavinia dozed in the armchair in her living room with her long legs stretched out and feet propped up on the ottoman with ankles crossed. Her hands, with fingers locked, lay at the top of her belly. The alarm on her cell phone sounded to tell her it was time to get ready for dinner, and Lavinia jumped, knocking the phone off the arm of the chair and to the floor.

She grunted as she stretched to reach the phone. Three

missed messages from Lucas. Chicken emoji. Palm tree. Avocado. She didn't quite understand the game, but she matched him three-for-three. Sleepy face emoji. Airplane. Thumbs up.

Lavinia rose slowly and stretched. It always took her a while to get going after a nap, like a pump that needed priming. When the water was finally flowing, she checked her makeup then grabbed the plastic tray of crème-filled sandwich cookies from the kitchen counter and carried them to the car, pressing the loose plastic wrap to the bottom of the plate as she walked. Instead of heading to Senior Central, she drove a quarter mile to the other side of Cypress Shores.

There were three sections of the retirement community. After the private villas for active seniors came the upscale assisted living facility that resembled a five-star hotel. Further down the winding paved road was *the home*, the literal end of the line, reserved for those unwillingly sent back in time to a state of dependence—some who even had to be fed and cleaned like infants. She sighed thinking about it. Lavinia had a special place in her heart for these patients. Maybe it was because she could have been one of them. If the stroke had been worse, or if time hadn't been as kind, she could have been at the home instead of her villa. It seemed like nothing more than luck of the draw. They had a bad hand, and she had a royal flush. Maybe she sympathized because she knew her luck could change any day.

Lavinia visited the home at least once a week, usually to see Rosie—a long-time resident with a pleasant smile and kind eyes. Rosie could get around as well as Lavinia, maybe better, but she never spoke. Somewhere along the way, her brain had stopped delivering words to her mouth. And it made Lavinia contemplate which was worse—a strong mind trapped in a feeble body, or a strong body trapped by a feeble mind.

Sometimes, Rosie gestured to communicate. She nodded *yes* and *no* on good days. But mostly, she whistled. She whistled waiting for breakfast; she whistled during checkups; she whistled walking on the main lawn with her private daytime nurse—a pretty little girl from Florida, as Lavinia recalled.

Lavinia arrived at the home and signed Rosie out at the front desk, with a promise to bring her back right after dinner.

"You have fun now, Miss Rosie," the desk nurse said with a smile.

Rosie gave a whippoorwill call in reply.

The nurse turned back to Lavinia. "It's nice of you to take her with you, Mrs. Lewis. Most of our patients *never* go out in the evening."

"Well, Rosie is a special friend. Aren't you, dear?" Lavinia patted Rosie's hand.

Rosie puckered and produce two staccato tones that resembled *uh-huh.*

As they arrived at dinner, Lavinia was happy to find that Sylvia and Henry had saved seats for them. Lavinia helped Rosie get settled in, then she placed her tray of Oreos on the dessert table and headed toward the main spread. Skipping over a couple of mystery dishes, she found Henry's pot roast and scooped heaping, still-warm servings onto two plates before adding a few of her favorite sides to each.

As she placed the plates on the table, a familiar face caught her attention from across the room.

"What's Gordon doing here?" Lavinia said in hushed tones, slapping Sylvia's hand. "He never comes to the monthly potluck."

Gordon sat at a table by himself, even as people walked by searching for a seat, their foam trays on the verge of collapse beneath the weight of old-school southern cooking.

"He's checking you out, Lavinia. What did I tell you?" Sylvia's tone had a hint of smugness at being right. Lavinia ignored her. Rosie paid no attention to either of them, but she stopped whistling the theme song to *Bonanza* to take a bite of Salisbury steak.

Other than Gordon's presence and Rosie's occasional whistling, it was like all the other potlucks. People talked and laughed as they ate their meals and indulged in dessert, testing the effectiveness of their diabetes medications. Then the happy scene was interrupted.

"Lavinia!" a woman's angry voice rang out.

Lavinia looked up from her forkful of macaroni salad, startled. Rosie tensed up next to her as Gladys Smith, Lavinia's backyard neighbor, marched toward them, holding a half-eaten Oreo in her hand. Gladys was an anomaly in that her bouffant hair matched the color of the outside of the Oreo instead of the middle, though it had never been dyed.

"You did this!" she yelled, waving the remainder of cookie.

"What are you talkin' about, Gladys? *Did what?*" Lavinia rose from her seat to face her accuser.

"You replaced the cream in the middle of these with toothpaste. About made me gag when I bit into it."

"But I didn't—"

"You did bring Oreos, *didn't you?* I saw you carrying a tray of them in, and it was the only one up there!"

"Yes, but they were straight out of the pack. I didn't do anything to them, Gladys. I promise." Lavinia was calm. For once, she was innocent.

People in another part of the room started spitting and sputtering. Some laughed and took a drink. Some cursed. Gladys stood there, waiting for an explanation that Lavinia didn't have.

"Lavinia, look," Gladys's tone softened. "I like most of your jokes. You keep things lively around here. But this kind of prank needs to stop. That mint and baking soda ruined my dinner. I was so caught off guard by the taste I nearly threw up."

"Gladys, I'm sorry about that, but it wasn't me."

Gladys's face turned an even deeper shade of red.

"I'm telling you what, Lavinia!" she shouted. People that hadn't noticed the commotion before looked up from their plates. "Marvin is going to hear about this! I'm fed up!"

Lavinia would have worked harder to defend herself had it not been for Rosie. Her friend's face was contorted with distress and her eyes filled with silent tears. Henry tried to comfort her, while Sylvia sat perched on the edge of her seat. She looked ready to jump in if Gladys started throwing punches.

"Oh, c'mon sweetheart," Lavinia said to Rosie. "Let's get you outta here." She took Rosie by the hand, shot Gladys an *I-hope-you're-happy* look, and left her there wagging her finger at nothing.

By the time they were back at the home, Rosie was calm again, and Lavinia didn't say or hear anything else about the potluck until the next morning.

"Did you hear about Wendy Wisengood?" Sylvia said through the telephone. "She had to go to the emergency room last night by ambulance! She's real bad off, Lavinia. I heard it might be something she ate at dinner."

***

"So, you weren't aware that Mrs. Wisengood has a rare allergy to fluoride, Mrs. Lewis?" The tall officer who had started off as the nicest suddenly turned gruff, and his eyes accused her. "You had no idea that contact with fluoride toothpaste could make her extremely ill?"

"No! I've never heard of such a thing!" Lavinia said. "And I certainly didn't know anyone at *Cypress Shores* was allergic to toothpaste."

"Well, it is extremely rare," the other officer said. He looked at Lavinia with understanding. "Probably one in ten million."

"And potentially deadly," said the tall one. He gave her a hard stare. "Causing someone to ingest something harmful without their knowledge is very serious, Mrs. Lewis."

"It was toothpaste!"

"Is that a confession?"

"No! I mean, I didn't do it. It wasn't me this time." She leaned against the back of the couch and placed the back of her hand against her forehead as beads of perspiration erupted from her pores.

"But you do enjoy playing pranks, right? We were told that you've been known to do things like this before."

Lavinia wiped her brow, sat up straight, and addressed the officers, willing herself to stay calm.

"Yes, I've played that prank before. But this time, it wasn't me."

The young officer smiled sweetly. "You know, my grandma liked a good joke," he said. "You remind me a lot of her. Do you have grandchildren?"

"Two boys, nine and twelve." She couldn't help but smile thinking of Dylan and Lucas.

"I have a file here from her doctor," the older cop interrupted. He slapped a brown folder against the table while still holding onto it, and Lavinia's smile went away. "His report confirms that Mrs. Wisengood's illness was caused by consumption of fluoride." He rose from his chair and approached Lavinia. He leaned one hand on the arm of the couch and loomed close to her face. "There are two factors that will play a big role in how this case goes, Mrs. Lewis." His coffee breath overwhelmed her, but she sat like a statue. *"Two. Factors."* He paused, obviously for dramatic effect. "Whether her poisoning was *intentional* or accidental, and whether she pulls through this or not."

Chapter Five

Tuesday afternoon, October 16

"Vinny, I don't know what to say."

Lavinia's son-in-law stroked her hand as they sat on his living room sofa. The gesture was comforting, except the way the thin skin of her hand slipped this way and that with each stroke. It used to stay in its place. How long had it been like that?

Lucas sat on the floor in front of her, rubbing his hands back and forth on the plush carpet. Not once had he checked his phone since Lavinia got there.

Dylan sat on the other side of her, perched on the edge of the sofa. "I don't like it when you're this quiet, Nana," he said. "It's not normal."

She patted his knee but couldn't find the words to reassure him. The reality of her situation had hit hard, all at once.

When Marvin had shown up at her front door earlier that day to deliver the news, Lavinia handled it without tears, in part because, even though he had *threatened* to kick her out at least a half dozen times, there was remorse in his voice, and she felt sorry for him having to evict her.

"Just until the investigation is over, Lavinia," Marvin had said. "I'm sure you'll be back in no time, keepin' us all on our toes."

She told him she understood and that she would be out by the next day. He agreed to give her that much time and promised to be as discreet as possible about her reason for leaving.

The night before she was forced to leave her home, Lavinia had considered setting off the car alarm on Marvin's Miata at 3:00 a.m. and watching him run out of his apartment in his boxer shorts in a panic; not because she was mad, but as a farewell prank for him to remember her by, in case, for some reason, she didn't get to come back.

I should have done it, Lavinia thought. She came back to herself when Lee spoke.

"You know you're welcome here as long as it takes to get this cleared up," he said. "But we're going to help get things back to normal. I know how much you enjoy it at Cypress Shores."

"I don't mind sharing my room with Dylan, Nana," Lucas said, his baby blues shining up at her. "Not for you. If it was anybody else, I'd be cheesed off."

"Lucas," Lee scolded.

Lavinia pursed her lips to keep from smiling.

"Well, I would be. But I'd share a room with Dylan for the rest of my life to help Nana."

She winked at Lucas and leaned her head over on Lee's strong shoulder. Lee was built so much like her Samuel—tall and broad shouldered. She glanced up at his face so close to her and was startled. From that angle, seeing his profile, he even looked like Samuel. She'd never noticed before. She sat up straight again.

"My boys have always been so good to me," Lavinia said. Her head felt off-balance as she spoke. "I'm so lucky to have you."

Lavinia looked at both grandsons and drank in the adoration in their eyes. They were so devoted to her, as if she had done something special just by loving them the way that she did, the way she was supposed to; as if she were more than just their mother's mother. She didn't deserve them.

Both joy and pain pulled at Lavinia, and the struggle between the two tipped the scales in pain's favor. The events of the day crept back into her mind. Circumstances flexed their muscles and pushed out reassurance from her family. She replayed all that had happened, and her heart began to beat faster, forcing the blood through her veins with increased intensity.

"You know what the hardest part was?" she said. She didn't give anyone time to guess. "Gordon Proctor, standing there watching you carry out my suitcases, with that smug look on his puppety face."

Lee's brow wrinkled, but he stayed quiet.

"I just refused to look at 'im! And I wasn't about to give him the satisfaction of seein' me upset," Lavinia said. She slapped her palms down on her knees and gripped them until her knuckles turned white. "Oh, he was dyin' to say something. I know it. If I could get ahold of him, I'd..." The wide eyes of her grandsons made her pause, then she ended the rant with a short growl.

"I just wonder if everybody knows what's going on. I'm *sure* they do. There's no way to keep a secret like this. And, if they don't know, my bridge club will find out when I don't show up tonight, because Sylvia, bless her heart, can't keep a secret. She'll crack under the pressure. Then once Bridge Club knows, everybody else will, too. Then all of Cypress Shores Retirement Community will believe I'm a criminal miscreant!"

If Lavinia were a tea kettle, she'd have been just before whistling.

"Almost eighty years as a law-abiding citizen, and now I'm being investigated for a crime! And poor Wendy! Fighting for her life in the hospital! I guess I should be grateful I'm on this side of things instead of on hers. I just hope she doesn't think I'm the one that caused it, if she's even conscious. But it could have been me! *Oh, Lee! It could have been!* I played that toothpaste-in-the-Oreos prank at a bridge club meeting three months ago. But I never imagined it could hurt anybody! She wasn't there that afternoon, but I know she heard about it, and of course, she'll think it was me again this time. But it wasn't. I swear, it wasn't!"

Dylan wrapped his arms around hers and squeezed as he buried his face against her shoulder.

"We believe you, Vinny," Lee said. He patted her on the back. "That's one thing you don't have to worry about."

"Do you, though? Do *all* of you believe me? Amy Lynn can hardly look at me."

"No, she's just stressed out. She's got a lot going on at work. And now this."

"I could hear it in her voice on the phone last night. She thinks I'm guilty!" Her voice rose to a volume she didn't intend again. "Anyway," she said, composing herself for the sake of the boys, "all I have to do to prove I'm innocent, is to prove who really did it. Simple as that."

"But how are you going to find out who really put the toothpaste in the Oreos?" Lee said.

"That's easy. I already know who did it." Her bony pointer finger went into the air.

The boys inched closer, as if anticipating the reveal of the culprit in a detective movie. Nana sensed their excitement and delivered the news with fanfare.

"It was that dastardly Gordon Proctor! He wanted to get me kicked out! That's why *he* poisoned Wendy."

"DUN-DUN-DUUUUN!" Dylan added sound effects to the reveal, and for a moment, they shared a laugh as if nothing was wrong.

"Lavinia, do you really think so? And that he meant to hurt somebody?" Lee said.

She lowered her head. He'd found the hole in her theory.

"Well, maybe he didn't know she was allergic to fluoride,

like I didn't. But he still did it to get me in trouble. It probably had nothing to do with Wendy, but it was the kind of prank Gordon knew Marvin wouldn't like."

"Okay, Vinny," he said, switching back to her pet name. "I'm going to figure out a way to help you. Chief won't let me anywhere near your case, but I've got lots of friends we can call. I've been thinking about it, and I already called this lawyer who—"

"I know you'll do what you can, Lee," Lavinia said. She arched her back in a stretch. "But you know what? We've talked about it enough for now, dear." Her tea kettle of emotions had been moved off the burner. Her posture relaxed, and her tone softened, like a switch had been flipped. "I don't want to think about it anymore today."

Lavinia had always had at least three things in common with Scarlett O'Hara, her personal hero. She was sometimes childish, she loved a good party, and after a brief, cathartic fit of self-pity, she preferred to put off worrying until another day.

"Okay, Vinny," Lee said. "I'm going to go make you a nice dinner." He slapped his knees then stood and headed for the kitchen. "It probably won't be as fancy as what you're used to at the retirement community, but I'll do my best. And listen, we're not going to be upset tonight. *Okay?* We're going to celebrate that you're visiting with us for a while."

"I like the way you think, Lee. But what about Amy Lynn? Isn't she going to help cook?" The sun had set long ago, and Amy Lynn was normally home by now.

"No. She said to go ahead without her." His muscular frame filled the doorway. "She's going to be a little late. But I've got this. Spaghetti and meatballs, a nice salad, garlic bread. You just relax. Everything's gonna be okay."

Lee left the room and Lucas soon followed, announcing that he was headed to play video games until dinner. Dylan stayed with

Nana. He'd been studying her intently ever since she got there.

"So, baby boy, what do you want to do this evening? We can read a book or play Scrabble. Your papa and I use to love to play Scrabble together."

"Is that the one you play on your phone?"

He snuggled up to her on the couch, and she wrapped an arm around his shoulders. Lavinia cherished the closeness. Some nine-year-olds had already outgrown cuddles, but not her youngest grandson. At twelve, Lucas could be persuaded on occasion, but Dylan didn't have to be.

"Well, sorta," Lavinia said. "But this one is on a board, and you play sittin' across the table from one another, where I can look into those pretty brown eyes of yours."

"Sounds like fun. But, Nana?"

"What is it, baby?"

"I've been thinking. And..." He dropped his head.

"Go ahead, darlin'."

"You're in a lot of trouble, aren't you?"

The question made her head hurt. "I don't rightly know yet, Dylan," she said in a weak voice. "But I guess I could be."

Dylan grabbed her hands and squeezed. He closed his eyes tightly.

"I know what we need to do, Nana." He took a deep breath. "Dear God," he said, "please help my nana get out of trouble with the police." His voice was solemn and reverent. "And please help Mrs. Wisengood get better real soon. And please help Mama believe that Nana didn't do anything wrong. Thanks for listening, God. Amen."

Seldom had Lavinia been so impressed with another person. His honesty, his boldness, his unapologetic faith—it made her proud and put her to shame at the same time. His prayer was simple, yet so powerful. Goosebumps erupted on the tender skin of her jiggly underarm, just below the short sleeves of her sweater. She grabbed Dylan in a big hug.

When was the last time she had prayed? More than just a passing thought? Too long, she knew. But it had been a while since faith seemed necessary. And she was forced to face the truth—she'd been relying on things she could control, namely the jokes. The jokes distracted her from things she couldn't change.

"Thank you, Dylan. That was a beautiful prayer."

"I hope it helps."

"I'm sure it will, sweetie. I'm sure it will." She stroked his long locks. "Hey, where'd you learn to pray like that?"

"Daddy's been taking me and Lucas to church on Sunday mornings. Three weeks in a row!"

"*He has*, has he? And what about your mama?"

"She stays home."

"I see. Well, do you enjoy it?"

"Yep! I think I'm an Episcopalian now." Dylan beamed.

"Well, good for you, sweet baby! Good for you! One of your papa's vice presidents was an Episcopalian. He was a very nice man."

Lavinia and Dylan looked up at the sound of keys rattling. Dylan got up to open the door, but his mother opened it before he got there.

Amy Lynn carried two large tote bags, one hanging off each shoulder. Books and papers peeked out of the tops of both bags. She paused to free a strand of straight, shoulder-length brown hair from beneath one of the straps, but then dropped the bags to the floor with a thud anyway.

"Hey, baby," Lavinia said.

"Mama, did they help you get all settled in Dylan's room?" Amy Lynn asked, panting. She dug her cell phone out of her pocket and checked it while she picked up the bags and positioned them on the same shoulder.

"Yes, it's very comfortable. Thank you."

"Good. Let me know if you need anything. Dylan, did you do your homework?"

"Yep," Dylan answered.

"Good boy. Well, I'll be in the office if y'all need me."

"But you just got home. And Lee's cooking dinner. Aren't you going to eat with us?" Lavinia asked.

"No, Mama. I have some more work to do. I'll catch up with you later."

"Okay, sweetie." Amy Lynn didn't hear her. She'd already left the room.

Lavinia and Dylan sat in silence for a moment, then he spoke up. "She didn't even ask if you were okay, Nana."

Once again, surprising wisdom from a child.

"Yeah..." Lavinia took her glasses off and cleaned them with the bottom of her sweater. "Yeah, I noticed."

Chapter Six

Wednesday, October 17

"Vinny, if anyone can prove you're innocent, it's Neville McGrath," Lee said. "He's the best I've ever seen in a courtroom. He's always so confident."

"I sure hope so," Lavinia said. "The sooner I can put this mess behind me, the better."

"He's a good guy, too, and he hasn't lost a case since before he moved his practice here to Southport in ninety-eight."

"Sure, but how many has he defended? One per decade?"

"Trust me, Vinny. He's good."

The boys were at school, and so was Amy Lynn. Lee had the night shift, so he'd taken Lavinia to lunch at her favorite Mexican restaurant out near the Walmart. It was the first time Lavinia had eaten a meal alone with a man since Edgar died.

As they neared the attorney's office, Lavinia hoisted her giant bag into her lap, reached in, and dug around, feeling for something she couldn't find.

"Now, Lavinia, no pranks with Mr. McGrath. Okay?" Lee said, sounding suspicious.

"Of course. I know better than that. I'm just looking for a stick of gum to get rid of this salsa breath before we go in. My fajita had a lot of onions. *Oh*, but it was tasty." She finally located a pack and pulled it out. "Here, want some?"

Lee reached over and started to take a piece sticking up out of the pack.

"Oh, wait," Lavinia said, pulling it away just before he touched it. "You're driving. That might not be a good idea."

She put the electric zap gag pack back in the bag and pulled out the real gum.

"Here you go," she said, and she placed a stick of wintergreen in his open palm. He looked at her with a mix of amusement and disapproval.

"Thank you," he said dryly, with a hint of a smile. "I'm going to have to start inspecting that bag like the TSA."

She giggled like a schoolgirl.

Lee had always been so patient with her. Theirs was not the typical relationship between a mother-in-law and son-in-law, and she presumed it had to with the fact that his own mother died five years before he and Amy Lynn started dating. Lavinia had always tried, in some meager way, to fill the empty space in his heart. She knew all too well about voids.

Lavinia popped a piece of gum into her mouth. She'd been truthful about her original intent to banish bad breath, but when she found the fake pack first, she couldn't help herself.

Lee's tan hands gripped the wheel at ten and two until it was time to turn left by the Surf Shop onto Eighth Street. He steered the pickup truck into the graveled lot beside the office, next to the auto detailing shop and the hair salon. He parked and got out, then walked around the car to help Lavinia step down out of the giant truck. Getting out was considerably easier than getting in.

They entered the little house-turned-office, and the smell of a linen-scented candle greeted them. The candle flickered inside a jar on the receptionist's desk. Lavinia noticed the doilies on the accent tables, and, comparing them to the receptionists embroidered collar, deduced she was also the office decorator. The entire front room had a feminine touch.

"Hello, Officer Davenport!" Shirley greeted.

"Hi, Shirley," Lee said warmly.

"And you must be Mrs. Lewis." Shirley stood up from the desk and reached her hand toward Lavinia.

"Hello, dear," Lavinia said. She took Shirley's hand and squeezed gently in place of a shake. "You have a lovely office."

"Why, thank you! I try to keep it nice for our guests. When people come to visit Mr. McGrath, it's normally for, um…a not-so-happy occasion, so I want it to be as pleasant here as possible."

Lavinia gave her a *don't-I-know-it* nod.

"Let me tell him you're here," Shirley said.

Before Shirley reached the closed office door, Neville opened it and waved them in with his cane.

"Lee, it's good to see you," Neville said. He shook Lee's hand.

"You, too, Neville," Lee said. "I haven't seen you since I busted that guy with prescription pills who claimed he was a doctor. And you argued that he actually believed it."

"Not guilty by reason of insanity. Two months in a psych ward sure beat the alternative."

Shirley followed behind Lee and Lavinia with a laptop and a notepad. She took a seat in an armchair in the corner of the room while Lee guided Lavinia to one of the two chairs directly in front of the lawyer's giant cherrywood desk. Neville walked around the desk and sat down in the cushiony leather chair, reclining slightly. He propped one elbow on the armrest. The other arm was extended onto the desk with fingers drumming.

Neville had yet to acknowledge her. Lavinia wriggled in her seat, trying to get comfortable, positioning and repositioning her pocketbook on one side of her lap then the other before she settled on resting it at her feet. Neville didn't look away from Lee as they reminisced about past cases.

"Remember that time that you walked into the courtroom and found out your defendant had brought—"

"His pet hamster!"

Neville slapped the desk with his finger-tapping hand.

"I was so glad I was the arresting officer on that one. Do you know how many times I've told that story? They found him in contempt for the hamster, but you got the charges dropped on a technicality."

Laughter rang out on both sides of the desk, while Lavinia and Shirley sat, observing. The merry sound gradually dwindled to a breathy chuckle.

"Neville, thank you for taking time to talk to us about my mother-in-law's situation," he said. "We really can't believe this is happening to her."

"Well, I've already talked to Officer York, and I've read the report. She's the only person of interest right now. Normally, they wouldn't have moved so fast on something like this, but they have witnesses who saw her carry in a tray of cookies, it was the only one on the dessert table, and apparently someone tipped them off about a history of disruptive pranks at the retirement community."

Neville locked his fingers in front of his chest and leaned back in his chair. Lavinia sat in silence while Neville talked *about* her.

"But why haven't they charged her yet? If they thought a crime had been committed, they should have already charged her with something," Lee said.

"My guess is that they're trying to establish a motive."

"This is crazy! She didn't do anything wrong."

"Lee, you're too close to this to be objective. You know how investigations work. Let's say she did put toothpaste in those cookies. Best case, it was a prank gone wrong. She had no intention of harming anyone. They can, possibly, still charge her with a crime. If not, a civil suit is very likely. Now, if they dig up some kind of motive, then they will definitely be able to charge her for making that woman sick."

Lee slumped back in his seat and shook his head. "I know."

Lavinia reached into her bag and took out her phone. The icon for her word game had a little red circle on top. Her finger hovered over the screen. She wanted to find out if Wilmer had taken the lead.

Lee looked over at her. "Lavinia, you're awfully quiet. What are you thinking?" He looked at the phone in her hand then pointed to her bag with a small jerk of his head.

"*Hmmm?* Oh, are you talking to me?" She was flippant. "Well, I think...I think he's a hundred and two!"

She placed the phone screen-down on her leg and gave Lee a hard stare.

"Well, you're no spring chicken yourself!" Neville shot back.

"You're right about that," she said. Lavinia dropped the phone in her bag and shifted her weight in the seat. "Forgive me for being rude, Mr. McGrath. *Please.* But I didn't expect to meet someone as...as advanced in years as I am here today. I'm in a bit of a jam, you see, and I need someone with lots of energy to take up the cause of helping me out of it."

"*Energy?* Mrs. Lewis, you don't know anything about how much energy I have."

"Not as much as you used to, I bet. Same as me."

"Here's all I want to know. Did you do it?"

"Of course, I didn't do it! I wouldn't be here asking you to prove me innocent if I did it!" Lavinia wagged her pointer finger until she caught herself, then she tucked the offending finger away beneath her other hand and rested them in her lap in a more ladylike pose. "Mr. McGrath, I enjoy a good joke. I like having fun. And in the past, I have ruffled some feathers with my gags. But I've changed. I only play *little* jokes now."

Neville studied her for an uncomfortably long time before speaking again.

"When the officers searched your home on Sunday afternoon, they found this," he finally said. He opened a file on his desk and took out a photograph of Lavinia's bathroom. "They're running tests to determine if the brand of toothpaste found in the cookies is the same brand found in your bathroom."

"How did the police even *get* the cookies? Did they go through the trash?"

"When Mrs. Wisengood bit into one of the cookies and realized she'd possibly been exposed to fluoride, she wrapped it up and put it in her purse."

"Let me see that picture." Lavinia leaned forward and slid the picture on the desk toward herself, then glanced upward to see Neville studying her. The pictured showed an open bathroom drawer and a mostly empty tube of toothpaste that Lavinia didn't remember buying.

"Where did this come from?" she asked. "That's Dentashield toothpaste. I only buy MegaWhite brand, with Baking Soda."

She flashed her pearly whites at Neville and pointed to them. "MegaWhite keeps you clean and bright." Lavinia quoted the slogan from the commercials with her teeth still together. "Do you think I get a gleam like this with discount store *generic* toothpaste?"

Lee leaned forward and studied the picture with Lavinia.

"She's been set up, Neville," he said.

"It sounds that way," Neville admitted. "Although I can't imagine why."

"I know why, and I know who did it. My next-door neighbor has never liked me. He wanted to pull a prank that would get me kicked out. Wendy just happened to eat the wrong cookie at the wrong potluck."

"But, Vinny, what about one of the maids? It makes more sense that someone with access to your bathroom is responsible."

"Sure, it makes sense, if Gordon put 'em up to it." She sat up straight and put a hand over her mouth. "Oh, I hope it wasn't Francesca. That would break my heart. But that Kimberly does seem a little sketchy now that I think about it."

"Well, I do have some good news. I've already interviewed Mrs. Wisengood's doctor," Neville said.

"Neville, you're amazing," Lee said. "I called you just a couple days ago. I had no idea you had already jumped into an investigation."

"I like to strike while the iron is hot." He directed his gaze to Lavinia. "At any rate, the doctor painted a bit of a different picture for me than the officers apparently painted for you, Mrs. Lewis."

"You mean they lied to me?" Lavinia clutched her pearl necklace.

"I wouldn't say *lied*. But they may have been a little overzealous in their assessment of the situation. There aren't too many poisonings reported in Southport, and it's gotten people a little excited."

"Well, what's the good news?" Lee said.

"I believe you were told that Mrs. Wisengood had a severe allergic reaction to the fluoride found in the cookies that she ingested at the potluck." Lavinia nodded. "That's not entirely accurate," Neville said. "Mrs. Wisengood is apparently one of many people in the world with a fluoride *hypersensitivity*. She experiences fluoride toxicity at much lower levels of exposure than most people. Some people with her condition have skin reactions to the toxicity. In her case, like many, the symptoms are…um…varying levels of…gastric distress."

"So, it just made her sick? She'll be okay?"

"More than likely, she'll recover in a few days."

"Oh, I'm so glad she's not as bad off as they made it sound. I've been worried plumb sick about her."

"The officers *did* have reason to believe her illness is potentially life-threatening. They interviewed a doctor at Cypress Shores. Mrs. Wisengood had exaggerated her condition to him and a lot of other people. Also, the doctor at the hospital said the reaction was more severe than previous reactions because she was already dealing with a bout of"—he leaned forward and checked the notes in the file—"colitis."

"Oh, bless her heart. My mama had that. No fun at all." Lavinia shook her head from side to side, remembering her poor sick mama.

"So, Mrs. Lewis, you at least don't have to worry about a murder charge. But we still need to clear your name and help you get moved back into your home. That is,"—Neville leaned back in his chair and flashed a sly grin at Lavinia— "if you think I have enough energy to help you out."

Lavinia looked away. Her cheeks grew hot.

"Well, since Lee speaks so highly of you, and you've already put some time toward it, I guess I should give you a chance."

"Okay. Just give me some names of people to talk to at the retirement community. Some character witnesses. And I'll call the director for information on all the maids and other staff that have access to your place."

Lavinia rattled off names and Shirley scribbled them down on the notepad quickly.

"Now, tell me more about this next-door neighbor you believe framed you," Neville said. "I'll talk to him last."

***

Shirley came back inside from walking Lavinia and Lee to their truck and marched toward Neville's desk.

"What just happened?" she said. She folded her arms across her chest and squinted at him.

"*Huh?* What do you mean?"

"I *mean*, I thought you were going to tell Officer Davenport that you didn't want the case. You said you were gonna help him by sharing what you'd already found out, then let someone else take it from here. That's what you told me this morning."

Neville looked around the room, but there was no one there to answer for him. He shrugged his shoulders and put his hands in the air and back down again.

"Oh, yeah. Well…I changed my mind."

Chapter Seven

Lavinia napped on top of a Spiderman comforter, fully dressed including her watch, rings, pearls, and tasseled loafers. Her body sank into the fluffy softness of the bedding. Emotionally exhausted from the meeting with Mr. McGrath, her head and limbs bore the effects.

Sensing a presence in the room, Lavinia opened one eye as Dylan grabbed something off his dresser then tiptoed out and closed the door gently. She closed her eye again, then, as if it were an off switch, felt her body powering down.

Lavinia's mind raced, even in slumber, and the surreal took over. At a carnival, she stood beside a colorful carousel. On the first rotation, only two riders sat atop the polished horses—Edgar and Samuel. As the carousel spun around a second time, her husband and son were suddenly joined by her son-in-law and two grandsons. The grandsons were the only ones to wave. The rest held on to the brass pole and looked straight ahead, stalwart. The next time the carousel went around, three more men rode—two men in police uniforms and Wilmer. Though she'd never seen him, she was sure it was Wilmer.

The music slowed and the carousel slowed with it. It spun around one last time to show a new man—Neville McGrath, only he was sitting on a bench seat instead of mounted on a horse, and he was smiling, a cat-who-ate-the-canary smile, looking straight at her, his wavy gray hair tousled slightly.

Lavinia smiled back in the dream, then someone she couldn't see took her by the arm and led her away. Lavinia kept her gaze locked on Mr. McGrath as she walked, until the carousel disappeared in a thick fog. She found herself standing in line at a booth, where people took turns throwing cream pies at someone sitting in a wooden chair. When the seated person wiped the cream away with a white shirt sleeve, she saw it was Marvin Mickle, the director of Cypress Shores. He motioned for her to take his seat, and she did so without question. Lavinia settled into the chair, and someone launched a pie at her. She didn't see who it was at first, because the thick fog rolled in and concealed the face of the thrower. The pie traveled in slow motion through the air, giving Lavinia time to anticipate the impact. When it was halfway to her, the fog cleared, revealing the thrower as Wendy Wisengood. Lavinia looked forward to the taste of the whipped cream, but when it smacked her face and she licked her lips, the fluffy substance had the same flavor as MegaWhite toothpaste.

Lavinia opened her eyes and stared at rows of red and white airplanes lining blue walls.

That's not my gardenia wallpaper.

Her head felt like a hundred-pound bowling ball, but she made it turn enough to see a swing set outside through the window beside her, instead of her boxwoods and cherub fountain.

This isn't my bedroom. This isn't my house. Where am I?

The moment she realized where she was, Amy Lynn opened the door. An overwhelming smell of baby powder came into the bedroom with her.

"Mother! Why?" Amy Lynn yelled.

Lavinia sat up too quickly. Her daughter stood tapping her foot ineffectively on the carpeted floor, while Lavinia waited for the vertigo to subside.

"Mother!" Amy Lynn yelled again when Lavinia looked at

her squarely.

Despite the lingering dizziness and hint of sleepy confusion, Lavinia burst out laughing. She couldn't help herself. The top of Amy Lynn's head looked like a yeti. Amy Lynn shook her body like a wet St. Bernard, only to create a cloud of floating powder above her head, and Lavinia laughed even harder.

"What if I had been running late for work? What if Lee had used the hairdryer instead of me, to dry a spot on his uniform? And you made *him* late for work, or he had to leave for an emergency covered in baby powder? Do you ever stop and think about what trouble you could cause?"

Lavinia stopped laughing.

"I'm sorry, dear. It was just a joke. Maybe I did use a little too much powder in the hairdryer, though."

"It's all too much, Mama! All your jokes are too much! You're staying here because a prank of yours went wrong and has landed you in serious trouble, but you haven't learned anything at all from it."

"Now, wait a minute!" Lavinia's indignation pushed her to jump out of bed with the agility of someone twenty years younger. "First of all, I am still your mother. And I deserve a little more respect." She hadn't heard that voice come out of her in years. "Second of all, that wasn't my prank. I've told you that."

"I know, Mama. But it seems a little far-fetched that someone swapped out your tray of cookies for the ones that made somebody sick."

"*Far-fetched?* You're standing there calling me a liar. How can you say that?"

"Look, I know you didn't put toothpaste in cookies trying to hurt anybody. I don't think that for a second. But when you look at the facts…"

"I can't believe what I'm hearing."

"Mama, it was your tray. It came from your house."

Lavinia's mouth gaped.

"Why, I never." She sat back down on the edge of the bed, somewhere between needing smelling salts and needing someone to restrain her from slapping her own daughter.

Amy Lynn sighed, then with both hands, rubbed her hair vigorously to shake the powder free. Lavinia didn't laugh at the cloud this time.

"Ever since Daddy died, you've been different," Amy Lynn said. "Just out of control. And then Lucas got that stupid book of pranks at the library, and you two started cooking up all kinds of gags together. It was cute at first, but the schemes are getting old."

"Shenanigans," Lavinia interrupted. She'd managed to tuck her hurt and anger away neatly for the moment.

"What?"

"You should say, 'The she-*nana*-gans are getting old.' Because I'm a nana, *get it?* Isn't that clever? Dylan came up with it. He's such a smart boy." She pushed against the cuticle on her ring finger with her thumbnail.

"Mama, you're not listening."

"I don't think *you're* listening. You really think I started tryin' to make people laugh and to enjoy life more just because I'm missin' your daddy? I do miss him something terrible. Every single day." Her volume and pitch rose and fell like the waves of the ocean. "But that's not why I enjoy a good joke, darlin', and I don't play pranks because of some book. It's like you don't know me at all, Amy Lynn."

"Do you have a different explanation? You went from a straitlaced debutante to some kind of Bozo the Clown wannabe. You've taken the reputation Daddy spent his life building, and you've thrown it out the window." Her hands waved in the air like a losing coach on the sidelines. "He was a respectable businessman, a pillar of the community, and his legacy deserves better than for his widow to be running around acting like a teenage boy with too much free time."

Lavinia took every emotional blow like a boxer paid to take a dive.

The hands Amy Lynn had raised in the air came down slowly and her expression softened. Her tone was markedly more tender. "Mama, the therapists told us there might be some long-term...changes after the stroke. And if that's what this is, I understand that you can't help it. But I hope you'll try."

Amy Lynn couldn't have said anything worse. It was the first time she'd accused her of having lost her faculties.

"That's...*not*...it." Lavinia's top teeth pressed tightly into the bottom ones.

"But, Mama...how would you know?"

Lavinia sat down on the bed again, in slow motion. She hadn't considered it. If, in fact, she wasn't normal, because of side effects from the stroke, she could be totally oblivious to the fact for the same reason.

"Just stop with the pranks, please, Mama. At least while you're here. I don't have time for them." She turned her back on her mother, but Lavinia's words stopped her.

"You don't seem to have time for much of anything. Not your husband or kids, not for me, not for church."

"I spend plenty of quality time with Lee and the boys. And where do you get off bringing up church? When's the last time you went to church?"

"I go to chapel at Cypress Shores on occasion," Lavinia said. She fidgeted with her pearls. Her voice got quieter. "I need to do better, sure, but so do you. Dylan prayed a beautiful prayer for me, Amy Lynn." She smoothed out the rough edges of her tone with even more sincerity. "His praying made me think about how I've neglected my faith. And, honey, we both need to make more time for what matters."

Amy Lynn turned her back and slammed the door as she left the room.

Lavinia swallowed hard and stood, with significant effort. She shuffled to the mirror that hung above Dylan's dresser, then she examined her distraught persona and replaced it with her Scarlett face.

"Speaking of making time," she said, with her head held high, "what time is it? I guess I should leave, too. I don't want to be late meeting Sylvia and Henry for dinner."

***

"So, does everybody and their brother know why I left Cypress Shores? Please pass the butter," Lavinia said.

Henry obeyed, and Lavinia peeled back the foil lid on the little container. Hushpuppies were always better with butter.

"I didn't tell nobody, Lavinia," Sylvia said. "I promise I didn't."

Lavinia questioned the answer with her expression.

"What?" Sylvia said defensively. "You're my best friend, besides Henry. I'm not gonna run around telling people all your misfortune."

"And I sure didn't either. Can you hand me the salt?" said Henry. He doctored his baked potato with plenty of salt, pepper, butter, and sour cream. Steam from the foil-wrapped vegetable rose up and fogged his glasses.

Henry and Sylvia were part of that strange phenomenon— married people who start to look alike over time—and the resemblance grew stronger as the years passed. He had the same squatty neck and round face of his wife but sported a crew cut.

"But they all know, *don't they?*" Lavinia said.

"Well, I don't think *everybody* knows," Sylvia said. "You know how it is. People are so wrapped up in themselves they've barely got time to notice who's there and who's not, much less to care why somebody mighta left."

"You oughta be grateful that most of us aren't as savvy on those smartphones as you are, Lavinia," Henry said. "If everybody at Cypress Shores used their high-tech gadgets for much more than callin', word would get around a lot quicker."

Lavinia saw right through it, but her friends were kind to deal with her so carefully.

The short drive over the bridge from Southport to her favorite seafood restaurant on Oak Island had given her a chance to clear her mind. Now here she was filling it up again, worried about what her neighbors, or rather, former neighbors, thought.

"Well, it doesn't matter anyway, does it?" Lavinia shifted focus as she started in on the second half of a giant piece of flounder. "What's really important is, have you heard any update on Wendy?"

"As a matter of fact, I did. I've jus' been waitin' to tell ya," Sylvia answered. Her tone was gossipy with a hint of regret. "Martha Minotti went to see her yesterday, and she told me that Wendy swears up and down that she's a'havin' to stay in the hospital because of fluoride poisonin'."

"Oh, my. I guess that's not good for me, but if she's well enough to carry on a conversation, that *is* good to hear."

"Oh, you bet she is. But git this. A nurse came, and while Martha was waitin' out in the hall, she overheard her talkin' to Wendy about her bad colitis spell, nothin' more. Said the nurse told her she hoped she wouldn't have to come back a third time with this same problem."

"I don't get it, Sylvia," Lavinia said. "If toothpaste is only a small part of what made her sick in the first place, why are they houndin' me over it so?"

"I don't know, honey. But Wendy has a lot of money. She's one of the hospital's largest donors. Her first cousin sits on the city council. That's why she moved down here, to be close to some cousins. She practically paid for the mayor's re-election." Sylvia punctuated each statement in the air with her fork. "If she wants it to be fluoride poisonin', that's what it'll be."

Lavinia put down her fork and locked her fingers on the edge of the table, studying their lines. The low-hanging light fixture above the table cast a glint off her perfectly polished mauve fingernails and the gold band she still wore on her left hand.

"I get it that she's mad at me for playing a prank." Lavinia hung her head for a moment, then looked at her friends again. "But if it didn't really hurt her, why take it this far? It was just a joke."

Both Henry and Sylvia's faces changed at the same time, then they looked at each other and back to her.

"Lavinia?" Sylvia said, leaning forward.

Lavinia didn't know how or if she was supposed to respond. She picked up her fork and looked at Sylvia, letting some silence pass. "What dear?" she finally said.

"You just talked like...like you did it. Like you did put toothpaste in them Oreos."

"What? No, I didn't say that."

The waitress came to refill their tea glasses, and they all sat quietly, waiting for her to finish and leave.

"You said Wendy is mad at you for playing a prank," Henry said when the waitress was gone.

"I did?"

"Yeah, honey. You did," Sylvia said.

Lavinia put her fork down again, for the last time, and put her hands palms-down on the table. She drew a deep breath, and her eyes searched the empty space between her and Sylvia and Henry.

"Well, I meant…what I meant to say was…I meant she's mad at me because she *thinks* I played a prank. She *thinks* I did. You know I didn't *actually* do it! Not this time." She relaxed and focused on her friends again.

"Okay, Lavinia. We understand," Sylvia said.

"When Marvin told me to tone it down, I toned it down. No big jokes. Just harmless gags. Harmless. Like with you the other day, Sylvia. The snake. And like getting you with that fake rat in your golf cart, Henry. It's all silly. I know it. But I'm not hurtin' anybody."

Sylvia and Henry took turns nodding at Lavinia. Each vertical bob of their heads reminded her that they were on her side.

Lavinia changed the subject, telling them about meeting Neville McGrath and how Lee assured her he could help.

"He's pretty sharp, I tell you. Lee said he's never lost a case. I gave him your names as character witnesses. He'll probably be callin' soon." Lavinia dipped another hushpuppy in the butter and used it to point across the table playfully at her friends. "Now y'all better not make me sound too bad. I'm not askin' you to lie, but I need all the help I can get."

"You know we'll help you any way we can, Lavinia," Sylvia said.

"Yeah, oh, yeah. Surely, we will. Any way at all," Henry said.

Lavinia popped the rest of the hushpuppy into her mouth and reached across the table. She patted both of them on the hand, with a grateful smile.

"It sure is nice to have good friends like you. It sure is nice."

***

By the time she was back at her daughter and son-in-law's

house and had turned in for the night beneath the Spiderman comforter in Dylan's room, Lavinia had nearly pushed the fight with Amy Lynn out of her mind. She nestled into the pillow and decided to get a good night's sleep by pretending she was back in Wilson with Edgar, in their old house, in their old bed, and there had never been any pranks, or Cypress Shores, or Wendy Wisengood.

To her conscious mind, Lavinia's method worked, but the next morning, the only memory from her dreams was one in which she ate Oreo after Oreo, mountains of them, until she threw up.

Chapter Eight

Thursday, October 18

"You have a lovely home here, Mr. and Mrs. Baxter."

Sylvia and Henry, in lockstep, led Neville from the square of foyer and around the sofa that separated the living room and the breakfast nook.

"Thank you," they said in unison.

"Have you ever considered living in a retirement community, Mr. McGrath?" Sylvia said. She sat down on the flowery sofa beside her husband and bounced a few times to get situated. Sylvia was fidgety from the start. Overly chatty and giggly at their introduction. "It's just a dream come true, really it is. I can't say enough good things about Cypress Shores and the staff. It is top notch. Just a really nice place to be."

"Well, no, I've never considered a retirement community," Neville said. He took the chair Sylvia offered across from them. An oak coffee table sat between them. On it, a burning candle that filled the room with the tempting smells of Neville's childhood home when his mother would bake pies. The scent of pumpkin, nutmeg, and sugar overwhelmed him.

"So much better than having a big house to worry about and a yard to take care of," Sylvia said.

"Oh, for sure," Henry agreed.

"The only problem is that they feed us too good around here. But I guess you can tell that, can't you?" Sylvia let out a big laugh. She slapped Henry on the leg, and he joined in the laughter.

Neville smiled politely, settled back into the chair, and crossed his feet at the ankles. Henry and Sylvia seemed none too quick to get down to business. He might as well get comfortable. He surveyed the room and the adjoining breakfast nook. Cypress Shores did offer nice homes, and the Baxters had given theirs a decidedly welcoming country feel. A garland of fall leaves was draped across the mantle. A realistic plastic pumpkin adorned the dining table.

"And there's always something to do at Senior Central. More card games and craft times than you can shake a stick at. That's fer sure!" Sylvia said. "Sometimes I'm almost *too* busy. This retirement life is like a job of its own kind."

Neville's ears perked up. Retirement being like a job was a strange concept. At least they weren't sitting around letting themselves rot. Still, cards and crafts sounded like summer camp activities for children, not a meaningful use of time for adults.

"I worked real estate when I was in the business world," Sylvia said. "Did real well with land. Mostly Christmas tree farms."

"Interesting," Neville said.

"She was good," Henry praised his wife. "And now, two of our four children sell real estate like their mama did. I had my own business as an accountant, but they didn't want to follow in my footsteps."

"Seems like a lifetime ago, now. Do you have any plans of retiring soon, Mr. McGrath? If you don't mind me asking," Sylvia said.

"I...uh...well, I...I don't...no. No, I don't have any plans to retire." Neville locked his fingers and twiddled his thumbs. "I enjoy my work. I see no reason to give it up."

"You know who you remind me of?" Sylvia changed the

subject, saving Neville from the question he'd been struggling to answer for months. "I think you're a regular Ben Matlock," she said. "You know he was raised up not too far from me?"

"Ben Matlock?"

"No, silly! Andy Griffith." It took Neville a moment to make the connection. "You look a lot like him, too. Kind of a mix between him and that Hal Holbrook. You know, he played a lawyer on *Designing Women.* Did you ever see that show?"

"Yes, I believe I did."

"You remind me so much of them two lawyers. Except, they both had a southern accent and you...well, you don't. You're not from around here, are you?"

"No. But I've lived here quite a while."

"Do you live close by?" Henry said.

"I have an apartment not too far away—"

"Oh, that's nice. Apartments are nice. Aren't they nice, Henry?" Sylvia said.

"Oh, yes," Henry said.

The interview was not going at all like Neville had planned. He decided to let them chat for a minute more, to be cordial, then he would take charge of the conversation.

"We love our little condo, or townhouse, or whatever you call it here," Sylvia said.

"Villa," Henry said.

"That's right. *Villa.* Where do they come up with these fancy words? I'd just call it a little house if it was me. But whatever it's called, it's home now. And we love living so close to Lavinia," Sylvia said.

"Oh, yes, yes. She's terrific," Henry said.

Now they were getting somewhere. Neville jumped in while he had the chance.

"Yes, Mrs. Lewis said you are good friends to her. I'm glad

you were willing to talk to me about her case." He sat up straight then leaned forward in the cushy armchair. "If she's charged, and if this goes to trial, she's going to need excellent character witnesses. Basically, people who can vouch that she's not a criminal. People other than her relatives who can speak to her good character."

"Well, Lavinia's a character all right," Henry said. "This one time—"

Sylvia shot him a *shut up* look, and he quickly pursed his lips.

"It's okay," Neville said. "I want to hear it all. Feel free to share as much about Mrs. Lewis as you can. I'm not the judge."

Henry looked at Sylvia for permission. She nodded, but he must not have trusted it. He waited for a second nod from his wife then continued.

"She keeps things lively, that's all," Henry said. "It's a good thing. She makes us all feel young again."

Neville scooted forward in the chair to hear better. As he did, both knees cracked like a wishbone after Thanksgiving dinner. He motioned for Henry to go on with his story.

"This one time at the swimming pool, on a really crowded day—I think it was the fourth of July last year—she tried to convince everyone that maintenance had put some chemical in the water that would turn it a different color if somebody went to the bathroom in the pool. Of course, nobody believed her. But she had a bottle of red food coloring and"—Henry snorted before he could finish the story—"she kept sneaking up on people and hollering 'See! I told you!'"

Neville smiled in spite of himself.

"Oh, that was funny," Sylvia said. "And did you know that stuff isn't even real? That's a myth. There's no such chemical."

"I didn't know that," Neville said.

"Oh, gracious, where are my manners? Mr. McGrath, can I

get you something to drink? I just made a gallon of sweet tea. Or, would you like some water?" Sylvia said.

"Water would be good. Thank you."

Sylvia hoisted herself off the sofa and waddled to the kitchen, in sight of the living room.

"Tell me, Mrs. Baxter—" Neville said.

"Please, call me Sylvia."

"Sylvia, does Mrs. Lewis have lots of friends here at Cypress Shores?"

She made her way back to her guest and handed him a cold bottle of water, and she brought a glass of sweet tea to Henry, even though he hadn't asked for one.

"She has lots of people who are friendly to her," Sylvia said, "but not too many close friends like me and Henry. She has pockets here and there."

"And do you think there's any certain reason for that?"

Sylvia dropped herself back onto the sofa.

"Mr. McGrath, I promise you that Lavinia is a good woman. She's a terrific friend, and a good mama, and goodness gracious, does she love those grandsons. But I have to admit, she's not everybody's cup of tea."

"How so?"

"Lavinia plays by her own set of rules, that's all. And they're kind of all over the place. Like…she sticks to no white after Labor Day, except if it's above seventy-five degrees outside. Yet she'll jump right in a swimming pool after eating. Best I know, she always makes her bed. But she never writes thank you notes unless the gift came in the mail. She says when someone hands you a gift and you thank 'em to their face, there's no reason to do it again."

Neville grew impatient. "All that is very interesting, Sylvia, but I'm not sure it helps the investigation."

"I guess what I'm trying to say is, she's too lax for the stuffy crowd and too stuffy for the lax crowd. She's got money, no doubt. But she's down-to-earth, not hoity-toity like some around here. And she don't put on airs for nobody. She speaks her mind more often than some, but never to be hurtful. Her intentions are always good."

"It seems you know her very well."

"I like to think I do. She's a dear friend."

"So, in your mind, there's no way she intentionally hurt Wendy Wisengood by putting toothpaste in the cookies she brought to the potluck?"

"Why, heavens no! Never! Not in a million years!"

"And in your mind, is there any way she could be lying about playing the joke, even if she didn't mean to hurt anyone?"

"Well...I don't think so." Sylvia hesitated. "I mean, *no*, I know she wouldn't lie."

Neville studied how she rocked forward and backward on the sofa, her hands clasped together, making a sling for her substantial belly. He played an old lawyer trick, staying completely silent without breaking eye contact with Sylvia, until she got so uncomfortable that she elaborated without even being asked for more details.

"I just mean that, Lavinia's like the rest of us around here. She's not as young as she used to be. And...well, if she ever gives you any wrong information, it won't be because she's lying. She forgets sometimes. Normal stuff. I do it, too."

"Of course," Neville said. "I understand."

They talked for another twenty minutes, the conversation eventually landing on Gordon Proctor. "So, do you agree with Lavinia's theory that Gordon framed Lavinia to get her kicked out?"

"I think it's possible," Sylvia said. "He does come off mean. But then again"—she paused in thought—"I had almost decided maybe ol' Gordon was cross with Lavinia because he likes her. To get her attention, you know. So, I'm not sure what to think." She had finally relaxed and spoke freely to Neville without rambling, but Neville wanted to know more about this new topic.

"And if that's the case, that he has feelings for Mrs. Lewis, it would be unrequited?"

"Oh, law, yes. Lavinia wouldn't look twice at Gordon Proctor. Besides, she's still grieving her husband. It's been two years, but I know she still grieves."

"I see."

The interview drew to a close, but not before Neville had declined a glass of tea for the second time. He shook both of their hands and left the villa, leaving his truck in their driveway to find his next destination on foot.

Neville knocked on two more doors in the community, looking for friends to vouch for his client. No one was at home either place, so he left a card in the doors. What he lacked for in signage at his office, he made up for with business cards. They were of the highest quality cardstock, thick and glossy with raised lettering. Such a professional presentation usually payed off. Even back in the early days, he splurged on the nicest cards, though it meant buying one small box at a time. Quality over quantity.

At Gordon Proctor's residence, Neville knocked, waited, then knocked again. He was about to leave a business card in Mr. Proctor's door, too, when it finally opened.

"Hello, sir," Neville said. "I—"

"Are you lost?" Gordon snarled.

"*Lost?* No, I'm here—"

"The home's back that way if you've wandered off. Though you'd be dressed pretty sharply for one of those blank slates."

"Mr. Proctor, my name is Neville McGrath. I'm an attorney representing Lavinia Lewis."

Gordon sized him up.

"I've already talked to the police."

"Well, I wondered if you'd take a minute to tell me about what kind of neighbor Mrs. Lewis is. That's all."

Gordon's wrinkly face wrinkled more.

"What kind of neighbor is she? An annoying one. That's what kind she is."

"So, you're glad she's gone then? You were happy to see her get kicked out of Cypress Shores?"

"I don't know if I'd say that." Gordon crossed his arms. His face softened the slightest bit. "It's been considerably calmer around here, though. I don't have to worry about any more plastic flamingos in my yard." He gestured to a pair of the bright pink painted birds standing, facing each other on the small square of lawn between his house and the street. Neville turned to see them and felt a sharp pain run from his hip down his leg. His sciatica was acting up again.

"So those were her doing, huh?" Neville said, wincing.

"Well it sure wasn't mine."

"Maybe she was only trying to make you smile?" Neville surprised himself with the question.

"She did it to aggravate me. And it worked."

It was obvious that Mr. Proctor had no intention of inviting him inside.

"If you don't like them, why'd you leave them out there?" Neville said.

"Huh? Well, I just did." His tone was thick with resentment. "Haven't had time to throw them in the trash yet."

Neville gave him the same long, silent stare he'd used on Sylvia.

"Look, I told you, I've already talked to the police!" He grabbed the door as if to slam it but held it still. He was bluffing. Neville looked down at the legal pad in his hand, pretending to read his notes as he often did when he was formulating his next move. But Neville decided he didn't feel like pushing the man, and he was tired of standing.

"I'm sorry to have bothered you, Mr. Proctor. Maybe we can speak another time."

Neville turned to walk down the driveway. He was halfway to the decorative lamp post on the left and the mailbox on the right when Gordon called after him.

"Hold on a second. You look familiar. Do I know you from somewhere?"

Neville stopped and pivoted in a slow shuffle step.

"I don't think so, Mr. Proctor. Unless you've ever been in trouble with the law or know someone who has."

Gordon's disposition returned to its original state, face contorted in disgust. He stepped back into his villa and slammed the door. Just then, Henry and Sylvia pulled up to the curb in their golf cart. Sylvia was at the wheel.

"Hello, again!" she said. "We're on our way to dinner. Is there anywhere else in the neighborhood we can take you?"

"No, thank you. I think I'm done for today. I'm headed home."

"Okay, then. Again, it was nice to meet you. And you remember now, if you ever do decide to call it quits with that lawyerin' business, there'd be plenty of things to keep you busy here at Cypress Shores."

"I'll keep that in mind."

Sylvia and Henry said goodbye and waved as Sylvia turned the cart around in the middle of the street and headed the other direction. Neville stepped off the curb and began walking, leaning heavily on his cane. With every step, the pain in his knees grew from a minor annoyance to a nearly intolerable obstacle, and he regretted not asking for a ride back to his truck.

Chapter Nine

Neville poured himself a drink, a strong one. The familiar smell of the clear liquid rose to his sinuses and alerted his brain that rest was coming. He loosened his tie with one hand and picked up the short, diamond cut drinking glass with the other. One tiny sip before setting the glass back on the counter and reaching into the cabinet above him. Neville brought down a plastic box full of bottles he wished he could live without. He struggled to open the first one. *Stupid childproof caps.* He sat each pill on the stovetop while he replaced the caps and put the bottles back into the box. One, two, three, four. Blood pressure, thyroid, calcium, pain. He scooped them all up, popped them in his mouth, and washed them down with a different kind of medicine, though the labels on the pill bottles recommended against it.

One heavy foot in front of the other, he made his way to the living room. He plopped down on the end of the sofa, sloshing a drop of his drink onto his shirt, and a giant puff of dust and cat hair escaped from the cushions and floated into a beam of late-evening sun coming from the front window. He leaned his head back against the plush couch and let his lids blanket his weary blue eyes for half a minute.

I didn't even walk that far today.

Neville forced his head forward thirty degrees and reached for a stack of file folders on the side table. There were three—his current clients. *A traffic ticket for Mr. Green, a DUI for Miss Perkins, Simple Assault for Mrs. Lewis.* He opened Lavinia's file and looked over the police report again, there with the retainer check from Lee that he had yet to deposit. He'd not even mentioned the word *assault* in front of her in his office. He hoped he could help clear her name before any formal charges were ever filed.

Alibi hopped up in Neville's lap and walked across the folder, shuffling the papers with his paws. The flat-faced animal purred loudly, begging for attention. Neville sat the drink down on the table so he could pet him. Just a few minutes was enough, and Alibi reclaimed his favorite spot on the back of the chair.

The sun set lower in the sky. Neville reached to switch on the lamp beside him. He looked at the photograph of Lavinia's bathroom in the file. One lonely toothbrush, like his.

Neville's cell phone rang loudly, like an alarm bell to hinder his thoughts. He looked at the display. Maine was on the line.

"Hello, Donald," he said.

"Hi, Uncle. How've you been? You didn't return my call. I was starting to worry."

"Well, you know that if you ever can't reach me, you can call Shirley to check. But if I keel over, you'll be the first she calls anyway."

"Uncle!" Donald said.

"You know it's true."

"I know, and I'm glad you have Shirley and Chuck. It would be sad to be there with no family at all. But hey—" Donald seized his chance—"if you come live with me, you'll be with real family. And we can go fishing every day."

"Donald, I live on the coast. I have the perfect place to go fishing here."

"Yeah, if you weren't working all the time. When's the last time you took a day off to relax?"

Neville let out a noise between a huff and a sigh.

"Besides, if you're here with me," Donald said, "it'll be a lot easier for your only nephew to get to your inheritance when you do kick the bucket."

That's what Neville needed to hear. It was much easier when things weren't so emotional.

"Yeah, yeah, yeah. I know."

"I'm glad you can take a joke, Uncle. I know I've been hounding you a lot lately about moving. The truth is, as much as I love this place, it gets pretty lonely up here."

There they were, back to emotional again.

"I think having you here would be good for both of us," Donald said.

"I know, son, but what if you decide to find a woman you'd like to live with instead of a crochety old uncle? You'd throw me out on my ear, and I'd have nowhere to go."

"C'mon, uncle. You know better. I've been divorced twice. I'm not trying that again." Donald cleared his throat and his voice turned solemn. "Uncle Neville, the cabin is great...really...but, out here away from town, by myself, it isn't quite what I thought it would be. I'm thinking about selling."

"*Selling?* You can't be serious. I thought it was your dream."

"It was, it was. It is. But I didn't think it all through. A person can only spend so much time in the woods by themselves before they start to go a little stir crazy. And I'm so far away from things. I don't get out very much. But if you decide to move up here, I think it would be different. We could keep each other company."

"I didn't know it meant so much to you that I come. I thought you were just worried about me being alone down here." Though Neville had no children of his own, a feeling of paternal responsibility gripped his heart. Donald was fifty-eight, but he still needed someone, and Neville seemed to be his only option.

"Well, that's part of it, too," Donald said. "I do worry about you. Listen, I'm not trying to guilt-trip you. I mean it. I'm a big boy. I can manage on my own. If you want to come, great. If you don't, well..."—his volume dropped—"I'm going to list the property by the end of November. Look for something closer to town. Maybe while I'm looking, I can come visit you. I might even stay for Christmas." Donald laughed, obviously to lighten the mood.

"Okay, buddy. I'm still considering it. I just can't give you an answer yet."

"I understand. How 'bout this? I won't mention it anymore. You let me know when you decide, but I won't talk about it again."

Neville was off the hook for an answer, but nonetheless guilt stricken.

"That'll be good, Donald. But I promise to let you know something soon."

"Well, how's things? Any good cases?" Just like that, the subject was dropped.

"Yeah, I've got one that's pretty interesting. Not quite like anything else I've ever done before. Definitely one of my most unique clients, too."

He wanted to talk about it, to tell Donald about Lavinia and about Wendy's unique allergy. But Donald didn't ask.

"Just make sure you're not working too hard. Remember, you're eighty years old. Nobody would blame you for taking it easy for a while."

"That's what I'm afraid of, Donald—taking it easy. If I let the old motor idle, it might never rev back up again."

When Neville ended the call, he went to the kitchen to pour another drink, taking Lavinia's folder with him. He hoisted himself into the tall chair at the bistro-style table, pausing for a moment. Sciatic nerve pain again. The table was made for a patio, but it was the only one he could find that was small enough for his apartment.

He only needed room for one plate anyway.

He looked over the notes from his call with the officer earlier that afternoon, straining to read his own scribble. If only he could squint hard enough to change the words on the paper to something better.

I think I'll call and give her the news.

Only a half ring later he heard her voice.

"Hello-o."

"Hello, Mrs. Lewis. This is Neville McGrath. You certainly answered the phone quickly. Did you know it was me?"

That sounded conceited. I didn't mean it that way.

"Oh, no. I had the phone in my hand. I was playing a word game with my friend Wilmer. He's up by thirty-five points."

"I'm sorry to interrupt your game," he said, chuckling under his breath, "but I do have some news about your case."

"Already?" Lavinia breathed loudly into the phone. "Okay. I'm ready to hear it."

"The good news is, I think you have some very good character witnesses, if it comes to that. We're ahead of the game there."

"Sylvia and Henry said they enjoyed meeting you. Aren't they just the best?"

"Very nice people," he agreed.

"Yes, I do have good friends at Cypress Shores. Okay, Mr. McGrath, go ahead and tell me the rest. Is there bad news?"

The inside of Neville's mouth was a desert. He absentmindedly raised his glass, forgetting it wasn't water, and took a too-big drink. He coughed the liquid down and cleared his throat with an unpleasant, guttural sound before he could move the phone away.

"Are you okay, Mr. McGrath?" Lavinia said. Her voice was maternal, comforting, like a bandage on a wound or a child's stuffed bear in the dark.

"Excuse me, Mrs. Lewis. Excuse me," he said, coughing and embarrassed. "Yes, I'm fine." He held the phone away and coughed some more. "Anyway…a lab report came back, a lot sooner than I expected."

"And?"

Neville drummed his fingers on the metal tabletop.

"The toothpaste in the cookies was the same kind found at your house."

"Oh, dear." The line went quiet.

"Lavinia,"—he surprised himself using her first name without permission—"I don't want you to worry about this. They still can't prove anything. Lots of people use that brand of toothpaste."

"I didn't even buy it." Her voice trailed off.

"I did have them run fingerprints on the tube, in hopes of showing that someone planted it there, if you hadn't touched it."

"Let me guess. I touched it, didn't I?"

"There was only one tube of toothpaste in the drawer. If someone switched your regular brand, you probably didn't notice."

Neville was struck by the oddity of his own words. If they were true, it had to be the first time in history someone had planted toothpaste in order to implicate someone else in a crime.

"Well, whaddaya know. I guess generic does work as well as the leading brand."

Neville chuckled again, then he realized Lavinia hadn't meant to be funny.

"Lavinia, I believe that you didn't play the prank, or even buy the toothpaste. So, I see two angles here. Either someone was trying to get you kicked out of Cypress Shores as you suspect, or someone really was trying to hurt Mrs. Wisengood and you made the perfect fall guy, um…fall girl…fall woman." Awkward silence.

"One more thing. Gordon Proctor wouldn't talk to me, so I'll have to find a different approach."

"I'm not surprised, the weasel. If you ask me, that proves he's got something to hide. So, what's next?"

"I think it might help for me to get to know you a little better, ask some more questions."

"Now?"

"Oh, no. It's getting late, and I should let you get back to your word game."

Alibi jumped to the empty chair then onto the table. He walked to Neville and began rubbing against his shoulder over and over like an addict looking for a fix. Fine hairs stuck to Neville's shirt, and some floated down to the tabletop.

"Okay, would you like me to come to your office tomorrow?"

"Actually, I was thinking of a more relaxed atmosphere. Maybe we should discuss your case...over a meal."

"Oh...well...okay."

Neville turned in his chair to avoid the distracting cat. He held his hand out lazily as an attempt to appease him. Alibi ran his body underneath Neville's extended hand twice, then hopped down from the table, bored with the counterfeit attention.

"Will tomorrow night work for you?" Neville said. "I haven't been to The Provision Company in a while. It's my favorite. Meet me there at seven?"

"Oh, that's my favorite place, too." She hesitated. "Okay, Neville. I'll meet you there."

"Um...one more thing. I guess my cell number came up on your display. Just call that number if anything comes up, and feel free to call anytime...if you need me."

She agreed and said good night, and Neville flipped the phone shut, feeling accomplished. But the feeling was quickly replaced by a less pleasant emotion.

"What did I just do, Alibi?" Neville said. "What did I just do?"

Chapter Ten

Friday, October 19

Neville stood in the gravel parking lot. A dirt drive separated the lot and the restaurant. From the outside, the Southport landmark was little to be desired, although it adorned many a postcard and visitor guide. The entrance—a swinging, wooden framed screen door—would fit in fine on a farmhouse back porch. To the right of it, outside, were the doors to the bathrooms. Most noticeable about the façade was the giant, rectangle sign on top, with a beautiful replica of a marlin mounted to the front.

The appeal of The Provision Company was three-fold, starting with the magnificent view that awaited patrons once inside. The alfresco dining area sat on top of the Old Yacht Basin, and many customers arrived by boat, pulling right up to the dock on the back side of the building. The other draws were a variety of deep-fried delicacies, fresher than fresh seafood, and a *Cheers*-like atmosphere that always made you want to stay a little bit longer.

The sun was almost gone from the sky. Only a faint glimmer illuminated the water. Neville looked at his watch. *6:59*. Then he looked down at his suit.

Maybe it's too formal. But it is a business meeting. A business meeting over food. Just another client. Why shouldn't I dress professionally? But what if she thinks I dressed up because it's a date? Why would she think it's a date?

How many dates had he been on in the last sixty years? The lines blurred so often, between business and friendship and something more. It was hard to identify the primary intent of every meal or outing he'd shared with a member of the opposite sex, but for certain, the number of actual dates since his late teens was few. He'd made sure to keep it that way.

At exactly seven o'clock, Lavinia's Buick pulled into the lot and parked askew beside Neville's pickup.

"Good evening," Neville said as Lavinia opened the car door. *Good evening? Who says good evening?* he thought.

Lavinia swung one leg then the other out of car. With both feet firmly on the ground, she pushed herself up slowly with both hands on the car seat, then reached back in for the giant pocketbook.

"Hello there, Mr. McGrath," she said. Her accent was charmingly, over-the-top southern.

She looked back at the Buick. There were no lines by which to gauge it, but next to Neville's truck, the parking job was noticeably bad.

"Could I be more cattywampus?"

"Excuse me?" Neville said.

"My parking—it's terrible! I used to be so good at that, too." She shook her head. "I don't know what happened."

"Don't worry about it. It's not really that bad," he lied.

Neville felt suddenly uncomfortable. He didn't remember ever taking a client to dinner before. Lunch, yes. But the evening meal seemed somehow different. He didn't worry about the suit anymore, though. Lavinia wore a short-sleeved, taupe cardigan and a long, flowy black skirt with little flowers that matched the sweater. He noticed the same pearls she'd worn to his office. Based on appearance, people would never get the impression that Lavinia Lewis was any sort of jokester. Even her posture and mannerisms had an air of class and sophistication.

She took the lead crossing the road, and he held the door for her to enter. She ordered a chicken sandwich at the counter and whipped out her debit card, before an awkward question about who was buying could arise.

"Would you look at those Halloween decorations?" Lavinia shook her head, pointing at the cobwebs and spiders in the corner. "*My, my*. All that spooky stuff is not my cup of tea."

Neville ordered the steamed shrimp and paid the cashier.

"A holiday for pranks? I assumed you'd love it," Neville said with a smile.

"Oh, well, of course, I enjoy that part. But that's every day for me. I don't need a holiday." Lavinia laughed as they made their way out to the patio. It was full of people, despite a nip in the air.

They sat at one of the many white, weatherproof tables that filled the space.

"I just don't like scary stuff," she said. "But I do love dressing up! One year when my daughter was little, I went as a marshmallow, my husband, Edgar, went as a graham cracker, and Amy Lynn made the cutest little square of chocolate."

"S'mores!" The imagery of the family costumes amused him.

"It was so much fun. What about you? Do you ever dress up?"

Neville scratched at his thinning hair line, and the loose skin of his scalp moved with his fingers.

"I remember one party, a few years back," he said, straight-faced. "I went as a lawyer." Neville surprised himself with his own wit.

"Oh, now," Lavinia laughed and waved a hand at him.

The waitress brought out Lavinia's sweet tea and Neville's water. They sipped their drinks, and Lavinia looked around, waving and smiling in greeting at somebody different every few moments.

"Do you know everybody in here?" Neville said.

She gave the place a three sixty sweep.

"No, not *everybody*. You know there's always a lot of vacationers here," she said. "Oh, hey, Barbara Jean!" Lavinia smiled and waved to a lady across the patio. The lady had her hand in the air moving side-to-side.

"How do you know so many people? Have you lived here all your life?"

"No, actually. Only a few years."

"I've been here twenty years and the only people I know besides my assistant and her husband are other lawyers, police officers, and criminals."

"Well, I like to talk to people, I guess. Like Barbara Jean over there. I met her at the hair salon. She was gonna go with a pixie cut, but I told her she didn't have the right bone structure for that. Not many people can pull that off. And wouldn't you know it, she took my advice. A total stranger. I think I saved her a lot of heartache. Doesn't she look cute with that bob?"

Neville looked at the lady and agreed with Lavinia, then refocused his brain from the distraction. It was all too informal, too familiar. He inched his chair closer to the table, making a scrubbing sound on the concrete floor, and sat up straight. It was time to get to the point. He took a miniature steno pad and a pen from his breast pocket to convey it to Lavinia.

"While we wait on our food, how about I ask you a few questions?"

"Of course, I'm happy to answer your questions, but I've already told you, it was Gordon Proctor."

"I understand, but just humor me."

He asked about any enemies she might have other than Mr. Proctor. Zero. He asked how many warnings she'd received about playing pranks in the community. Lavinia answered, "a few," in a high-pitched voice as she squeezed a slice of lemon to death over her glass.

A cool breeze blew across the table as the waitress returned with their food. She was a young twenty-something with permed hair and a tiny diamond stud in the side of her nose. She wore heavy eyeliner and a big, eager smile.

"Here you go," the waitress said. She sat the meals down in front of them, in plastic baskets lined with red and white checked paper.

"Ooh, that looks good," Lavinia said, eyeing Neville's food. "Next time I'll get that." She turned to the waitress. "Thank you, dear. Hey, I don't believe I've seen you in here before."

"Yes, ma'am, I'm new. Been here going on three weeks. And can I just say, y'all are the sweetest-looking couple. How long have you been married?"

Neville froze. Lavinia laughed.

"Oh, we're not married. We're not even dating. He's my la..." She stumbled on the nature of their relationship. "I know him from...he's a friend."

"Oh, I'm sorry. You remind me of my grandparents. They've been married for sixty years. And when I saw the way he made you laugh a second ago—"

"It's okay, dear," Lavinia said. "I *was* married for a long, long time, too. But he passed."

The waitress nodded and patted Lavinia's shoulder before turning to leave the table.

This was a bad idea, Neville thought. *I should have had her meet me at the office, during the day, with Shirley there, and Lee.*

Recovering from embarrassment, Neville fired away with questions, in between bites, hoping Lavinia wouldn't mention the waitress's mistake. She answered about her daily routine, her relationships outside of Cypress Shores, and even about her friends and family back in Wilson, while Neville scribbled away with his right hand and brought his food to his mouth with the left.

After a lengthy interrogation, Lavinia looked down at her tray. Three-quarters of her sandwich remained. She looked at Neville's tray.

"I think I should eat and let you be the one to talk for a while," Lavinia said.

"I'm not the one being investigated."

"But you are the one who's almost finished with your dinner." She picked up her sandwich.

He looked down at the one steamed shrimp left in the basket and dropped the pencil, then rested his hands on the table with fingers intertwined. His mind went suddenly blank, and he could only play a mental game of connect the dots with the dark brown age spots on the back of his hands.

"Do you always wear suits?" Lavinia said.

Neville looked up. It was a strange question.

"Just trying to give you something to talk about so I can eat," she said.

"Actually, yes. Most of the time, I do. Except when I'm sleeping or fishing. Fishing's the only time I wear blue jeans. Blue jeans and my lucky fishing hat."

"I like to fish, too" Lavinia said. "Haven't done it in a long time, though. Edgar and I had a pontoon and a good crappie lake back west."

"Is that so?" She nodded, her mouth full of food. "Oh, I've loved it since I was a boy. I guess it's really my only hobby. Haven't had a chance to go in a while either, though."

Neville ate the last shrimp and settled against the chair back. One hand rested on his leg, and the other held the foam cup of water. His suit jacket fell open in his relaxed posture. The bottom of his tie rested on the summit of his belly. Though he felt calmer, there was still nothing to talk about other than the investigation. Weather was cliché. Everything else was too personal.

Lavinia took a big bite of her sandwich, and all he could do was sit there while she chewed. She held a napkin over her mouth and waved to someone nearby. Time passed and the silence got louder.

Lavinia had just bitten into a french fry when Neville blurted out another question.

"Do you have any secrets?"

"Come again?" she said, before the fry was down.

"I ask all my clients, so no surprises come out in court. I mean, in case we have to go to court. It's good to know."

"Do you *really* think I'll be charged with a crime?" Her calm had faded away. The worry crept into her voice and showed on her face.

"Well, I don't know, but I'm preparing for all possibilities."

"I don't think all this interrogating is even necessary. All we have to do is figure out how Gordon swapped those cookies. I bet if you search his trash, you'll find some evidence. Are there any security cameras you can check to help catch him?"

"I think you're avoiding my question, Lavinia. Are you hiding something?" He was half serious, half teasing.

Lavinia looked around the restaurant, like a spy with top secret information. She drew a deep breath then spat out the words in a loud whisper.

"I wasn't born in the South."

Neville pursed his lips to keep the laughter from spilling out. He waited for her to elaborate, but she stayed quiet.

"Well, where were you born?" he said.

She held a hand to the side of her mouth and whispered it, as if hiding a curse word from a child.

"New Jersey." Her gaze dropped to her lap. "Not even Sylvia and Henry know that."

"That's not incriminating information."

"Maybe not to you." She dabbed at the corners of her mouth with a napkin. "My father was an engineer, and his work took him north, so I was born there. Mama tried to be supportive of his work, because she loved him so."

A smile crept across her face, and she had a wistful look in her eyes. Neville was struck by their intense color—a shade of gray somewhere between fog hanging over the marsh at dawn and wafting smoke from late night cigarettes over case files.

"But he saw she was miserable," Lavinia said. "He brought her back when I was six months old, just before the war started."

He drummed his fingers on the table, turned his head to one side, and smiled.

"I'm a Midwest guy, so...I don't understand this Mason-Dixon issue."

"Midwest?" Lavinia said. "So, what brought you here?"

"I guess it was an attempt at retirement. My practice in Des Moines made me enough money to live out my golden years, so I picked somewhere warmer, where the fishing was good, and packed everything up."

"How long were you retired?"

"Two months."

Lavinia smiled a curious smile. She brought the lipstick-covered straw to her mouth for a drink and raised her eyebrows in a question.

"Couldn't stand it," he said. "I'm not good at staying still."

"I see."

"Speaking of, I haven't heard back from your other character witnesses, so I'll drop back in tomorrow and try to speak to them."

"But tomorrow is Saturday."

"And?"

"You should take a day off."

"I told you, I'm not good at staying still. Besides, I'd think you'd want me working as often as I can to help you out."

"Well, listen. Since you're going over there...,"—Lavinia leaned in close—"I want to go with you. I called, and Marvin said it's okay as long as my attorney is with me."

"They kicked you out. Why would you want to visit?"

"I need to see my friend, Rosie. She's so used to my visits every week. I hate to let her down."

Neville leaned back and rubbed his chin.

"I guess that would be fine," he said.

Lavinia's phone on the table made a beeping noise. She turned it screen-up, then she explained that it was a message from Lucas, asking if she could take him and Dylan to the park tomorrow.

"One of our special places," she said. "He's been tryin' and tryin' to spot a gator there so he can snap a picture. I guess I'll take them after I visit Rosie with you."

The crowd had dwindled to only a handful of people that seemed like regulars. Neville's thin skin soaked in the chill of the night air, but he fought hard to hide it.

"Neville, before we leave...I want to say, thank you. Thank you for what you're doing to help me." She patted his hand quickly. "I want to get back to the way things were, and I believe you can help me get there. I want to go home and be near my friends, enjoy my jokes, and live life. That's really all I want."

***

Lavinia's glasses lay on the nightstand. She could barely see the phone screen without them but was too tired to reach and put them back on. The familiar chime of her word game rang loudly, and she hoped it didn't wake Lucas and Dylan.

Squinting and holding the phone close, Lavinia feared

Wilmer had taken the lead when she first noticed a ten-point *J*. His word was *joy*. No, only fourteen points. Not too bad. She was still ahead by twenty.

"Great day in the morning," she whispered when she realized his mistake. "He could have played that word for triple points!"

She decided she'd send him a message in the morning. Wilmer had put his *joy* in the wrong place.

Chapter Eleven

Saturday, October 20

Large pots of yellow mums adorned the expansive brick porch on the front of *the home*. Inside the building, pretty orange, red, brown, and yellow decorations, symbols of the season, covered the front desk—pumpkins, squash, leaves galore. A sign that read *Welcome Fall, Y'all* in shades of brown and muted cranberry hung on the wall near the desk. There was nobody there to greet them, only the sign.

Turning down a new hall, the decorations changed from cheerful to macabre. Flowy specters dangled from the ceiling, peering down with evil eyes at Neville and Lavinia as they made their way to Rosie's room.

"Why on earth would somebody want to hang those ghastly things?" Lavinia shook her head in disgust. "Somebody actually took time to climb up there for that, all down the hall. Nonsense." She clicked her tongue disapprovingly.

"I'm surprised it bothers you so much."

"Listen, life is frightenin' enough as it is. There's no need to heap extra spooks on top of the everyday scary."

Lavinia slowed her pace to walk side-by-side with Neville. The end of his wooden cane made an echoey sound in the empty hall each time it met the tile. Room after room, the doors looked the same. And there was the smell—the same one in all such facilities—

an unidentifiable, nearly repugnant odor that hung in the air even after the walls and halls were freshly scrubbed.

They reached Rosie's room, and Lavinia swiftly put the treat she carried behind her back as she entered. Rosie didn't notice her guests. She sat on the edge of her bed, staring at the television screen, glued to some kind of children's program with singing puppets. She swayed back and forth with the rhythm of the music.

"Hey there, Rosie!" Lavinia said.

Rosie jumped from the bed and made short, quick steps toward Lavinia. The broad smile on her face pushed her eyes into a squint, then her mouth opened wide in excitement, though no sound came out. She threw her arms around Lavinia's neck in an unusual display of affection. Lavinia reciprocated the hug with her free arm. *Mmmm, mmmm, mmmmm,* Lavinia hummed. It was southern speak for 'that's a good hug.'

Rosie stepped back and Lavinia presented the gift. Rosie grabbed the brown paper sack and peered inside to find it full of candy she loved—caramels with crème centers.

"I went to Bull Frog Corner to get them, just for you."

Lavinia could have bought the candy at a gas station. It would have been more convenient. But she looked for any excuse to visit the downtown shop. Big barrels of candy and filling up those brown paper sacks with sweets made her feel like a kid again. She had even browsed through the toys while she was there, admiring each themed nook, reminiscing about the joy and excitement over a new dolly or trinket.

Rosie hugged Lavinia one more time, stepped back to look at her squarely, and began to whistle a familiar tune. Her fingers reached up to brush Lavinia's wrinkled cheek, as joy drops formed in the corners of her eyes. The song was a message.

"Is that "Happy Days are Here Again"?" Neville spoke up from the doorway.

"It's unmistakable, isn't it? She's got a real gift." Lavinia stroked Rosie's cheek. "I'm happy to see you, too, friend. And I'd like for you to meet Neville."

Rosie turned toward him and dropped her head as Neville made careful steps closer. She whistled softly, meekly, a light, happy tune. Lavinia and Neville stood still and looked at one another, trying to make out the new song.

After a few measures, Lavinia had it. "It's from *The King and I*," she said. "I think she's saying 'nice to meet you'."

Lavinia smiled at Rosie who had raised her head but still wouldn't make eye contact with Neville. Lavinia and Rosie both snapped their heads in his direction when a soft baritone voice filled the room.

"Getting to know you, getting to know all about you. Getting to like you, getting to hope you like me," Neville sang.

Rosie's face lit up, and she whistled with renewed passion, her eyes focused on Neville as he continued singing. Lavinia's mouth hung open slightly. It seemed to her like a scene from a movie—an unexpectedly sweet gesture from someone who hadn't come across as the *sweet* type.

"Getting to know you, putting it my way but nicely. You are precisely, my cup of tea."

Neville's singing voice was rich and charming, though it wavered a bit from the unsteadiness of vocal cords that comes with age. It swelled with confidence at the end of the line.

Rosie motioned eagerly for them to take a seat near the window, and she sat down near them in the single chair.

The small room looked the same as all the other rooms on the hall—adequate, comfortable, but nothing fancy. Storm cloud-colored paper dressed the walls—a drab shade for people who didn't get out very much. Lavinia wished all the walls in the home weren't gray. Peach or periwinkle would have been much nicer for Rosie. The room did have a big window with a seating nook, but it didn't help the mood in the room today. The sky outside matched the wallpaper.

"Oh, I have one more thing for you," Lavinia said. "Hang on. Where is it?" She dug around in the abyss of her bag. "Oh, here it is," she said. She drew out a container in the shape of a Pringles can with a similar snap on lid. Rosie clapped her hands then took the container from Lavinia.

"Don't worry," Lavinia whispered to Neville. She patted him on the knee just as she might have done to Dylan or Lucas. "She knows what it is."

Rosie pulled the lid off the top of the container, spurning a rain shower of stuffed, fabric snakes. Rosie's face shined with bliss as she experienced the anticipated fun.

"You always love that old gag, don't you, sweetie?"

Rosie nodded.

"Oh, Neville. Did you see that? She's talking a lot today. I think she likes having you here."

Rosie nodded again, and Neville smiled.

"Alright now. I guess I should clean these critters up." Lavinia grunted as she heaved herself from the seat, locking her knees to stay balanced. Rosie and Neville got up to help.

As Neville bent down to pick up a snake, he froze and grabbed at his knee. Lavinia sensed his hesitation and went to help. Just as she leaned down to pick it up, he rallied and reached for it himself. Grabbing the toy at the same time, they looked up at one another with their faces two inches apart. Lavinia stood up quickly and stepped back as Neville handed it to her.

"Thank you, both," she said, recovering from the awkwardness as she stuffed the snakes back into the can. She put it into her bag and sat down again.

"Where's your nurse, sweetie?" Lavinia said, looking around. "What's her name? Jenny?" Lavinia spoke to Rosie as if she could answer in complete sentences.

Rosie managed a response in her own way, with a furrowed brow as she made music. This time, Lavinia couldn't make out the tune, so Rosie tried again.

Wee wee wee we woo. Wee wee wee we woooo.

"Hmmm. I don't think I know that one, honey," Lavinia said.

Rosie grew agitated, and she whistled the song more loudly.

A large, mocha-skinned nurse with kind eyes peeked her head into the room to check on Rosie. Noticing the guests, she smiled, and popped back out again.

"Excuse me," Lavinia called.

The nurse came back, and her kind eyes brightened as she recognized Lavinia.

"Hi, there. You're a resident of Cypress Shores, aren't you? Over in the villas?"

"Well...yes, Tricia," Lavinia said, looking at the woman's badge pinned to her pink scrubs. Lavinia hoped to avoid an explanation about being a resident but not being a resident.

"I know I've seen you visiting before. I'm sorry I don't remember your name."

"Lavinia Lewis."

Kindness didn't leave the nurses eyes, but it was suddenly accompanied by a new awareness.

"Oh," Nurse Tricia said.

Lavinia pretended she didn't notice Tricia's surprise.

"Does her private nurse have the day off?"

"Uh...no, ma'am. She quit. On Monday."

Rosie started whistling again, the same tune as before.

"Rosie, you're still singing that same song?" the nurse said. "She's being doing that all week."

"I don't recognize it. Do you know what it is?" Lavinia said.

"I can't place it either, but I think it's from a Disney movie."

"Hmmm...well, maybe it will come to me. It's very familiar."

"Rosie, is there anything I can get for you while I'm here?" the nurse asked.

Rosie kept whistling.

"Okay then." Tricia headed for the door but paused and turned around. "For what it's worth, Mrs. Lewis...I think they're being too hard on you. Even if you did put the toothpaste in those cookies, I know you didn't mean any harm in it. They ought to let it go."

A lump formed in Lavinia's throat, as gratitude welled up in her chest.

"Thank you, dear," Lavinia said. "Thank you, sincerely."

***

Lavinia wrestled a hodgepodge of emotions as she walked to Neville's car. Seeing Rosie had lifted her spirits, but she'd come down hard when Rosie became agitated. The nurses face when she told her who she was brought Lavinia even lower, but her kind words as she left the room brought her back up again. The rollercoaster was enough to make anybody dizzy.

As they walked, Lavinia spotted a familiar bald head from across the parking lot. The face was pointed toward the ground, but the slick dome was unmistakable. No more roller coaster; she was in a plane losing altitude fast.

"Unlock the door!" Lavinia yelled in a whisper as they reached the truck.

Neville looked confused, but he obeyed, opening the creaky driver side door and climbing in, not fast enough. Lavinia kept her head down as she waited for him to lean across the bench seat and pull the lock upward. The door finally unlocked, she scrambled inside, breathing hard.

"What's wrong, Lavinia?" he said.

"It's Gordon Proctor. He's headed this way, and I don't want him to see me."

"Okay, okay. Don't worry."

Neville put the pickup in reverse and backed out of the parking space as Gordon approached on the sidewalk carrying trekking poles and wearing a red sweatband around his head.

"Keep your head down. Don't look at him," Lavinia said.

"What's he gonna do?"

"I know it's silly, but I don't want him to see me. And I don't want to face him. He's the reason I'm in the mess that I'm in. I just need you to prove it."

As Neville drove Lavinia back to her car where she'd left it outside the guard station, a tone rang out from her pocketbook.

"Was that Porky Pig in your bag?"

"That's my new text message tone. Isn't it darling?"

Th-th-th-that's all folks! The phone sounded again.

"One of those blasted things," Neville lamented.

"What do you mean?" Lavinia was indignant as she pulled the phone out of the bag and used her pointer finger to open the message on the screen and remove the red notification dot.

"They're taking over, that's what I mean. In your case, you probably went more than seven-eighths of your life without a device like that, and now I bet you couldn't do without it."

"I'd do just fine without it, *thank you.* I like to keep up with the times, that's all."

He gave her an *I-doubt-it* smirk.

"Don't think for a minute I've forgotten what it's like to dial a rotary telephone or to have milk delivered to the doorstep in glass bottles."

"Don't forget carbon copy receipts," Neville added.

"Record players and black-and-white televisions."

"Or no televisions. And making coffee in a percolator."

"Times have changed, that's for sure. But it really is for the better," Lavinia said in her honey-laden persuading voice. "This message here is from my Lucas, wantin' to know when I'll be there to get 'im. He can be miles and miles away from me and just hit a button, and *voila*, I get the message. Isn't it wonderful? Ah, what I would have given to get messages so easily from my Edgar when he was away on a business trip, travelin' all over the place for the bank."

Neville tilted his head to one side as if it were unbalanced by the information his brain had received. He didn't argue with her.

"Well, surely, you being a businessman, you must at least use email," Lavinia said. "You have to. It's the twenty-first century!"

"Of course, we have to use email. But Shirley takes care of all that. She reads them to me when they come in or prints them and hands them to me. If I need to send a message, I dictate it to her. It's a necessary evil, though, if you ask me."

"Oh, it's not evil. It's wonderful. On this little computer that fits in my hand, I can play games and meet new people even. My pal Wilmer is as nice as he can be. We chat every once in a while, and he's all the way in Sweden."

Neville drove by the little brick guardhouse and parked on the other side of it beside Lavinia's Buick.

"Just one sec. Let me finish sending this text."

She held the phone with her left hand while her right pointer finger stabbed the screen over and over, spelling out a message back to Lucas.

"There," she said. The phone made a swishing sound to signal the text had been sent. "I even like that noise. Like it just pushed my message through the air and on its way."

"Mmm-hmmm," Neville said. He sounded very unimpressed.

"Well, thank you again for taking me to visit Rosie. And what you did, singing her song, that was very, very nice."

"I enjoyed meeting her," Neville said.

"And I'm sorry you didn't get to speak with my other friends. They are on the go quite a bit."

"It's okay. I'm sure they'll call me back soon. And if not, I'll try again another day."

Lavinia had her hand on the door handle, ready to exit the truck, when an idea bubble burst in her brain and, before she knew it, came out of her mouth.

"Say, would you like to go to the park with the boys and me? Meet my grandsons?"

He put both hands on the wheel and stared out the windshield, speaking slowly and softly.

"I'm sure they are great kids, Lavinia, but I don't think meeting them will help me with the investigation."

"I know that. I just thought you might like to do something besides work for a little while."

Neville looked like a deer in headlights. And in the awkwardness of the moment, as he sat there silent and wide-eyed, mouth slightly ajar, Lavinia noticed for the first time that Neville McGrath was a handsome man.

Chapter Twelve

"Lucas, why don't you go play on the playground with your brother?" Lavinia said.

The pair sat on a green metal bench, under an overcast sky, facing the giant climbing structure at Dutchman Creek Park.

"I'm too big for that. I just like to come here and look at the water."

Nana wasn't buying it. The sadness in his eyes when he spoke told the truth.

"*Too big?* You're an average-sized twelve-year-old." She flashed a mischievous grin at him. The joke wasn't funny, but it didn't need to be. It only had to keep him talking.

"You know what I mean, Nana. I'm too old for that playground."

She looked up and gave a congratulatory wave to Dylan as he conquered the traversing wall. He grinned and pushed himself off the wall, landing masterfully on both feet. Lavinia gave him a thumbs up to assure him she had seen that trick, too.

"But look at how much fun your brother's having," she said.

Lucas picked at a loose string in the hem of his shirt, and Lavinia looked to the big grassy field behind the playground where a group of boys close to Lucas's age threw a football back and forth between them.

"*Hmmmm...*does your wantin' to sit here have anything to do with what those boys over there might think of you?" She pointed to the boys then poked her index finger gently into his chest.

"Kind of." Lucas shrugged. "I mean, maybe...I guess."

"I see. Well, baby, it's one thing for your little brother to want to ride in the front seat to feel more grown up. It's another thing entirely for you to miss out on having fun just because you think you're too big to play or because of how you might look to somebody else, especially people you don't even know." She reached over and pinched his cheek gently. "I still like to have fun, and be silly, even though some people don't like it."

"Like Mama?"

"Well, yes, like your mother."

Lucas wasn't persuaded.

"Okay, come with me," she said. She patted his back firmly.

Lavinia stood, stepped gingerly over the raised border of the playground, and traipsed through the mulch in her tasseled loafers.

"Where are we going, Nana?" Lucas asked as he followed.

Without answering, she walked over to the swings and claimed the one on the end. She carefully slipped her backside into the leather sling, took three little steps backward, and, lifting her feet from the ground, let it take her forward in a rush as she gripped the chain as tightly as her weakening grip would allow. The veins in her wrinkled hands protruded.

"Lookin' good, Nana!" Dylan yelled from the bouncing bridge of the play structure. He gave her a two-handed thumbs up. "Woohoo!"

"Woohoo!" Lavinia said in reply. "Thank you, baby!"

"Oh, alright. You've made your point," Lucas said. He looked around, smiled, and took a seat in the swing next to her.

"Life's too short, Lucas. Life is *too* short."

Lucas and Lavinia swung side-by-side for a short time, then Lucas put more effort into it and beat the height of Lavinia's swinging by double. Dylan came and joined them on the swing next to his brother. The sun pierced through and overtook the killjoy clouds that had threatened their time at the park. *Swoosh, swoosh.* The air whipped past Lavinia's ears. Almost seventy-one years separated her and her youngest grandson, but in that moment, the difference didn't matter at all.

Lavinia eventually stopped kicking her legs, keeping them straight and motionless to slow herself. The laws of physics prevailed and soon she was barely moving. As she stopped, someone pulled on the chains of the swing from behind her, lifting her gently backwards. Lavinia swiveled to see who it was as she swung forward.

"Well, you did make it," she said. "When you said maybe, I thought for sure you meant no."

"I decided a little fresh air might be nice," Neville said.

Lavinia stopped the swing carefully, letting her feet drag the ground for a while before she tried to stand. "Ooh, I'll pay for that later, I'm sure."

Standing, she introduced Neville to the boys, and they both used their manners, offering a 'nice to meet you, sir.'

The climbing structure, with its slides and bridges, fireman's pole and rock wall, finally tempted Lucas out of his inhibition. "That's the one who's going to help Nana not go to jail," Dylan whispered too loudly to his brother as they ran off to play.

Lavinia laughed, and the conversation immediately turned to the universal diffuser of awkward situations.

"Those clouds really cleared out in a hurry, didn't they?" Neville said.

"Why, yes. You're right. They did. And it's the perfect temperature out here."

"Just around seventy degrees."

The two stood and watched the boys playing. Finally, Neville suggested they sit. He didn't have his cane.

"How have I lived here so long and never visited this park?" Neville said. They found a bench between the playground and the shore. "Beautiful lawns and right on the water."

"Some people even fish from the bank right down there," Lavinia said.

"Is that right?"

"Yes, and the other day I saw a gentleman bring a kayak on a little contraption like a wheelbarrow. Toted it right down there by himself, took the wheels off, pushed the boat out, and paddled away with three fishing rods rigged up and ready."

"Man, that sounds like fun." Neville took off his suit jacket and laid it carefully over the back of the park bench. "You know, I never did any saltwater fishing until I moved down here."

"And where is that you came from exactly? Didn't you say Des Moines?"

"That's where I lived most recently, before moving here. But I grew up in Oskaloosa, Iowa."

"Good fishing in Oskaloosa?"

"Some of my best memories from childhood are fishing with my father. He was a coal miner. Worked six days a week all his life. But two weeks every summer he took vacation and took me to camp at Lake Red Rock. We fished from sunup to sundown every day."

"That sounds nice. My Daddy took me fishin' a lot, too. We used a cane pole in a little farm pond most often."

After conferring about something, Lucas and Dylan jumped off the climbing wall at the same time and walked over. "Nana, can we go down to the bank and look for my gator now?" Lucas said.

"You got your phone to snap a picture if you see 'im?"

"Yes, ma'am." Lucas patted his pocket.

"Y'all don't get too close to the water, and if you see one, keep your distance."

"Got it!" Dylan and Lucas said in unison as they ran off

toward the water.

Lavinia turned her body slightly on the bench to watch the boys as they explored the shoreline. After weather and fishing, the conversation with Neville lulled.

"So, last night at dinner, you asked some difficult questions. Now it's my turn." She gave a coy smile as Neville looked at her with a measure of concern on his face. "Do *you* have any secrets?"

"I don't think that's relevant."

"We're not in court."

Neville put his elbows on his knees and wiped his face with both hands.

"Hmmm…. okay, okay. Here's one for you," he said, sitting up straight again. "I hate to lose."

"That's it? Why, that's downright boring."

"Well, the real secret is, I win so many cases because I'm very selective. I only accept the ones I'm certain I can win. I have a sixth sense about it."

"So, you only accept clients that you know for sure are innocent then?"

He scratched the back of his head. "I didn't say that."

"Oh…I see. But do you think you can win mine?" she said.

"The thing is, you haven't been charged yet. And I haven't agreed to defend you in court yet. But my gut says yes, if it comes to that."

Lavinia patted him on the shoulder and breathed a thankful sigh.

"I suppose I should be honest with you, Lavinia," Neville said, "There's a chance I might not be here long enough to try your case anyway."

"Oh, no! Are you ill?"

"No, no, no. I don't mean like that. Although, let's face it, it's a possibility. What I meant was, I'm thinking about moving to

Maine to live with my nephew. He knows I don't have any family down here, and he's been on me about coming to live with him. He's got a cabin on this beautiful lake, and he fishes all the time."

"That sounds lovely. And it's so nice that he cares about you."

"Yeah, I guess."

"What do you mean?"

"Never mind. I think that's enough about me."

"Well, I'm sure you'll make the right decision about staying or going, though it must be difficult."

Neville only nodded. She could see the decision had him distressed.

"It'll be okay, Edgar," she said.

Lavinia didn't know she'd said it until she read the confusion on his face.

"Oh, I'm sorry, Neville." A heavy feeling settled on her chest, and a wave of heat washed over her.

"Don't worry about it," Neville said. He cleared his throat.

They got quiet again as they watched Dylan and Lucas scanning the sandy bank that dipped down just beyond the manicured lawn of plush, green grass. Only their heads and shoulders could be seen; and they bobbed this way and that, shielding their eyes from the sun with their hands and sometimes pointing.

Ah, Lavinia thought, *to be young again.* Just yesterday that was her, skipping along a sandy bank, playing hide-and-seek among the reeds with her brother. Only moments ago, she watched old people sitting on park benches and felt sorry for them, that they no longer played games and went on adventures. The years had seemed so long until one day they weren't. Just seconds in disguise, time had tricked her, dressing up as eternity. Now she found herself sitting on a park bench, calling a new acquaintance by her dead husband's name.

"Nana! Help! Help!" Lucas yelled. "It's got Dylan!"

Dylan's head disappeared from above the ridge.

It took a second for her brain to process what Lucas was saying. She couldn't sprint, but she moved quickly—much quicker than if she'd had to do it without adrenaline coursing through her body.

As she made her way across the lawn, she reached into her pants pocket for her phone, ready to hit the red emergency call button on the lock screen.

Dylan was screaming, a panicked, pained screamed that made Lavinia dizzy.

She reached where the edge of the lawn dipped off to see Dylan lying on the ground and wriggling in the sand with his eyes pinched shut. She yelled his name, nearly choking on her fear, then he opened his eyes and burst out laughing.

"We got you, Nana! We got you!" Lucas yelled. Instead of taking pictures of an alligator, Lucas was videoing her reaction to their prank.

"Boys! I oughta beat the both of you!" She bent over and put her hands on her knees, panting.

Neville caught up to her. "It was a joke? Oh, thank goodness!" he said.

Lucas stopped recording, but he and Dylan kept laughing. Dylan laughed until his face looked sunburnt.

Lavinia was still shaking. Neville bent down close to her and whispered in her ear. "Play along." Before she had a chance to respond, he called to the boys sternly. "You could have given your grandmother a heart attack, you know. Hey,"—Neville turned to Lavinia—"you don't look well. Your face looks kind of *gray!*" Neville's voice was overly dramatic.

Lavinia caught on and pressed one hand against her chest.

"Oh!" she yelled. "My heart! It couldn't take the scare!"

Dylan and Lucas stopped laughing.

"The pain! The pain!" she moaned.

Dylan jumped up from the ground and made it to her side just after Lucas.

"Nana! We're so sorry! Are you okay?" Lucas said.

"It was supposed to be funny," Dylan said.

Neville patted Lavinia on the back, pretending to comfort her, then she stood up straight. "Gotcha!" she said.

They both stared blankly for a moment, then the laughter resumed amongst all four of them.

"That's enough excitement for me today, I believe," Neville said as the laughter died down.

"I think for us, too," Lavinia said. "Boys, let's head back to the car. After the scare you gave me, you may have to carry me." She winked.

Dylan and Lucas looked at each other, then sprinted on ahead, probably hoping to get one more chance to slide before the old people caught up to them.

"So, I don't guess you're going to punish them for that prank?" Neville asked.

"I think we're even now, thanks to you. Besides, they get that kind of thing from me."

"I'm glad you caught on to my suggestion, but I have to say, you're a horrible actress."

Lavinia pretended to be appalled by his insult.

"What do you mean? I could have won an Oscar for that performance. I was every bit as good as Ingrid Bergman."

They met Dylan and Lucas just as the boys exited twin slides on the playground.

"Ready, boys?"

"Uh-huh," they both said. The boys were sweaty and red.

As they walked to the gravel parking lot, Lavinia began humming a bouncy tune.

"Hey, that sounds familiar," Neville said.

"I have it stuck in my head. It's that melody Rosie whistled for us. The one we couldn't figure out."

"I know that song," Dylan said. "It's from the dalmatian movie. Where the woman is after all the puppies."

"Yeah," Lucas agreed. "The song's about her, the villain. She's real evil."

Lavinia and Neville looked at each other as they passed through the exit, an open space between two white fence pieces.

"Rosie whistled that song when I asked about her nurse," Lavinia said. "Isn't that strange? You don't reckon that nurse was mean to Rosie, do you? I'd sure hate to find that out."

Chapter Thirteen

Tuesday morning, October 23

Lavinia floated, weightless. Everything around her was bright white, although her eyes were closed. Maybe she didn't have eyes. But she must've had skin, because the air caressed her gently, almost imperceptibly, as she went upward, pulled by an invisible force. The color changed all at once from white to brilliant gold, like precious metal mixed with daffodils and sunshine. She didn't question the change in state, but she began to perceive that she was headed somewhere, and she wasn't afraid.

"Lavinia," a deep voice whispered. "Lavinia, I need to talk to you."

Peace turned to a measure of fear. Eyes still closed, she found her voice. With mouth barely open she said, "God? Is that you?"

The voice called again—"I need to talk to you. Are you awake?"—and she realized her response to the initial call had only been in her mind.

"God? Is that you?" she asked again, aloud. The corners of her dry mouth cracked as they were forced to move.

"Lavinia. Lavinia, wake up. It's Lee."

"What?" Lavinia pulled the Spiderman comforter from underneath her chin, slowly lifted her head and shoulders off the bed, and propped on her elbows. Her eyes adjusted from the brightness of her dream to the reality of Dylan's bedroom.

Lee stood outside the room. The door was cracked, and only his nose poked in.

"I'm sorry to wake you," he said. "But Neville called."

"What time is it?" She rubbed her eyes and reached for the glasses on the nightstand.

"It's seven. Amy Lynn and the boys will be leaving for school soon." Lee opened the door a little further without peeking in. "I want to talk to you about Neville's call while they're still getting ready."

"Okay, Lee, I'll be right out."

Lee closed the door. Lavinia got out of bed and put on her cotton housecoat that lay draped across Dylan's chestnut dresser. She slid her feet into pink plush slippers and shuffled to meet Lee in the hall.

"Neville talked to the District Attorney late last night," Lee said. He ran his hands along the sides of his head and sighed. "Apparently, the DA has found some…circumstantial evidence. Something that might be used to suggest a motive. He wanted to press charges right away, but Neville convinced him to wait."

"*Evidence?* That's impossible! There can't be any evidence because I didn't do it. What in the world could it be?" Her voice cracked. The floor felt unsteady beneath her feet.

"I don't know. He didn't say. He was in a hurry. I think he just didn't want me hearing it at the station. But I'm going to see him on my way in later. I'll get all the details."

"I guess there's no sense in worrying until I know what there is to worry about then, is there?"

"I probably shouldn't have told you. I just got a little worked up about it."

"No, you should. I'm glad you did. Update me after you talk to Neville."

"I will, but I think we shouldn't say anything to Amy Lynn

yet, at least until we know more."

"Okay, sweetheart."

Lee went downstairs, and Lavinia stood alone in the hallway outside Dylan's room. She braced herself against the wall, gripping the chair rail molding to steady herself. With eyes clenched, she took three deep, cleansing breaths, then headed downstairs. No time to be upset; she had promised Dylan she'd have breakfast with him before school.

***

The house was quiet, and Lavinia was alone. She gathered the bowls from where her family had left them when they raced off to work and school. She dumped the milky remnants of cereal into the sink and sprayed them down into the garbage disposal. She loaded the dishwasher and wiped the table. It felt good to be useful, and it distracted her while she waited on news from Lee. She hadn't cleaned up after anyone else like this in years.

Lavinia was almost finished in the kitchen when the doorbell rang. Probably a delivery. She dried her hands as she went through the living room and was still holding the kitchen towel when she opened the front door.

"*Sylvia! Henry!* What a surprise," she said.

"I know we should have called." Sylvia's voice was weepy and her eyes bloodshot and swollen.

"No, it's fine. Come in. What's the matter?"

Henry had one hand on Sylvia's back and the other on her arm as they came inside and quickly took a seat.

"She's been so upset," Henry said. "I told her you would understand, but she just feels terrible about it."

"About what? What's going on?"

"Oh, Lavinia. I had to tell the truth. The DA asked me flat

out. I couldn't lie."

"Sylvia, what are you talking about? Now, pull yourself together," Lavinia said. She didn't want to have to slap Sylvia to get her to calm down, like they did in the movies, but she was prepared to if necessary.

"Okay." She tried to inhale through her nose, but the air met with resistance and she drew the rest of the deep breath through her mouth. Her ample bosom descended with the release of air from her lungs. "I had to tell him about your big fight with Wendy Wisengood."

"Sylvia, what *fight?* I've never fought with Wendy. We disagreed over what music to play during our bridge game a couple of times, but that wasn't anything serious."

"Lavinia, this is no time for jokin' around."

"Who's jokin'? I don't know what you're talkin' about."

Sylvia wailed, a loud siren shriek, as she leaned over and buried her head in Henry's shoulder for a moment. She removed her glasses and wiped her eyes on his shirt, then sat up again.

"It was about three months ago. About a month after Wendy first moved in. I believe it was her second week of playing cards with us." She was insistent. Frustration spilled out with the words. "You remember. She was being downright ugly that day, and you told her off!"

"Sylvia, are you sure that was me?"

"Do I have another best friend named Lavinia?" Sylvia planted her face in her hands, stifled a frustrated yelp, then looked up again. "Well, I knew you didn't mean what you said, so I didn't mention it to the police. But Janice Bumgarner did. Then the District Attorney called and asked me about it, and I had to tell him the truth. Oh, Lavinia, I'm so sorry!"

"Honey, you did the right thing. It's okay. I'm not mad. I just wish I could remember that argument. Keep telling me about it, and maybe it will come to me."

***

Lavinia and Sylvia flipped a coin like usual to see who got to sit *South* at the card table. Sylvia won, and Lavinia pretended to pout as she took her seat on the *North* side. Janice and the newcomer played *East* and *West*.

From the start, their normally friendly game of bridge was tense. The newcomer was bossy, opinionated. And, being from Rhode Island, she didn't seem amused by Sylvia and Lavinia's North and South jokes.

Senior Central was hot—not as bad as being outside, but unpleasant, nonetheless. One of the air conditioning units had surrendered to the fury of the July heat, and the remaining unit couldn't cool the space on its own. The HVAC contractor wouldn't be there to fix it until the next day.

Five teams of four soldiered on, fanning themselves with anything they could find, but the newcomer complained incessantly.

"We should reschedule the game. These conditions are ridiculous!" Wendy said.

"Oh, it's not that bad. And Marvin's on his way with a couple of fans," Lavinia said.

"Well, I don't pay the kind of money I pay to live here to sweat like this."

The loud woman brushed a midnight black curl away from her sweaty forehead. Unlike Gladys Smith and her fortunate genetics, Wendy's color hadn't been natural since Carter was president.

Wendy's mood declined even more as the game progressed. The sweatier she got, the louder her complaints became. She snapped at Melvin for taking too long with the fans; she whined about the chips and pretzels, saying bagged snacks were low class; and she didn't like the way Lavinia dealt the cards. Ten minutes in, Lavinia had had about all she could take. The drop of water that made the dam burst was a sideways remark about Sylvia's weight.

"Alright! That's enough!" Lavinia said, setting off a wave of breathy gasps through the room. She stood up. The ladies at every table stopped the games and stared.

"You know, Wendy, you've been hateful and nasty ever since you got here. Nobody's holdin' you hostage."

"Are you saying you want me to leave?"

"I'm sayin', if you want to keep throwin' temper tantrums, there's a nursery school right down the street. Better yet, there's a canine obedience school on the other side of town. And if you can't learn some manners there, they can at least give you a muzzle!"

***

"So, that's what Neville called about. Great day in the morning! This is not turning out well for me, is it?"

Sylvia placed one hand on Lavinia's knee. With the other hand, she pulled a tissue from her brassiere and dabbed at her leaking nose.

"We didn't know at the time that she was goin' through all that mess with her son—how he'd taken off to Florida with some floosy and wouldn't return any of her calls. That's why she was so sour, I bet. And she turned out to not be so bad, and y'all eventually became friends, sort of. So, of course, it didn't occur to me to bring it up. I just wish Janice had thought the same as me and kept her mouth shut."

"Well, how could it prove anything anyway?"

"I guess they could use the fight to say you had it out for her."

"But it's not true!"

"I know that, Lavinia," Sylvia said.

"And how can I not remember that? That's what bothers me the most."

The house phone rang. Lavinia picked up the cordless handset from the side table and answered it. It was Lee. She rose and walked to the fireplace, her back to Sylvia and Henry.

"I already know," she said before he could speak. "Sylvia and Henry are here." She touched the gilded frame of the largest portrait on the mantle—a picture of her and Edgar. Next to it was a picture of Amy Lynn and Lee and the boys taken in front of the ocean, all of them wearing white.

"Well, did they also tell you that Mrs. Wisengood claims you knew about her fluoride allergy?" Lee said. "She says she told you about it, that you had knowledge of it before the potluck."

Lavinia stayed quiet for a long time. Nothing made sense anymore.

"No. No, they didn't tell me that," she said somberly. "I just don't know what to make of all this."

"Neville doesn't want you to worry. Said to tell you he's got this under control. If the DA does press charges, you won't go to jail."

"But will I ever get my life back? My good name? When can I move back to my own house? This isn't fair, Lee. I'm innocent."

Lee hesitated. "I know you're not going to like this, Lavinia, but, if this goes to court, you may have to consider an incompetency plea. It might be the only way."

Lavinia's heart hit the bottom of her stomach. She had her answer, and it wasn't the one she wanted. If she were charged, if the case went to trial, she would not be getting her life back. Not the one she wanted. Not the one she'd planned.

***

Sylvia and Henry had left, and Lavinia was alone again. Her heart couldn't decide if she should scream or cry, but those were the only two options she had devised so far. One moment tense and jittery, the next despondent and melancholy, all afternoon she tried to process the news of the morning, and she began to feel the stress in her body. Her head throbbed, above her right eye, and her muscles ached. She tried to channel Scarlett's tomorrow-is-another-day moxie. Instead, she felt helpless, like throwing-a-vase-in-the-library Scarlett.

Lavinia needed a release. Punching a pillow wouldn't do, and she couldn't break any vases. None of them belonged to her, and she didn't want the mess to clean anyway.

Sitting in the living room recliner, Lavinia reached into her pocket to retrieve her phone. She unlocked the screen. A quick web search gave her the phone number. She repeated it over and over so she wouldn't forget it while she got to the phone screen. Lavinia pressed her fingertip angrily against the ten digits. Neville had advised her more than once not to do it, but she couldn't help it.

"Hello?" an old man answered the phone.

"Gordon, this is Lavinia Lewis. I just want you to know something. I know it was you that got me into the mess that I'm in. I know you're responsible for puttin' toothpaste in those cookies and makin' Wendy sick. And you're responsible for getting me kicked out of Cypress Shores like you've been wantin' to do for a long time. I don't know how you did it, but I know you did, and I have a good lawyer, and he's gonna prove it!"

The call would have been more satisfying back in the old days, when she could have slammed the receiver down to end it. But touching the red button with her pointer finger before Gordon had a chance to speak would have to do.

It helped at first. She exhaled hard, pushing out the tension. But she breathed it right back in again. The phone call hadn't accomplished anything. Maybe she *should* scream or cry. Then it occurred to Lavinia; there was at least a third option.

Chapter Fourteen

I know it's been a very long time.

It seemed like everyone at Waterfront Park could hear Lavinia's thoughts. She lowered the volume of the words in her brain.

After Dylan reminded me what I should do...he was such a good example...and, I still didn't do it.

A seagull dancing around in the grass nearby distracted her—a transient looking for a handout. It squawked at her, a high-pitched, ear-piercing plea. She had nothing to offer. It hopped closer, turned its head to the side as if studying her sad face, then flew away toward the water.

She tried again. *I'm sorry that it's been so long.*

She hugged the giant pocketbook in her lap. Her words felt vain, hollow. Like she was talking to someone on the other end of a misdialed phone call instead of to the Almighty. Maybe she did have the wrong number.

I didn't really mean that, did I? Let me try again. She breathed in through her nose deeply and out through her mouth. She closed her eyes. *I'm sorry.* With more expression. *I'm sorry.* More loudly in her brain. *I'm sorry that it's been so long.*

She wanted to mean it. She thought she did. But still she felt nothing. Wasn't she supposed to feel something? She couldn't remember.

Her one-sided conversation was interrupted by Porky Pig's

voice. She drew the phone from the bag quickly to check the message.

Where are you? Lee had texted.

My favorite place. She pecked out her response and hit send. She didn't try to pray anymore. She just watched the water and listened to it crashing against the shore over and over. Little bands of gulls cried out all around. The wind brought the sound of a whistle buoy to her ears, even though it was too far away to see. She tried to the let the breeze clear out her troubled mind like a can of compressed air blasting dust from a keyboard, only gentler. But not even her beloved Waterfront Park could soothe her. Maybe she should give up on the praying and go on a spree instead. Pranking, eating, or shopping, it didn't matter. In less than forty-five minutes, she could be at the big mall in Wilmington and accomplish at least two of the three.

She sat there until her backside was sore. In another hour and a half, the sun would dip below the horizon. The days were growing shorter and shorter, and in less than two weeks, daylight saving time would be over—another thing for Lavinia to be sad about.

"Hey," a deep voice said as Lavinia felt a hand on her shoulder. Lee came around and sat on the bench beside her, wearing his handsome blue uniform. She turned to see his patrol car parked nearby.

"What are you doing here?" she asked.

"I just wanted to check on you." His voice was tender and sincere. "Lucas texted me to say you weren't home when he got off the bus. Are you okay?"

"I'm fine, I guess. To be honest, dear, I…I came down here to…pray." She watched for his expression to change, to show a hint of surprise. But there was only kindness and patience in his eyes. "I'm afraid I'm not very good at it anymore," she said. "The words just don't seem to be enough." Lavinia hung her head.

Lee leaned forward and clasped his hands together with his forearms on his knees.

"Who says you have to be good at it? I think it's more important to just do it. Kinda like exercising, you know? Anything is better than nothing."

"I feel like I need to try. I don't know what else to do." Her hands went up and back down in defeat. "Lee, I'm starting to think I might really be in trouble. At first it all seemed so ridiculous. I thought there was no way they would ever charge a woman my age, for something that I didn't do. And over *toothpaste!*" She shook her head slowly from side to side. "But after today, I think I need help from a Higher Power to get out of this jam."

"Ah, I'm still not worried. But praying certainly wouldn't be a bad thing."

"I don't know what happened, Lee," Lavinia said. "I was raised in church. I sang in the choir. I won Sunday School ribbons every quarter for memorizing the most Bible verses. It was a big part of who I was. But somehow it got covered up, *you know?* It's still there. I know it. Buried under all the stuff I let get in the way."

"Seems like the *it* you're really talking about is *faith*, Vinny. And it sounds like you're on your way to unburying it." Lee looked at her sideways, with a twinkle in his eye, and smiled. She reached for his hand. He always knew just what to say.

"When Sammy was young, we dressed him up in his little suit and took him to church every week. He liked to stand out in the vestibule after service, right next to the preacher, and shake everybody's hand as they came out." She rolled her head back toward the clouds, wearing her first smile of the day.

"What made you stop going?" Lee asked. He sat up and leaned back against the bench.

She pondered it. It was an important question that she hadn't considered. Maybe she could dig out her faith along with the answer.

"I got lazy, I think. When Samuel was in high school and playing sports on the weekends, it seemed like a good excuse not to go as much. For Edgar, I think the more money he made, the harder it was to part with some of it in the offering plate, too." The leather of the pocketbook was warm on her lap. She let go of Lee's hand and sat the bag between them. Unrestricted, she turned her body slowly toward Lee and leaned back against the arm of the bench.

"After Samuel died, I only went at Christmas and Easter, and then it was only so I could remember being there with him on those special days." Lee made a good therapist. Lee and the soothing sounds of the Cape Fear. Alone, neither was powerful enough to pull her out of this deepest valley, but combined, they proved to be just what she needed.

"My grief was probably the real reason I pushed God away. I always knew it, but I never wanted to admit it." She nodded at the revelation. Yes, that was it. She'd allowed grief to choke out her faith, to snuff out the light within. She'd been blind to the fact for so long. Pain had transported her to an alternate reality, in which she was not the God-fearing person she used to be.

People passed by casually on the sidewalk in front of them. They walked alone and as couples. They walked with dogs on leashes. They walked as sight-seeing families. All of them unaware of the breakthrough taking place so close to them.

Lee said nothing. He just sat there as a sounding board and let her work through it.

"You know, I regret that we stopped taking Samuel to church as much when he got older. But he never lost his faith. And when Amy Lynn was born, he prayed for her every night. He prayed a lot because he hurt so, and he hurt for her. He wanted to marry Amy Lynn's mama, but her parents wouldn't have it. Instead, they moved away to start a new life where no one would know she'd gotten pregnant and had a baby."

"She never talks about her birth mother," Lee said. "But I think she has a picture of her somewhere."

"I gave her the only one I had of Samantha the day she turned eighteen. Samuel and Samantha. They made such a cute couple. I'd say they just made a mistake, but how could I call Amy Lynn a mistake."

"I think God is just that good—that He can turn even our mistakes into something beautiful." Lee smiled, wearing his love for Amy Lynn on his face.

"Well, Amy Lynn was right," Lavinia said, resolute. "No more pranks for me. I'm done with them. I'm innocent, but because of my reputation at Cypress Shores, everyone assumes I'm guilty."

"Aww, c'mon now. Your jokes are one of the things I love about you."

Lavinia smiled gratefully. She leaned her head to touch his shoulder then back up again.

"Lee, sometimes I feel like I'm losing it. I have more spring in my step than I did before the stroke, but…every once in a while, I feel like…like it could happen again. Or maybe there's something else wrong with me. Maybe I *am* senile. I don't remember an argument with Wendy."

"I know that bothers you, Vinny. But we all forget things sometimes. Don't worry. You're not crazy, and you're not senile."

"But how can a body be so sharp of mind one day, and feel like they have a head full of mush the next? Divine intervention may be my only hope." She took off her glasses and rubbed her eyes, careful to avoid messing up her mascara. She put the glasses back on and sighed. "I should have gone to church with you and the boys Sunday, instead of staying up so late the night before playing my word game. I did beat Wilmer three in a row, though." She giggled.

"You keep talking about going to church, like that's all you need to do. But I think you may be missing something. It's a great place to start, but church isn't the *most* important thing. It doesn't save you." Three pelicans flew overhead then dive-bombed the water in front of them with precision. "I haven't been going to church long at all," Lee continued. "The whole religion thing is pretty new to me. But I'm starting to figure out that it's about a lot more than a building or even a mindset. We'd love to have you come with us, though. We go with a friend of mine from dispatch. It's a really nice church. People are friendly. But I've been thinkin' of testin' out some others, too."

"Hold on a sec," Lavinia said. She leaned over to search her bag. "Mr. McGrath's secretary slipped me a card when we were in his office. For her church. I think her husband is a preacher or something. Let me find it."

She dug around in the big bag. She grabbed the rubber chicken by its long flimsy neck to move it out of the way while she searched.

"What do you do with that thing anyway, Lavinia?" Lee said.

"I don't know." She chuckled. "It's mostly to make the boys laugh when they want something out of my pocketbook. They ask for a mint, but I hand them this instead, like it's what they asked for, and they go absolutely hysterical." She waved it around in Lee's face, and he laughed like the boys always did. "See, it works!" she said.

"Oh, here it is," Lavinia pulled out the card.

The white card had *Solid Rock Church* printed in bold, black letters. "Hmmm…"—Lavinia repeated the name a few times—"It doesn't sound Episcopalian, does it?"

Lee shook his head.

"Shirley seems so nice. We should go visit her church together."

"Okay. We'll check it out if you want. We'll go tomorrow. But, Vinny…I think there's something else you need to do, too. I think you should try talkin' to Amy Lynn. Seems like it's long overdue."

As transparent as she had been with her son-in-law, now she feigned surprise. Her damaged faith was easier to admit than a broken relationship with her flesh and blood. Lee persisted, lovingly.

"Lavinia, you know I'm right. Y'all need to work some things out, and soon."

Chapter Fifteen

Sunday, October 28

"Amy Lynn, I need to talk to you."

Lavinia stood outside the office door. She was reminded of old times, when Amy Lynn lived under Lavinia's roof instead of the other way around. She'd be in her room studying, or listening to music, or talking on the telephone. Lavinia would stand outside the bedroom door waiting for permission to enter, so as not to evoke teenage wrath.

"What is it, Mama? I'm working on my State Boards and I have two weeks left to put my portfolio together." The teenage attitude was still there. She looked up from the desk and gave her mother unspoken permission to enter before redirecting focus to the computer screen.

Lavinia entered the small spare bedroom-turned-office only a few steps. The early morning sun cast a beam of light across the desk. Dust particles danced in the beam, just above the stacks of papers that Amy Lynn had been shuffling. A half-eaten snack cake and crumbs—remnants of Amy Lynn's breakfast—lay on a plastic wrapper on the corner of the desk.

She stood there, quiet, until Amy Lynn looked up again.

Lavinia was startled to suddenly realize how much her daughter had aged. Her once sparkling blue eyes were dim and fine lines had settled in around them. Her hair had thinned—so slightly that only a mother would notice. She kept the grays away with at-home hair dye and never took time for the salon. It hadn't been trimmed in months, evident from the split ends. Her hands were unmanicured, with nails of all different shapes and lengths, a couple of them chewed to the quick.

Not long ago, Lavinia had enjoyed *girl days* with Amy Lynn. After manicures and pedicures at the salon, Lavinia took Amy Lynn to the mall and she would get her makeup done at the cosmetic counter of the department store. Younger Amy Lynn loved getting all dolled up.

Despite her current imperfections, she was still Lavinia's beautiful little doll. The sun was setting on Amy Lynn's youth, but there was still daylight.

Noticing the changes in her daughter made Lavinia forget her purpose in Amy Lynn's office. She thought about her own thirty- and forty-something face, remembering how it had seemed to change every five years or so, overnight each time. She'd go to bed looking a certain way and wake up looking five years older. Now she saw it happening to Amy Lynn.

"Mama?" Amy Lynn looked impatient. "Mama, what is it? I'm busy."

"I'm sorry, dear. But I have something I need to tell you." She walked to the desk and stood with her fingertips pressed into the wood. She looked into Amy Lynn's eyes and paused to make sure she was ready to listen.

"Well, what is it?" Amy Lynn said.

Lavinia took a deep breath. "I came to tell you that it doesn't matter whether you believe me or not." Amy Lynn sat up straighter, her expression melting from impatient to surprised. "About the Oreos. About Wendy Wisengood. It doesn't matter. I love you regardless," Lavinia continued. "No matter what. I love you whether you support me or you don't. I love you whether you're proud of me or embarrassed. I love you whether you love me or not. I love you,

Amy Lynn. And there's nothing that can change that. That's all I wanted to say."

Lavinia turned to go, fully expecting that to be the end of the conversation.

"Mama, wait."

Lavinia stopped. Her right loafer did a careful pivot on the carpet until she faced Amy Lynn again.

Amy Lynn closed the laptop on the desk and leaned back in the office chair with her elbows on the armrests. Her fingers formed a tent in front of her mouth.

"I still don't know what to make of this whole mess," she said. There was a long pause. "It's all so crazy." She ran her fingers through her hair.

Lavinia licked nervously at chapped lips, anticipating Amy Lynn's words like a defendant waiting for the judge's verdict.

"But...Mama, no matter what...you know I love you, too."

The last words trailed off.

Amy Lynn seemed sincere, even if a bit annoyed at having been pushed into an emotional moment unexpectedly and in the middle of her work.

"I'll take it," Lavinia said with a grateful smile. Her posture relaxed.

They shared a *what-do-we-do-now* moment, neither of them moving or speaking. Then Amy Lynn broke the silence.

"Mama, the other day, when you said the jokes aren't about missing Daddy...you didn't say what they *are* about."

Lavinia walked over, took a seat in the glider rocker across from the desk in the corner of the small room, and leaned forward. She pulled in a long breath, hoping the air would find the right words somewhere down deep and bring them up on the exhale.

"Amy Lynn, do you know what it's like to lose who you are?" She paused to let her ponder, though she didn't expect a response. "When the stroke happened, I kept just enough of myself inside here"—she touched her pointer finger to her head above the temple—"to understand that I wasn't really me anymore. I was me, but I wasn't me. And that was agony. It was torture." She leaned back. "But I got a second chance, a gift. I recovered. Of course, that experience changed the way I see life. How could it not? I want to have fun with this second chance that I've been given, even if it means being a little less than dignified from time to time. It's not about missing your daddy, although I do miss him…so much. But it's about living." She paused, giving her words time to sink in. "There's a verse in the Bible that says, 'A merry heart does good, like medicine, but a broken spirit dries the bones.[2]' Amy Lynn, I don't wanna be a bunch of dried up old bones. What if it happens again? What if I lose myself again? And I've wasted the time I had being me by not enjoying it."

"But you're so different than you were before. Are you sure you're really *you* now?"

Lavinia sympathized with Amy Lynn. How strange it must have been to see her mother change.

"Baby girl, you've always known me just as your borin' ol' mama. But you didn't know who I was before…" She looked away, up to the window and that single beam of light.

"Before your son died."

"Samuel and I played jokes on each other all the time. It was our thing. And even before then, me and your Daddy use to get each other every year at April Fools. Your daddy was a jokester, too, you know. It was simple fun, something we all shared."

"That's hard to imagine, Mama," Amy Lynn said with a hint of a smile.

"I know it must be…but I hope you can understand, the

---

[2] Proverbs 17:22 (NKJV)

stroke made me forget who I was for a while, but then it helped me remember things I'd forgotten about myself."

"I guess I understand."

"And maybe I did show it a little more after Edgar died, but I promise you, he wouldn't disapprove. He wouldn't be embarrassed. If he were at Cypress Shores with me, we'd both be keeping everybody on their toes."

Amy Lynn had acceptance in her eyes, a look of peace. And had it not been for the desk between them, Lavinia would have leaned in for a hug.

"Mama, if you say you didn't pull this prank, I believe you. And...I'll support you."

One mountain conquered. A sense of accomplishment washed over Lavinia's soul. Happy tears begged to spill, but the feeling was fleeting. She wasn't finished with her mission. There were more mountains to climb.

"That makes me happier than you can know, baby. But while I'm here...there is one more thing...something else I'd forgotten about myself, up until I found myself in this trouble."

"What is it, Mama?"

"You know that second chance I was talkin' about?"

Amy Lynn nodded.

"I had forgotten where that second chance came from." Her voice was pained, as if recounting how she'd misplaced a diamond ring or a box of old photos. "It was a miracle, Amy Lynn. My recovery was a miracle. And miracles only come from one place, don't they?"

"I know..."

"I don't know how someone just forgets God, like He's not the One in control of us livin' and breathin' and movin' around on this earth. I don't know how the most important thing became so unimportant to me. I know it doesn't make sense, but it happened.

And I wanna fix it. I wanna make things right again. I remember who God is now. This whole mess reminded me…Dylan reminded me, and Lee reminded me…God reminded me."

Amy Lynn sat up straight and opened the laptop.

"That's good, Mama. I'm happy for you. If that's important to you, then I'm happy you're findin' it again." She wore a contrived smile that begged Lavinia to be finished talking.

"Amy Lynn, I know you're busy, but I'd really love for you to come to church with us this morning. With Lee, and the boys, and me. I did you a disservice by not taking you to church more when you were growing up, and baby, I don't want you to make the same mistake with those boys." Lavinia looked into Amy Lynn's eyes intently, searching her soul. "The time, it goes by so fast. You only have so much time to…to help point them in the right direction."

Amy Lynn looked at Lavinia as if she had her confused with someone else; someone who wasn't busy working on important things. She didn't utter a word, but the face said it all.

Lavinia was careful not to push. Pushing had worked on Samuel—he was mama's boy. But it had never worked with Amy Lynn. Girls were different with their mothers. They had to be dealt with carefully to avoid the power struggle. She'd learned that the hard way in the teenage years.

Lavinia remembered the stare-down trick Neville had taught her, and she decided it was worth a try. Complete silence for thirty seconds. Lavinia didn't flinch. She peered into Amy Lynn's eyes, attempting to touch her heart with an unspoken plea. Then she allowed her face to relax, and she held the stare blankly.

"Okay, okay." Amy Lynn huffed and closed the laptop again. "I'll go with y'all."

Amy Lynn left the room to go make herself more presentable, and Lavinia followed, looking upward and whispering a thank you on her way out the door.

Chapter Sixteen

Lavinia climbed into the front passenger seat of the minivan. It was last year's model and still had the new car smell. The leather seat cushioned her back nicely. She sat the large handbag between her feet and started scrolling through Facebook on her phone. As the rest of the family loaded into the van, she fought the urge to post a status update. She was so happy about the whole family going to church together, but she couldn't share it with her online friends. She had to lay low on social media until the investigation was over.

"I'm sitting next to Mama," Dylan called out in a sing-songy voice from outside the car.

"No, I'm sitting next to her!" Lucas said.

"Boys, how 'bout I sit next to Dylan on the way there and with Lucas on the way home?" Amy Lynn said.

"Okay." Lucas relented and got in the back, letting his mother and brother have the two seats in the middle row.

The whole exchange made Lavinia's heart overflow. The boys were so happy to have their mother with them, and in some way, she had helped make it happen for them. But having Amy Lynn come along was even more important to Lavinia. Like another second chance.

As happy as the boys were, they were not thrilled about attending a new church. Dylan was quite proud of his status as an Episcopalian and didn't see why he should be forced to give it up.

"I'm sure this other church will be great, too," Lavinia

reassured. "You can go back to being Episcopalian next week if you want. We just want to try this one. You'll like Ms. Shirley. She was the sweetest thing when I met her a couple weeks ago. I'm looking forward to seeing her again."

Lee drove ten minutes on familiar roads. When the GPS told them they had reached their destination, she was surprised. The church was hidden in plain sight—a converted warehouse on the main highway, with a small sign and a wooden cross in the sandy dirt in front of the building. They passed it often, and she had never even noticed it was a church.

Lee pulled into the gravel parking lot at three minutes before eleven. Amy Lynn, Lee, and the boys piled out of the minivan and stood waiting while Lavinia hoisted the giant bag onto her shoulder, glanced at her reflection in the mirror on the sun visor, and fluffed her hair. She picked up her right knee with both hands and dropped the leg outside of the van. Next the other. She used the door frame to support herself as she stood. Lavinia shielded her eyes from the light as she studied the small, unassuming wooden cross near the church sign. The sun was high in the sky and there were no clouds, but the light around the cross appeared different than the sunlight all around. Different in a way that Lavinia's brain couldn't make sense of.

The sounds of piano and drums pushed their way outside the church's walls and greeted the five of them as they walked toward the building. The style was different, but the song was familiar. The music reached into the recesses of Lavinia's mind and tugged at a memory. The memory tugged at Lavinia's heart and pulled her to another time.

***

Sunday, Summer, 1944

Rows of white lace on Lavinia's socks formed an umbrella over black patent leather shoes. Her chubby legs kicked and feet dangled from the church pew. The shoes were so shiny she could see her face in the toes. She leaned down and stuck out her tongue and pulled on her ears. The face made her giggle and had to be shared.

"Look, Daddy!" Lavinia turned to her father sitting beside her on the pew. She made the funny face again, and, since the service hadn't started yet, he was free to laugh aloud.

"Aren't you a funny one?" her father said. "You love to make people laugh, don't you? And you're so good at it!"

Lavinia snuggled in close to her father.

"Always keep your joy, Lavinia," he said. "And not just any 'ol kind. The joy of the Lord gives us strength." A light flickered through the weariness in his eyes. "That's what we should sing about tonight." He drew his watch out of his pocket and checked the time. "Be a good girl and sit still until Mama comes back with baby brother, okay?"

Lavinia nodded. Her father stood from the pew and made his way to the front, leaning on each pew as he went for extra support. The limp was pronounced but improving.

"Church, let us stand and sing a hymn of joy tonight." Lavinia returned to making faces at her shoes as her father's strong voice carried over the heads of everyone in the congregation. "Turn in your hymnal to page ninety." The piano player began playing without even opening the book. The bouncy notes caught Lavinia's attention.

"I know it don't seem like we got much cause for rejoicin'," Lavinia's father said. "There's no denyin' these are dark times." Voices echoed his sentiment throughout the room. "But we have a blessed hope that doesn't hinge on circumstances here." He jumped right into the chorus and the piano followed.

"It is joy unspeakable and full of glory,

Full of glory, full of glory;
It is joy unspeakable and full of glory,
Oh, the half has never yet been told."

Lavinia sat, captivated by the music—not only her father's strong baritone voice or the piano's driving rhythm—but the lyrics of the hymn. There had been so much sadness around her. People talked about fighting and boys not coming home. And her daddy had been gone for such a long time then came back with a bad leg. Yet there he stood, singing about joy unspeakable. If he could do it, surely, she could carry that same joy around with her everywhere. Surely, it was the kind of joy that would last for all eternity.

***

There were no pews in the old warehouse, just rows of cushioned chairs in three sections. The music continued as they found their seats, and Lavinia was thankful for five chairs together. With Lee leading the way, the family sat two rows from the back on the right side of the church.

People offered friendly smiles and nodded at the newcomers, but they didn't overwhelm them with greeting as Lavinia had feared. It would have been fine with her if they did. She wouldn't have been bothered in the least if someone rushed to say hello and shake her hand, but Lavinia didn't want Amy Lynn to be scared away.

She recognized a ponytail of red curls near the front, in the middle aisle, and she smiled.

The music leader stood on the raised platform at the front of the building, welcomed everyone, and asked them to join him in song. There were no hymnals, but the giant screen behind the director held the words of the precious hymn her father had sung so many years ago. A joyous chorus of voices rang out, and an electricity immediately flowed through the room. She glanced at

Amy Lynn who wasn't singing but wore a peaceful expression.

The church was so different to Lavinia. Some people, like her, wore *church clothes.* For her own tastes, she felt slightly underdressed in her khaki skirt, sweater, panty hose, and dress flats. But others, like Amy Lynn, wore their everyday clothes. And the dress wearers and suit wearers stood side-by-side with the blue jean wearers, and it seemed that neither group had an issue with the other.

There were people of all skin colors and ages. An older Hispanic woman sat next to a white, teenage boy in front of them. To her left, in the middle section, was a couple with six stair-stepped children lined up beside them. A middle-aged black gentleman in front of them turned around during the song with a smile and slipped a handful of candies to the mother who smiled back gratefully. On the other side of the room, a woman left her seat, even as she sang. She slipped into a different row to stand next to a woman who appeared to be there alone.

Lavinia loved people-watching, and she couldn't help but think what a beautiful group of people it was. They reminded her of flowers, picked from all over the garden, bunched together, and placed in a crystal vase to make a gorgeous bouquet.

The song ended, and Lavinia dabbed at the tear of nostalgia in the corner of her eye as the band struck up another. The new song had a driving beat, and the drummer played enthusiastically, raising his sticks high between the beats. Two ladies with microphones joined the male singer on the platform. They had nice, soulful voices, and they sang the words on the screen over and over again.

"I don't know what this music is, but I like it!" Lavinia said to Dylan beside her. He nodded in agreement.

People all around her clapped, and they looked so happy about it that Lavinia joined them. She became lost in the music, but not in the notes and beats, and not in the emotion of the song. There was something else tangible about the worship. Heaven hung in the air and she breathed it in. A long-forgotten feeling swelled within her and begged to be poured out. She closed her eyes and tilted her head back toward the ceiling. In that moment, Lavinia connected with God in a way she vowed never to forget again.

When the music was over, everyone sat down and the young preacher took the stage. He had no podium or lectern. He held his Bible in his hands for the entire sermon. He was charismatic but genuine, and even Dylan and Lucas were fixated on his words. The entire stage was his workshop. He cut away at confusion and hammered out a message so plain. He smoothed each of his points and delivered them to the listeners with love. He didn't look like the preachers of Lavinia's day—with his blue jeans and spiky hair—but he sounded like them. He was fiery in a way that brought comfort, not condemnation, and the words of the message stirred her heart even more than the music had.

"Yea, I have loved thee with an everlasting love: therefore with lovingkindness have I drawn thee[3]," he read.

It felt so good, not only being there, but being there with the right attitude and the right purpose. Surely, she had been drawn, like the Scripture said.

Soon the dismissal amen was pronounced. People began filing out of the rows. Some milled about in conversation. Others hit the door fast, no doubt to be first in line at the lunch buffet.

As she side-stepped her way to the aisle, holding Dylan's hand for balance, a friendly voice called out. "Mrs. Lewis! Officer Davenport!" Shirley made her way toward them from the front of the church in double-time. "What a nice surprise!" she said.

"Good to see you, Shirley," Lee said. He reached out and shook her hand.

Shirley reached for Lavinia's hand next. "I'm so glad you

[3] Jeremiah 31:3 (KJV)

came!" she said.

"Well, thank you for inviting me." Lavinia introduced Shirley to Amy Lynn, Lucas, and Dylan. "We enjoyed the service. Didn't we, boys?" She tousled Dylan's hair as he nodded.

"You keepin' Neville straight this week, Shirley?" Lee joked.

"Oh, I'm doing my best. It's not easy," she answered playfully.

They chatted for a couple of minutes, then Lee and Amy Lynn said goodbye to Shirley and made their way to the door.

Lavinia lingered with Shirley. She grabbed her hand. "I do thank you for inviting us," Lavinia said. "This service was just what I needed today."

Shirley smiled warmly. "I'm so glad," she said.

"You did throw me off a little, though"—Lavinia winked—"with that first hymn followed by something so new and different."

"I can understand that." Shirley chuckled. "We are a little all over the place. But we try not to focus on style and format so much as pointing people to Jesus." She placed a firm, reassuring hand on Lavinia's back.

"I can see you are doing just that." Lavinia's voice was tender, appreciative.

"I hope you can come back again soon. Matt's our associate pastor. My husband Chuck preaches most Sundays. He's the head pastor."

"I enjoyed his sermon, and being here is...well...like I said, it's just what I needed."

Their hands were still joined, suspended in the air between them, with Lavinia's fingers curled around the tips of Shirley's.

"Oh, we're having a fall festival on Wednesday," Shirley said. "Maybe your family would like to come."

Shirley gave her all the details while Lavinia nodded with interest. It had already occurred to her that she'd miss all the festivities at Cypress Shores this year, but maybe a church festival would be a good alternative.

"You know," Shirley said, leaning in closer, "I invite Neville to the festival every year, hoping he'll come since it's not regular church. But he's a tough nut to crack. I have to be very careful not to push him away. I can get him to the Moose Lodge for Bingo, but he draws the line at church."

Lavinia's brow furrowed. "It's a shame he feels that way. I wonder why."

Shirley shrugged and shook her head. "I wish I knew. He's been that way for as long as I've known him. Maybe one day we'll win him over."

***

On the way home from church, Lavinia was on cloud nine. *What investigation? Wendy who? Criminal charges—what?* Her circumstances seemed less consequential now.

If only Neville, and everyone else, had the same kind of unspeakable joy she carried with her out of those church doors, the lingering, sustaining peace that settled over her. Lavinia's time at Solid Rock Church made her happier than a boatload of gags. The thrill of a good prank didn't come close.

Chapter Seventeen

Monday, October 29

"Wendy Wisengood is out of the hospital. I thought you might like to know," Neville said.

Lavinia breathed her relief against the smartphone screen. She sat in a lounge chair on the back patio of Amy Lynn and Lee's house, her long legs stretched out in the warm sunshine drying freshly polished toenails. Everyone was at work or school, so she had the place all to herself.

"Oh, goodness me," she said. "I'm so glad she's doing better. And it...it must be nice for her to go home." The slightest bit of resentment crept into her voice and into her spirit.

"Lavinia, I'm trying to get you back there, too. I finally got statements from your other character witnesses. They'll be very helpful if we need them. And, I think you'll be happy to know, I got my hands on Marvin Mickle's statement to the police. Listen to this...he vouched for you. He told them all of your antics have been, quote, good-natured and never harmful."

Lavinia smiled. Marvin really did like her after all.

"It didn't turn up any leads, but I've spent the last few days researching all the staff that had access to your apartment, though I didn't expect to find anything anyway. They all had background checks before they were hired. I talked to a couple of the maids, and I can tell you, they seemed really sad that you had to leave Cypress Shores. Especially Francesca, the one with the heavy accent. That girl actually cried over the telephone."

"Oh, she always has been so sweet to me. Bless her heart. And bless yours, too. It sounds like you've been busy!"

"There's another maid I'm still checking on. *What's her name?* Kimberly. Some of the others said she bad-mouths Mrs. Wisengood for being a difficult customer, really fussy about the way she likes things. I'd like to talk to her."

"She always did seem a bit sketchy, but, Neville, I would still bet my last dollar that it was Gordon Proctor. You just wait and see. I'm not tellin' you how to do your job, but—"

"I know, Lavinia. I called Mr. Proctor again this morning. He didn't answer, but I'll keep trying. The police said they had no reason to interview him, but we'll get him to talk."

"When?" Lavinia said.

Neville huffed into the phone. "I want to give him time to respond on his own. But if I have to, I'll subpoena him. Just be patient."

The whole mess hinged on getting Gordon to talk. Or somehow proving that he did it. That constipated-looking old codger should be brought to justice, and the lack of progress was like driving behind a school bus on the interstate. Still, she had to be gracious. Neville had practiced law for a long time, and she had to trust him. Even more than that, she had to trust God to work it out. Her renewed faith insisted it; it required the mammoth task of believing that every situation's outcome was somehow good and right, even if it didn't seem like it on the surface, and even if it seemed anything *but* good.

"It's only been a little over two weeks since the incident," Neville said, as if reading her mind. "And we have time." He paused. "Listen, I probably shouldn't tell you this, but...not to get your hopes up, but..."

"What? What is it?"

"I think the DA is a lot of talk. Chances are, by the end of November, he'll realize that he's making too big of a deal out of this thing, and he'll drop it. Then you'll just have to worry about a possible civil suit. But I can help you with that, too. And Marvin says he'll let you come back if you're cleared, or if the investigation is dropped."

"Oh, Neville." The admiration in her voice surprised her. She said nothing more, but celebrated silently, until a long silence prompted her to switch gears fast and spit out the invitation she'd been chewing on since Sunday.

"Neville, I really appreciate your call. And since I have you on the phone, did Shirley mention that I saw her this weekend?" She tried to be as casual as possible.

"Yes, um, actually, she did. She said you visited her church."

"My whole family visited there. It was very enjoyable." What came next? Where was she going with this? Lavinia's brain stumbled on the memory of her dream the night before, in which she showed up to a potluck at Cypress Shores wearing only her brassiere and panty girdle. Her mouth went dry and her free hand shook. Not quite a lie, she went with a question to which she already knew the answer. "Have you ever been to Shirley's church?"

"No, I haven't, Lavinia." There were ice cubes in his voice.

"Well, you should think about going sometime. Oh, I'm so sorry, Neville. I think one of the boys needs me. I should go. Thank you again for calling."

There was the lie. She ended the call right after the fib slipped out. She hadn't meant to do it, but she had panicked. Like always, she took herself to the woodshed right away. She had to make it right or she wouldn't be able to sleep tonight. She sat up and put her bare feet down on the warm concrete. She shielded the phone screen from the glare of the sun and tapped the little green square with the white handset silhouette on it, then she touched on the number at the top of the *recents* list. She put the phone to her ear and pushed her glasses higher on her nose. At the end of each ring, Lavinia considered tapping the red square on the screen before Neville could answer, but on the third ring, it was too late.

"Hello?"

"Neville, this is Lavinia again. I'm sorry, but I need to tell you that I lied earlier. The boys weren't calling me. I...I...well, I just needed to go."

"Oka-ayyy..." His voice was a mixture of confused and curious.

Another awkward silence threatened to make Lavinia hang up without saying another word, but she fought through it.

"I called back to tell you..." Once she shut down the nerves, her words dripped with southern sweetness. It came out instinctively. She'd inherited the gift through observation, from studying, as a child, her mother and grandmother as they wielded their own powers of feminine persuasion.

"I, well I...I know this might sound a little strange...but, I had a really nice time at church yesterday, and in fact, it was so enjoyable, that I really think you should go, too...and I know you've told Shirley no in the past, but I think you should go this Wednesday because it isn't really church, it's a harvest festival, and there will be food and games and a costume contest, and I think you would have fun." Lavinia gulped a silent breath. Her plea had been persuasive, even if a bit lengthy.

"Interesting." He cleared his throat, then spoke slowly. "Are you inviting me to go with you?"

Was there hopefulness in his voice? *Was* she inviting Neville to go with her? Obviously. That had to be why she'd hung up before—she was nervous about asking Neville to go on a church date with her and her family...on a date with her and her family...on a date. The invitation to the park had felt different, friendlier. The nerves came back, and with good reason. Now coupled with the possibility of rejection was the fact that she'd never asked a man on a date before; never even been on a date with anyone besides her husband. Edgar was her every first; he'd been the only; and, she assumed, the last.

"Yes, well, with me and my family. Lee will be there." That seemed to reduce the awkwardness. "You see, it's like this. We've decided to get theme costumes, and we're missing somebody." Lavinia relaxed back in the lounge chair.

"Okay. What are you going as?"

"We-ell..."

Neville chuckled. "That bad, huh?"

"No, no. It's just...you might think it's silly."

"Try me." He didn't shoot her down right off the bat, so that was a good sign. The afternoon sun was blinding, so she stood and paced the patio to escape it. Her steps helped drive the conversation.

"Amy Lynn is going as Dorothy. Lee is Toto. Isn't that funny? Lucas is the Cowardly Lion, which is ironic—he's really a brave kid. And Dylan is the Scarecrow, which is also ironic because he's always been a smarty pants."

"And who are you, the Wicked Witch?"

Lavinia might have been offended if not for Neville's playful tone.

"No, silly. I'm Glinda the Good Witch, of course."

"Of course." He paused. "Hmmm...if I know my classic movies, then that means you're missing...a Tin Man, *right?*"

"Yeah, the one that needs a heart. Fitting, isn't it? The lawyer going as the Tin Man? Some people say lawyers are heartless, don't they?"

"Oh, c'mon now. Nobody says that."

"You keep telling yourself that, Neville." She laughed.

Things were going much better than Lavinia could have

hoped for. Her attempt to get Neville to church seemed to be working. She reminded herself that was the goal.

"But, how on earth am I going to get a costume in two days?" he said.

"Oh, don't worry about it. We're not going all out. Our costumes are simple. Just wear a gray shirt, and I'll help you with a little bit of silver face paint and a funnel hat. And we'll make a little heart to pin on your shirt. I'll even find an oil can for you to carry. You'll look great! I mean, uh, you'll look the part."

"So, it's not *church?*"

"No, Neville. It's a harvest festival." She was bolder now. "But if it *was* church, may I ask why would you be so against it?"

"No, you may not."

"Okay then. Fair enough. So, you'll come?"

"It would make your grandsons pretty happy to have the whole cast of characters there, wouldn't it?"

"Oh, yes. Definitely."

"And I'd be making Shirley happy too, I guess."

"Without a doubt."

He sighed loudly. "Okay, then. I guess I'll see you Wednesday."

When they ended the call, Lavinia sat back down sideways in the lounge chair as fast as her creaking knees would allow. Slowly, she moved her shaking legs up to the chair, then she dropped the phone into her lap, laid back, and threw her arm over her face in dramatic fashion, quite amazed that she'd convinced him to go and wondering how she'd ever convinced herself it was a good idea to ask him in the first place.

Chapter Eighteen

Wednesday, October 31

The costumes turned out even better than Lavinia had hoped. With only a wand and wings from the dollar store, some glittery eye shadow, and a flowy white skirt from her summer wardrobe, she felt like the good witch, and like a little kid again. A store-bought lion mask and brown sweats for Dylan, and a flannel shirt, floppy hat, and some straw for Lucas, and her grandsons looked straight out of Oz. The laziest costume was Lee's. He'd printed a picture of a Toto-looking dog from the internet and glued it to a popsicle stick to make a mask. Thanks to Amazon Prime, Amy Lynn had the only complete, purchased costume. It made her look positively adorable and at least five years younger.

The family stood in the parking lot of Solid Rock Church waiting on Lavinia to finish Neville's getup. The boys chased each other around the van and Amy Lynn and Lee stood hugged up against the driver side door like teenagers.

"I can't believe you talked me into this," Neville said, with only a hint of amusement. "How long have we known each other now? Two weeks today, I think."

"*They law!* Is that all? It seems like so much longer."

"I don't know how to take that." He pretended to be offended, and Lavinia slapped playfully at his shoulder, barely brushing the fibers of his shirt with the tips of her fingers.

She dipped a wedge-shaped sponge into a small, circular

container of costume makeup then dabbed lightly at Neville's cheeks. The process was uncomfortable at first. They were close. She could smell his aftershave. And she was reminded that he could probably smell the onions she'd had on her burger at lunch. After a few strokes on his cheeks, the closeness wasn't as awkward, and Lavinia relaxed.

Neville wore a hat Lavinia had made by spraying a funnel, which had also come from the dollar store, with silver paint. Amy Lynn had hot glued a piece of stretchy cord to it, which sat under his chin like a birthday party hat. It was the first time Lavinia had seen him without a suit. He wore a gray polo tucked into gray slacks, with a black belt, and it made him seem so different—more relaxed, more approachable.

"Not too much, okay?" Neville said.

"Of course not. Too much makeup is a fashion no-no." She giggled. "Just a little more here on your nose."

She rubbed the sponge softly on his face to smooth the silver makeup. Her makeup skills had adapted over the years, as she learned how best to apply buff beige number two over the lines and sags of her own changing face, but she'd never put makeup on a man before.

"Okay, here's your oil can." Lavinia handed Neville the prop. It was a miniature watering can, but it served its purpose.

"I think we're ready!" Lavinia announced to everyone. The setting sun cast a pink hue over the parking lot. The air was calm and the temperature still mild enough for short sleeves.

"Oh, wait!" Lavinia said. "I need to give you my heart." She reached into the open passenger seat of the van and into her bag, then pulled out a red piece of felt she had cut herself. She admired the heart before handing it to Neville. Slightly lopsided, but overall it looked nice.

"Here, I'll let you do it," she said. She passed some safety pins to him with the heart.

"Thank you," he said. His voice was thoughtful.

He fumbled to pin it on. He poked himself in the chest once and winced. The second time was his thumb and he cursed under his breath. Lavinia fought the maternal urge to scold him for cussing in the church parking lot. Then she fought the urge to jump in and pin the heart on for him. Eventually, he managed.

"There. How's that look?"

Lavinia stood back and admired her handiwork.

"You look great, Tin Man."

"Thank you. Now, let's go to a non-churchy harvest festival."

"Don't you need your cane tonight?"

"No, I'm feeling a little spring in my step. I'll leave it in the truck."

Lavinia left her bag, and even her smartphone in the van, too.

The parking lot was full of vehicles, and families streamed inside the large building. They were directed through the sanctuary and through a door at the back that led into another room just as large. Games were set up all along two walls of the room. Near the back of the room were tables for Bingo. One corner was dedicated to the cake walk. There was a serving window where ladies handed out hot dogs and bowls of chicken stew from a kitchen on the other side of the wall. Tables were spread out in the center of the room.

"Let's play a game," Dylan said. "I call bowling first!"

"How about we eat dinner first, kiddo," his father said.

Lucas pouted, though he hadn't been the one to ask.

Amy Lynn led the group toward the serving line. Lavinia and Neville brought up the rear, and she surveyed the room as they walked.

Halfway to the food, Shirley approached and stopped dead in her tracks, her mouth open.

"You told me you were coming, but you didn't tell me about

this. Oh, my goodness, Neville McGrath!"

"I wanted to keep it a surprise," Neville said.

"Well, I'm certainly surprised! You look great! Y'all get together and let me get a picture."

Neville held up his hand. "No photographic evidence, please," he said, even while he posed with Lavinia and the family. After the picture was taken, Lee, Amy Lynn, and the boys got in line while Neville and Lavinia chatted with Shirley. She gave Neville a quick side-hug and told him she was glad he came.

"You look great, too, Mrs. Lewis," she said.

"Thank you, Shirley. And so do you!"

"Arrggh! Thank ye, matey!" With her one uncovered eye, she looked down at her puffy blouse and brown short pants. "You should see Captain Pastor Chuck. I'm his first mate! Go get yourself some food now. He's getting ready to give a quick message after everyone gets seated."

Neville gave Shirley a *you-tricked-me* look then turned to Lavinia with the same raised eyebrow expression. Shirley put on a sheepish grin, and Lavinia raised her eyebrows back at Neville and shrugged her shoulders, smiling.

Shirley left to help the women in the kitchen, and Lavinia and Neville got their plates and joined the family at a table in the center of the room. The boys scarfed down the hot dogs at an unhealthy pace while the grown-ups savored the comforting fall favorite in their bowls. Crushed saltines and an extra dash of pepper made the chicken stew just right to Lavinia.

The pirate pastor called everyone to attention, and Lavinia sensed Neville tense up in the chair beside her.

"Thank you all for coming," Chuck said. "I hope you're enjoying your dinner. While you're eating, I'd like to share some thoughts with you. We talk about this every year around this time, about how Christians are like pumpkins."

Chuck's voice was warm and engaging. He had all the childrens' attention, standing there in his pirate costume, eyepatch and all, holding a carved pumpkin.

"You see, someone had to pick this pumpkin from the vine. First, God picks us. We've been chosen of God. How cool is that? Then he cleans us up, like whoever picked this pumpkin from the patch probably had to knock a bunch of dirt off of it. But the really yucky stuff was inside. So, just like we have to cut the top off of this pumpkin and scoop all the guts out, Jesus cleans us up on the inside." He paused and scanned the room. "How many of you have handled pumpkin guts?" He raised his hand. "They're pretty yucky, right?" He nodded as he spoke. "I can tell you, my sin was much yuckier than pumpkin guts before Jesus cleaned me up on the inside." A couple of older people said 'amen.' Neville squirmed in his seat, stared hard at the table, and cleared his throat. Lavinia silently prayed that he wouldn't leave.

"But that's not all," Chuck continued. "See how this jack-o-lantern shines? When we get saved, Jesus puts his light in us so that we can shine for Him. And you see how this pumpkin looks? See that smile?" Some of the kids giggled at the happy-faced pumpkin. "That's how being cleaned up and having the light of Jesus makes us feel. So, you remember that whenever you see a jack-o-lantern sittin' on a front porch. Okay?"

As people clapped then went back to eating, Chuck walked over and set the pumpkin on Lavinia's table, closest to Dylan.

"You can take this guy home with you if it's okay with mom and dad," he said. Dylan and Lucas looked to their parents who both nodded, smiling.

"Thanks, pastor," Lucas said.

Chuck nodded in response.

"Good to see you here tonight, Neville!" Chuck reached out to shake Neville's hand.

"Good to see you, Chuck," Neville said.

After Chuck's mini-sermon, Lavinia worried she'd pushed Neville too far. But the rest of the evening, he looked much more at ease. He and Lavinia played two games of Bingo while Amy Lynn and Lee walked around with the boys playing games at all the different stations. At the cake walk, when the music stopped and number seven was called, Lavinia won a giant slice of pineapple upside-down cake and Neville gave her a thumbs up.

"Let's sit down, Lavinia," Neville said after the cake walk. "Boy do I hate to admit it, but sciatica and arthritis have decided to tag team me all of a sudden."

"Do you want me to go get your cane?"

"No, no. Let's just sit for a while."

They returned to the same table where they had eaten dinner. Amy Lynn waved to them from the football toss game where it was Lucas's turn to throw. Lavinia waved back with her wand then laid it down.

"Did I tell you I've finished my other cases?" Neville said as he plopped into the seat.

"No, you didn't. That's good, I guess?"

He cupped his ear. The music from a game of hokey pokey on one side of the room and the radio being used for cake walk made the room loud.

"Yes, it's good. It means you're my only client at the moment, and I can start spending more time on a strategy to prove you're innocent, in case the District Attorney does go through with his crazy scheme." He waved his hands reassuringly. "I still don't believe he will, but just in case." He began to drum his fingers on the table, just like at the Provision Company. After only two weeks, Lavinia had spotted his nervous habit.

"Plus, I'm...well, I'm clearing my schedule a bit. Not taking any more cases until I decide about the move."

"Oh. Oh, yes. I'd nearly forgotten about that. Maine, is it, that you're considering?" She scanned the room—a sea of zoo animals, caped crusaders, cartoon characters, and the occasional pumpkin—trying to avoid his glance.

"Yes, Lake St. George."

"Well, that makes sense, I guess, to reduce your workload in case you decide to go." She tried desperately to hide the disappointment in her voice.

"I am a little concerned, though, Lavinia."

The way he said her name made her turn toward him.

"I don't want to be a heel," he said. "When I take a case, I see it through. I agreed to help you, and if you're charged, I'll stay here to defend you in court. I mean…I probably wouldn't leave right away, anyway, if I decide to move. Or maybe I could come back for a while, for court, if needed."

"Oh, that's too much travelin' for someone your…our age," Lavinia said.

Neville didn't argue.

"Lavinia, I don't mean to make you worry. But I'm too fond of you not to be straight with you."

"You're…you're what?" She sat up straight and grasped the sides of the chair's seat.

"How could I not be fond of you?" he said. "You're a very charming woman, Lavinia. And I do want to help you clear your name and move back to Cypress Shores. All I need is one break, one lead."

Neville's face showed worry for the first time. The suddenly furrowed brow and weary eyes spoke his concern. She put her hand on the table and found it creeping toward his, a centimeter at a time. She wanted to comfort him and show her gratitude, but the right boundaries had to be kept. What *were* the right boundaries in a relationship like theirs? *Just* an attorney wouldn't care so much. If he were *only* legal counsel, he wouldn't be there with her. Somewhere in the span of two weeks, Neville had become, at the very least, a friend.

The crowd began to thin, and Lavinia checked her watch. *8:02.* People made their way past the pair, on the way to the exit. Absent-minded children, hopped up on candy, bumped Lavinia's chair as they passed. Neville's head was down, his eyes locked on his own clasped hands. Lavinia's timid hand drifted along the smooth tabletop. It came within two inches of Neville's and stopped as an excited young voice called out to her.

"Hey, Nana! Look! I won a whole cake!"

"Wow! Would you look at that?" She faced Dylan who stood holding a two-layer chocolate cake covered in plastic wrap on a cardboard disc.

"Hey, Mama! Ready to go?" Amy Lynn said as she approached.

"I guess we've had all our fun for tonight." Lavinia used the table and the back of the chair to push herself into a standing position.

The group made their way out with the rest of the throng, and Lavinia and Neville were separated in the shuffle. Outside the church, Pastor Chuck and Shirley approached Lavinia and her family.

"Mrs. Lewis," Chuck said, "Shirley tells me you're going through a rough time right now, some unfair legal trouble."

Lavinia was surprised by his directness. Most people avoided the subject; they danced around it. But he brought the nasty, shameful business out into the light.

"Would it be okay if we prayed with you about it?" Chuck said. His words were better than a warm embrace. They seemed prompted by genuine concern and compassion.

"Of course," Lavinia said. Her family gathered around.

Chuck took Lavinia's hand to pray as Neville walked up on the group and froze like a deer in headlights. From over Chuck's shoulder, she saw him and graciously dismissed him with a nod. Neville looked around, then ducked into the shadows as Chuck began to pray.

"God, we thank you for our new friends. We know you can help Mrs. Lewis through this hardship. Let the truth come out. Let justice be done in her case. Give Neville the wisdom to defend her well. Lord, let Your will be done for the both of them."

Chapter Nineteen

Saturday, November 3

They spent part of the morning with Rosie. Her eyes lit up when she saw them, but she didn't whistle this time. She stayed quiet while her new nurse did all the talking.

"She's been eating fine," Nurse Regina said. "She prefers oatmeal for breakfast. I have a hard time getting her to eat as many vegetables as I would like for lunch, and of course, I'm not here for dinner, but the nightshift nurses say she loves banana pudding for dessert." The large woman sat on the edge of the chair holding her hands in her lap. She wore a uniform, which was different than Rosie's previous nurse.

Lavinia and Neville sat in the window seat. Lavinia sat cross-legged with her elbow on her knee and her head propped on her fist. Her eyes were wide as she listened, to stay awake. She nodded and held her mouth in an *'Oh, is that right?'* pose every few moments, pretending Rosie's diet was as interesting as her favorite daytime soap.

"She gets weighed every week, so we'll know right away if her nutrition needs to change," Regina said.

Rosie sat in the bed, staring at the television that was turned down so as not to disrupt the conversation. The chef on the program diced an onion, added it to the pot, then stirred the soup. Rosie seemed content to watch without sound.

"I take her vital signs twice during my shift. They're all

logged here in this book." The nurse patted a white binder on the nightstand.

Lavinia looked over at Neville who had started to nod off.

"It's seems like you're certainly taking good care of her," Lavinia said. "But when I asked how she'd been doing, what I really meant was, has she been in a good mood? Does she seem happy?"

"Oh..."

"You can tell, generally, by the songs she whistles. She'll let you know if she's happy or not."

"Yes, I've heard her whistling some, but not very much. She's been fairly quiet. Like I said, my first day was Monday, so we're still figuring each other out."

The nurse reached over and patted Rosie on her toothpick of an arm.

Lavinia stood and walked around to the other side of Rosie's bed. Rosie pressed the power button on the remote.

Sitting down on the bed, Lavinia gently took Rosie by the shoulders to get a good look at her. Rosie smiled faintly.

"Let's hear some "Yankee Doodle"," Lavinia said.

Rosie stayed silent.

"How about "She'll Be Comin' Round the Mountain"?"

Lavinia didn't want to push. She knew there were days when Rosie didn't communicate much. But something seemed wrong.

"Have there been any other changes for her that you know of?" Lavinia asked the nurse. "Since her other nurse quit?"

Regina put a finger to her lip. "*Hmmm,* let me see. I don't think so. But the night nurse did tell me this morning that the previous nurse came by last night. Said it was past visitin' hours, but she wanted to check Rosie's room for something she mighta left."

"Interesting." Lavinia looked back at Rosie. "Did Jenny find what she came lookin' for, Rosie?"

Rosie locked eyes with her but didn't whistle or nod.

"Was it nice to see your other nurse again? Did she stay a while?"

Rosie dropped her head. The whistle started with low pitch and volume, and it caught Lavinia by surprise. After a few notes, Rosie looked up and continued with a more confident-sounding melody.

"Hey, I know this one," Lavinia said. She looked at Neville who was now wide awake and listening intently. "She's whistling the grinch song, from the Christmas movie. I used to watch it with Amy Lynn every year."

"Well, listen at her! Say, she's good," the nurse said.

Neville walked to the bed, and Rosie stopped whistling. He reached toward her, and she offered her hand. As her bony fingers wrapped around his rough hand, a hollow, airy sound escaped his pursed lips.

"It's like our own game of name that tune," Regina said.

"And I know that one, too," Lavinia said. Her face beamed up at Neville from the opposite side of the hospital bed.

After a few measures, Neville stopped whistling. "I know that you understand our words just fine, Rosie," he said. "But I wanted to try your language. We're going to figure out what you're trying to tell us about Nurse Jenny."

On the way down the hall as they left, and across the parking lot, Lavinia had the song stuck in her head. And when Neville cranked the old pickup to life, they shared a moment of shock. James Taylor's voice rang out from the truck speakers, singing Neville's song to Rosie—"You've Got a Friend."

***

They spent the afternoon at City Pier.

"You keep talking me into things that no one else can,

Lavinia," Neville said.

"I don't believe I had to twist your arm, mister," Lavinia said. She slid a slimy piece of shrimp over the end of a hook. "You told me you enjoy fishing, and it's a nice day for it. And I figure I could do worse for company."

"Well, of course, I enjoy it. But I wasn't *planning* on fishing today. I normally make plans instead of just *doing*. I had to drive all the way home, change clothes, and come back here." He smirked. "Oh, and you certainly *could* have done worse for company, but probably not by much."

It hadn't taken him long at all to swap his suit for jeans and meet her there with two rods, bait, and a small tackle box.

"Maybe we should have tried the pier on the island," Lavinia said. The pier was crowded, but a young couple had given up their claim to one of the few benches so that Lavinia and Neville could sit.

"No, this is fine," he said.

Lavinia cast the line into the water, aiming for the silhouette of Old Baldy. She shielded her eyes with one hand for a better view of the Bald Head Island lighthouse in the distance, then she looked around at all the people on the pier as she sat back down.

The crowd was only part of the reason Lavinia second-guessed the location. That pier had belonged to her and Edgar before he died. It was their favorite place. From the corner, where it shifted into an *L* shape, over to the right, she could see part of the house they had shared. It was their dream retirement home, with a facade straight out of *Architectural Digest*. It was much bigger than the two of them needed, but form had won out over function.

"I'm glad you talked me into this," Neville said. "I have a feeling I'm going to catch a fish for the first time in a long time."

"Well, you know you have to put the line in the water first, right?"

"Ha, ha. Very funny." He pulled at the line to tighten the

knot above the hook. "You can question my methods, but I make sure everything is rigged up *just right.* Nothing worse than losing a whopper because of a bad rig." He stood and stepped over his cane, which lay on the wooden boards of the pier, then hauled back and let the bait fly through the air before it hit the water with a satisfying *plunk.*

"You know, I don't know why I don't come out here more often, really. I guess I just always preferred boat fishing. But I had to give it up. Too hard to get in and out of my little pontoon with these knees."

"Getting older is certainly…interesting," Lavinia said.

It was nice talking to Neville about their shared experiences. She was still in decent shape, but she sensed that Neville, like her, believed his good health was nearing the end of its limited warranty.

Aging had never troubled Edgar. He was strong of mind and body right up until the moment his heart gave out without warning. But Lavinia had lived in constant expectation of death since losing Samuel, and even more so after Edgar—not fearfully or with sadness, and not hopefully; but with a general awareness of the eventuality. Like a guest that had responded to an invitation for a floating party, she knew it was coming; she just didn't know when.

"Are you closer to a decision about moving?" Lavinia said.

"Not really."

"My husband Edgar always said, if you're torn between two choices, have someone else pick it for you. Once you hear their choice, your gut will tell you if it's the right one or not. Just a little way of tricking yourself into knowing what it really is that you want."

"Oh, that's ridiculous! No offense to Edgar. A man should be able to make up his mind without all that psychological hooey."

"Why don't you try it," she said.

"Nah, I'll figure it out." He shifted on the bench.

"But how?"

"It'll come to me. I don't have to give him an answer until the end of the month anyway."

"Now you're sounding like me. Putting your worries off 'til another day."

"Yeah, I guess I have two deadlines to worry about, though." He drummed the fingers of his free hand on his knee. "Answering Donald, and the DA's *supposed* deadline to press charges."

"No pressure, huh?"

"Shirley says once I decide about Maine, maybe I'll stop having all these crazy dreams. More psychological hooey if you ask me."

Lavinia leaned closer to him. "What do you dream about?" she said.

"Oh, the wackiest things. Most of the time Donald is there. Like, we're riding motorcycles in a forest and a moose jumps out of the woods holding a surfboard."

"You're kidding!"

"No! Or Donald driving me to the hospital in his car, but it has a siren like an ambulance and when we get there, they've turned the hospital into a roller rink."

"*Oh, my, Neville!* I think Shirley might be right! That, or maybe…"

"Maybe what?"

"Maybe you dream those things just because you're stressed out from working too hard. And you need to spend more time on City Pier with good company throwing a line in the water."

There was no mistaking the twinkle in his eye. "Maybe you're right," he said.

Over the wind and waves, Lavinia heard Porky Pig coming from her bag. She reached down to retrieve the phone.

"It's Amy Lynn. Oh, my word." Lavinia said, looking down

at the message on the screen.

"What is it?"

"I can't believe it!" she said, holding her breath.

"What?"

"Don't that beat all!"

"Woman, will you tell me what it is?"

Lavinia finally refilled her lungs. "She says the video of Dylan and Lucas pranking us about the gator at the park has gone viral."

"Viral? Does that mean it got infected with something?"

"No, silly!" She gave his shoulder a gentle swat.

"I'm just teasing. I know what it means."

"Here, look! Amy Lynn helped Lucas post it to YouTube."

"Twenty thousand views?"

"Yeah! So much for keeping a low profile. But isn't it fun? No tellin' who's seen it! We mighta made the president chuckle. Or the Queen of England."

"I kinda doubt that."

"Well, I'm sure somebody found it at least amusing, and I think that's special."

"I guess you're right. It is pretty special."

The tip of the rod in his hand suddenly bent downward, and Neville stood and leaned on the railing of the pier to better manhandle whatever creature was on the other end of the line. He set the hook with a quick jerk, wound up the slack, then began to steadily reel in the fish.

Lavinia stood up, too, ready to help him if needed. Bystanders and other fishermen watched them, waiting to see what prize Neville would bring up from the hidden depths. It was like a magic act. Sometimes a cutup piece of shrimp went into the water and a big fish came out.

On the pier, everyone was the same. Titles and status

disappeared the moment shoes hit the wooden boards. Neville wasn't a lawyer there; he was a fisherman, just the same as the guy a few feet away who wore a striped, button-up shirt with his first name embroidered on the left breast pocket. There was a kinship between all the people. They weren't young or old. For their time on the pier, they were each under the timeless spell of the sea, connected by its power and the desire to reel in a whopper.

The fish that put up such a fight wasn't as big as Lavinia expected, but it was a decently sized red drum, and Neville looked as happy as if it had been three times the size. She took her phone out and made him pose for a picture with the fish. A few people complimented him on the catch as they strolled by.

After he returned the fish to the water and wiped his dirty hands on his blue jeans, Neville sat back down with an *umpf.* He held onto the rod but didn't cast it again. Conversation went back to the viral video.

"One thing about the internet…doesn't it bother you being *out there?* What about privacy?"

"Well, for one thing, I don't put all my business online for the world to see. Some people just kill me talkin' 'bout every little thing that ails 'em or what they had for breakfast, lunch, and dinner. And so many get on there and talk about their ex and a hundred and one reasons he or she is a deadbeat and why they called it quits. I just don't get it. But even if I did share too much, it's not like I have any dirty laundry anyway. No deep, dark secrets to worry about." He gave her a knowing look. "Well," she said, "except for that one thing you know about. And that's not bad. It's just not something I volunteer. But I still think the good of all this new stuff outweighs the bad of it. I wouldn't have met Wilmer if it wasn't for this gadget." She patted at the phone in her pocket. "And you sure can learn a lot about people on the internet. Although, sometimes a lot more than you wanna know. Let me tell you."

"I bet. I'll admit, I appreciate the technology. Shirley does online research for me all the time. I'm not against the technology. I'm against the way people are addicted to it. We've forgotten how to think for ourselves."

She'd gotten so wrapped up in conversation, she almost forgot about her line in the water. When she finally got a bite, she hollered, and Neville laughed. She reeled it in while Neville stood by. Another drum, this one larger than the one he had caught.

"Do you want help with that? Or do you want to take it off the hook yourself?"

In response, she grabbed the fish by the gills with her left hand and twisted the hook from its lip with the other. She handed him the rod, though, so she could pose for a fish selfie.

Lavinia rested her elbow on the pier railing to help keep her balance. The fish dangled in front of her as she held the phone up high. Neville laughed as she posed like she'd seen all the teenage girls do. Chin up, cheeks sucked in. After getting the reaction she wanted, Lavinia relaxed into a posture more befitting a woman her age and snapped the picture. Thanks to technology, she'd have help remembering the day she landed such a great catch.

Chapter Twenty

Sunday, November 4

"Can you believe it's still warm enough to sit on the patio and paint nails?" Lavinia said.

Amy Lynn put the last stroke of Rum Raisin on the little finger of her mother's left hand.

"Now, now, Mama," she chided playfully. "You *paint* a barn. You *polish* nails."

Amy Lynn's laugh was priceless, and coupled with the gleam in her eyes from the afternoon sun, it nearly brought Lavinia to tears of joy.

"Oh, *excu-use* me. Polish," Lavinia said.

For the first time in years, they enjoyed time for just the two of them. No husbands, no children. Just mother and daughter and the simple joy of attractive, unnaturally colored fingernails.

"Maybe the difference is that we get them polished at the salon, and at home we paint them. But this is much better than going to a salon. Don't you think?" Lavinia did jazz hands to speed the drying time.

Amy Lynn smiled at her mother and nodded in agreement.

"I had such a nice time at church with my family this morning," Lavinia said. She leaned back in her chair and held her hands up, still now, her elbows on the armrests, in a *being-robbed-at-gunpoint* pose.

"The boys seemed to enjoy it, too." Amy Lynn browsed

through the collection of bottles in the little white basket, looking for the right shade for fall. "Mama, I hope you know I don't plan on going every week, but...it was nice today. And last week."

Lavinia ignored the negative. Amy Lynn had admitted that she enjoyed being there. That was enough for now.

"I love the music," Lavinia said. "A good mix of older and newer." She chuckled. "Kind of like me and you. Older and newer."

"I'd hardly call myself *newer* anymore, Mama."

"Well, if that's true, then what does it make me?" Lavinia laughed. "I'm practically a relic."

"Oh, Mama."

Amy Lynn settled on Dusty Rose and handed the bottle of polish to Lavinia who carefully inspected her own nails before taking it. Amy Lynn spread her fingers apart and put her palms on the glass tabletop.

"How long has it been since I did this?" Lavinia said. "I used to do it all the time when you were little."

Lavinia's hands shook with the first stroke, but gradually she steadied them.

"I think the last time was for my junior prom. I was so nervous about my date I couldn't do them myself, and we sat at the kitchen table for you to do it for me."

"I remember that. Timothy Singleton. He was a cute little fella."

"Of course, I had no way to know he was gonna be as nervous as I was and step on my dress and rip off the bottom half of the skirt before we even got out the door!"

"I shoulda had it hemmed for you."

"No! That was the style! Oh, he was so embarrassed."

"Definitely one you won't forget." She finished the first coat on one hand and started the other. "I guess by the time you were in high school, I was already an old woman to you, wasn't I?"

"*Well, Mama,* where on earth did *that* come from?"

"Oh, I don't know. Just thinkin'."

"You weren't old, Mama. At least, I never thought of you that way. You were just *Mama.*"

"It's funny. I know I'm old now—eighty in a little over two months—but it doesn't feel like I always thought it would. In my head, I'm the same person I was at my own prom. The same person but with a lot more experiences and memories."

"I guess I've never really stopped to think about it."

"Oh, you will. You'll ponder it for yourself one day, and I bet you'll reach the same conclusion."

Lavinia tightened the bottle on the polish as Lee stepped out the back door carrying two plates, each with a slice of pumpkin pie with a dollop of whipped cream on top.

"The boys and I were having some. I thought my two favorite ladies might enjoy some, too."

The pie looked delicious, and they made a big fuss over how nice it was for him to bring it. Lavinia had always espoused that the best way to encourage good behavior in men, just like with children, was to praise them consistently, no matter how exhausting it was.

He handed Lavinia a plate with a generous serving of the store-bought dessert, then he set Amy Lynn's plate down in front of her and leaned in for a quick kiss before heading back inside. He and the boys had been watching football most of the afternoon.

Lavinia's nails were dry, so she dug right in. Amy Lynn waited.

"I sure am glad you married Brett instead of that Timothy Singleton kid," Lavinia said after the first swallow. She had started to put another bite in her mouth when she noticed the look on Amy Lynn's face and stopped with her fork in the air. It was her teacher face. The one she gave when she talked about a student flunking a test. Lavinia lowered her fork and wrinkled her brow, waiting on

Amy Lynn to speak.

"His name is Lee, mother," Amy Lynn said.

"Well, of course, I know that. What did I say?"

"You called him Brett."

Lavinia laughed at her brain hiccup.

"I'm sorry, dear," she said. "How silly. Brett's the name of the boy you dated before you met Lee.

"No, Mama," Amy Lynn said. She held on to the same disappointed expression.

Lavinia's brain began to spin, trying to interpret the look. Had she gotten something else wrong? Had she somehow hurt her feelings without meaning to? Amy Lynn was sensitive and temperamental about a lot of things. Maybe she shouldn't have brought up Brett at all. Maybe it revived bad memories.

"Mama, the boy I dated right before Lee was named Stephen. Remember? Stephen Fields. His parents owned the mini golf back home. Everybody thought we'd get married, but I met Lee and knew he was the one instead. *Remember?* Brett is the name of the principal at my school. I never dated a Brett."

Stephen. That didn't seem right. The activities director at Cypress Shores was a Stephen. But she was sure Amy Lynn had never dated one. What *was* that boy's name? He came to Thanksgiving one year. Nice manners.

It didn't matter. Amy Lynn was married to Lee and that's all that was important. Amy Lynn didn't look happy, though, and Lavinia couldn't figure out why.

"Eat your pie, sweetie," she said. "It'll cheer you up. It's very good. I think I'll go give Stephen a kiss on the cheek for this."

"Mama, I'm going to go get us something to drink. *Okay?* You just finish your pie. I'll be right back."

Amy Lynn rose slowly, holding her fingers apart like they might still be wet. She backed toward the house, watching Lavinia as she walked, then quickly ducked inside.

Lavinia finished the pumpkin filling, savoring the last bite, then picked up the crust and rubbed it across the paper plate, leaving no traces of whipped cream behind. A shadow fell across the patio table as the October sun was suddenly overtaken by clouds. With the disappearance of the warm sun, fall stepped in and took its rightful place from summer.

Lavinia stood, picked up the empty plate and basket of nail polishes, then went inside to escape the chill. In the kitchen, she heard Amy Lynn's voice coming from the next room. She spoke in hushed tones, and she sounded upset. Lavinia had a split second to decide whether to make her presence known or to try to figure out what Amy Lynn was talking about. She tiptoed to the door that connected the kitchen to the living room, then stopped, staying still and quiet.

"I think you're making too big a deal out of this, honey," Lee said. "So, she got some names mixed up. It happens to everybody."

"No, Lee. This was different. Something is wrong with her. I'm starting to think Mama's going senile. And it scares me! How can we let her drive the boys around? What if she forgets where she is?"

Lavinia held her breath to keep from crying. Her lips were turned inward and pressed together hard, and her eyes were clenched. Her eardrums vibrated from the pressure in her head, blocking out the sound of Lee's response to Amy Lynn. She felt like a spring pressed down into a tiny box.

Could it have been that bad? Surely, Amy Lynn was getting all worked up over nothing. If only there was some way to hear herself. If their conversation had been recorded, she could prove she wasn't crazy. She'd only made a simple mistake.

Lavinia cleared her throat loudly. The chatter in the other

room stopped.

"It got cold outside. I'm going upstairs for a bit," she called out. Nobody answered.

Lavinia pulled herself upstairs with the stair rail. Hand over hand she fought to keep her emotionally wrecked body upright and climbing. And she was suddenly glad Edgar was dead. He'd never have to deal with his wife losing her mind.

***

Lavinia's second reaction to the painful realization that she was slipping, or at least her daughter thought she was, was to pray about it. Her rekindled faith wasn't yet strong enough for it to be the first line of defense. By the time Lavinia even thought about praying, she'd already made up her mind and packed her bags.

"Amy Lynn, Lee...I'm going to check into a motel this evening," she announced. She stood in the doorway of the living room with her suitcase at her feet. Lee put down his tablet. Amy Lynn closed her laptop.

"What on earth do you mean?" Amy Lynn said. "Why would you do that?"

Lavinia was careful to keep her voice down. The boys were in the den playing video games, and she didn't want them to hear.

"Amy Lynn, I'll be honest with you, though it hurts me to talk about. I know I got a little confused this afternoon and it worried you. I'm not mad," Lavinia said, though her tone betrayed her, "but, I think it's better if I'm not around quite so much to trouble you."

"Mama, we've been getting along so well."

"I know, baby. We have. And I want to keep it that way. That's why I should leave. If I stay, I'll be paranoid that you're questioning my sanity every time I forget the slightest detail or get the least bit tongue-tied. I'm already defensive enough about my mental capacity. I'm at least still sharp enough to realize that."

Lee put down the footrest of his recliner and stood. Without any words he walked over, gave her a gentle hug, and left the room. He understood her. He always knew what to say and what not to say. Amy Lynn pushed.

"Mama, don't go. The boys love having you."

"And I love being here with them. And with you and Lee. But this is for the best."

"But it's silly to waste your money on a motel when you can stay here for free."

"Amy Lynn, you know money isn't a problem."

"I don't know how much you heard of what I said to Lee, but I didn't mean to hurt your feelings, Mama. I really didn't."

"I know that, baby. And don't you worry about it anymore. Your mama's a tough old bird. I'll be all right."

***

Wilmer, I know you really don't know me from Adam, but can I get your honest opinion about something? You seem like such a nice, honest fella.

Lavinia lay on the motel room bed, propped up on both pillows, messaging her Swedish friend through the word game app. Another benefit of coastal Carolina living was lots of hotels and motels close by to choose from. She had considered a chain hotel near the interstate—one with room service and continental breakfast. It would have been like being back home at Cypress Shores. But she decided on a Southport landmark instead—a fixture so engrained in the landscape of the town it was often overlooked, a family-owned motel right on Howe Street, three blocks from Neville's office and a short drive away from Amy Lynn, Lee, and the boys.

Hi, Lavinia. Who is Adam? Wilmer responded.

Lavinia felt silly.

Never mind.

He messaged again immediately. *Lavinia, can I help you?*

She thought long and hard. How could he possibly help her? He wasn't a medical doctor or a psychologist. Not to mention the fact that he was over four thousand miles away. Would it help to tell him her daughter thought she was going nutty and she was scared to death that she might be right?

You're a young person, aren't you? Lavinia typed. Another odd question.

Youth is relative. I'm forty-three.

Funny. That's about what Lavinia would have guessed.

And how old do you think I am? In case he got the wrong idea, she quickly sent a follow-up. *I guess I ask because I'm feeling a little old and useless today. At least I can still play a decent game of Words, right?*

I'm sorry you're having a bad day, he texted back.

Lavinia played her word against Wilmer—*video.* The word made her think of Dylan and Lucas. They were playing video games when she told them she was leaving. She tried to downplay her sudden exit, but Dylan still cried.

A little blue speech bubble appeared in the corner of the screen to indicate a new message. She hoped he didn't trade messages out of pity. It would be inconsiderate to tie someone up. Especially someone too compassionate to tell you they were tired. It was after midnight in Sweden.

Every person is valuable, regardless of age or ability. And you do play a great word game.

Lavinia smiled. His words brought her comfort. A few moments passed, and another message from Wilmer arrived.

Remember, you're who God created you to be now. Before He made you, He designed you at every age. If He has the hairs on our head numbered, I'm sure He knows which ones are going to turn gray first and when it will be.

If he had been right there in front of her, in person, in real life, close enough to see and smell and touch, she would have kissed him on the cheek, whether he was forty-three or one hundred and three.

"Well, whaddaya know," she said aloud as she typed back a message of sincere thanks. Wilmer was a believer, too.

Chapter Twenty-one

Monday, November 5

Lavinia's heart jumped to her throat. The knock on the motel room door came just as she had slipped from dozing and into a real afternoon nap. She lifted herself off the vibrant comforter, moved her head from side to side to shake out the sleep, and stepped to the door quietly, careful not to let whoever was on the other side hear her. She might not want their company. She certainly wouldn't open it to a stranger, unless it was an employee of the motel, and if it was Amy Lynn, she didn't know what she'd do.

Barely breathing, she looked through the peephole. The distorted image of the person on the other side of the door caused a faint gasp of excitement to escape her lips. She touched the corners of her mouth, checking for drool, then went to the mirror to tame her bed head. When her hair was fluffed, Lavinia slipped on her shoes at the end of the bed and opened the door.

The skin under Neville's eyes appeared to have an extra amount of sag to it, and his muted blue tie was loosened a hand-width from his collar, but he wore a charming smile and had an unmistakable twinkle in his eyes.

"Neville! What are you doing here?"

"Well, you sounded a little down on the phone. I thought maybe some food would cheer you up."

He held out a white plastic bag with a foam takeout plate inside. Lavinia detected the aroma of seafood.

"Mercy me! How kind of you," she said. "What did you bring me?"

She stepped one foot outside the room, onto the concrete walkway, careful to hold the door open with the other foot. The key card was inside, and the door would lock automatically if she let it shut.

"It's from Provision," Neville said. "When we were there, you said next time you wanted to order what I ordered, so I brought you some shrimp."

"I can't believe you remembered that."

"In my profession, attention to small details can be important."

He handed the bag over to Lavinia. Grateful, and excited about the meal, she was also struck by the awkwardness of the situation. It would be rude to take the food and retreat inside the room alone to eat, and she didn't want him to leave, but she most certainly couldn't invite him in. It would be unseemly. Even if they sat on opposite sides of the room, even if no one saw him enter or leave, and even if no one ever found out that he had visited, it just shouldn't be done. If she even thought about being alone in a motel room with a man to whom she wasn't married, her mother, twenty years dead, would somehow know and most certainly would roll over in her grave.

"You know what? I'm really going to enjoy these for supper. I had no idea what I was going to do for a meal tonight. But…it's a little early yet. Would you like to…maybe we could…go for a walk? I can put these in the fridge for now and warm them up later."

Neville's truck was parked right in front of them, but a walk around the motel was the only thing she could think to suggest.

He looked up at the overcast sky. "I think the rain will hold off. And it's not too cold out here. Let me grab my cane from the truck."

"And I'll get my sweater."

Lavinia stepped back into the room and put the plate, still inside the bag, into the mini fridge. She pulled open the bureau drawer and retrieved an oversized oatmeal-colored sweater with clear buttons then put it on. The key card went into her sweater pocket, but she left her phone on the table and went to meet Neville outside.

The motel was on the main road that led in and out of downtown Southport, the one that ran straight to the waterfront and was lined by sidewalks. Just a few steps across the parking lot they made a right, and Lavinia began to regret the suggestion. Neville moved slowly, and the cool temperature had her joints aching. She looked back at the rocking chairs on the covered porch of the motel. *That would have made more sense,* she thought. But it would seem flighty to turn back.

"I get so tired of these signs all over the side of the road," Lavinia said. She pointed to a farm of political campaign ads. The signs were packed in so tightly around a stop sign that the names were a jumbled blur of letters. "They make the place look trashy. And do candidates really think someone's going to vote for them just because they put their name on a sign?"

"You're right." Neville refilled his lungs. "I've never gotten to the voting booth and said, 'You know what, I think I'll vote for him because he had a nice-looking sign.'"

Lavinia laughed. Neville was as witty as he was handsome.

"Maybe some people care that little about our country and its future," she said, "but I want to know what my candidates stand for. I read and research and talk to people. It's important."

"Maybe you and I are just old-school like that," he said. "I wish more people felt the way we do."

"Hey, look at that one!" she said. The names became clearer as they approached the intersection. "I've got a Sharpie in my bag back in the room. We could fix that sign up right."

"What are you talking about?" Neville stopped and leaned on the handle of his cane.

"That one right there. Elect Todd Tinker. We should add an *s* to it, and people will be tryin' to vote for Todd *Stinker!*"

Lavinia laughed at her own joke, starting softly and building into a loud and carefree expression. She laughed away pain she hadn't realized was there, and she laughed away the fear of going to jail *and* of going crazy.

Neville's face morphed from a look of confusion into a look of genuine amusement, and his smile, combined with her own laughter, made Lavinia's face warm despite the cool autumn air.

"Say, that's pretty good," he said. "But as your lawyer, I must advise against it. Tampering with campaign signs is a crime, you know." He started walking again.

"Oh, I know. I was just kidding, *Mr. Lawyer.* You have to admit, it would be pretty funny, though." Lavinia reached the corner then turned back, and Neville followed. "But I probably wouldn't do it," she said. "Even if it *was* legal. It doesn't seem…well, it doesn't seem nice. And I don't play jokes to be hurtful. I do it to be funny. Doesn't matter if he's red or blue."

"What about that one?" He pointed to a sign in another cluster on the other side of the street. "It would take a little more work, but I bet you could change Vote for Friar to Vote for Liar. I know that guy. It would be fitting."

"Oh, Neville." She slapped at his shoulder playfully.

As they approached the motel, a gentle rain began to fall, and they hunched over, shielding their faces from the cold, wet drops. By the time they reached the shelter of the porch, the rain was a downpour.

"*Shoo,* that one snuck up on us, didn't it?" Lavinia said, panting. "Would you like to sit for a minute, Neville?" She pointed to the pair of rocking chairs a couple doors down from her room.

He answered by heading in that direction, leaning on his cane with each step.

"To be honest, I'm glad it started raining," he said, easing into the rocker. "I didn't feel like going any farther."

"Well, that makes two of us." Lavinia shuffle-stepped between his outstretched feet and the porch post to sit on the other side of him.

"I shouldn't be this tired." Neville drew in a deep breath and let it come out long and slow. "It's not like I worked much today."

"I was wonderin' about that. Since I'm your only client now, what are you doing with all of your time, if you don't mind me askin'? You're dressed like you've been to the office." Lavinia wiped at a raindrop that had fallen through her hair to her scalp and was making its way down her forehead.

"I have been. All day. I'm so used to doing the same thing every day—I put on my suit and go to the office. That's just what I do." His voice was like the coffee maker at Lavinia's villa, rumbly and low as it warmed up. "Shirley found some research work. We're helping another lawyer with a few cases. Mostly, I help Shirley study. Did you know she's enrolled in law school now?"

"Oh, that's terrific. And it's great that you can help her with schoolwork."

"I'm proud of her. Although, I still don't understand all this online stuff, or how she can get a bona fide education in jurisprudence through the internet. Seems like a scam to me."

"Shirley's a smart girl. I'm sure she made a wise decision."

"I guess you're right."

Raindrops bounced on the concrete in front of them, and a gentle wind blew down the corridor of the old motel building.

"Communication and education are so much different now. We have the world at our fingertips, you know," Lavinia said.

Neville shrugged.

"And...what about my case?" Lavinia made her voice gentle and bright, sweet and unassuming, like she was offering a slice of pound cake instead of discussing whether or not she might go to jail.

"Oh, so *that's* what you were getting at, asking about how I spend my time?"

"We-elll..."

He smiled, and she grinned back. Their playful back-and-forth seemed to come so naturally.

"I talked to Kimberly the maid today," he said. "She was the last of the staff I needed to interview. I'm pretty sure she didn't have anything to do with it, Lavinia. She hates Wendy Wisengood, and she didn't try to hide it. But she spoke highly of you. I didn't catch any hints that she was lying."

"That's good, but what about the person that I *know* did it?" Her sugary tone was gone.

"Oh, here we go," he said, rolling his eyes. He let out a huff that sounded much more annoyed than the amused look on his face suggested. "I know you're convinced of that, and I will check it out. I've called Proctor a few times now. Sent him two letters. If he hasn't responded by the end of the week, I'll ask for the subpoena."

"Very good," she said with a single, exaggerated nod.

She looked over at his slouched form in the rocking chair next to her. He drummed the fingers of both hands on the armrests as he rocked slowly. Past due for a haircut, little gray sprigs kissed the top of his ears. She looked away when he turned and caught her staring.

Neville's companionship was comforting, and Lavinia would have been content to sit in that rocking chair for the rest of the evening, until the moon was high in the sky, talking and laughing so much like she used to do with Edgar. She didn't want to go inside; never mind the shrimp. But the rain that soaked into her sweater before they reached shelter had absorbed into the layer below and the wet blouse gave her a chill. She decided to run back to the room and at least swap out the sweater for a dry top layer.

"I'll be right back," she told Neville. "Can I get you a bottle of water from the fridge?"

"No, I'm fine." Neville's voice was solemn, and he looked straight ahead into the fast-darkening sky.

As she neared her room, a faint tapping sound met her ears. Was it Neville's cane on the cement? She didn't turn to see. With a swipe of the key card, the door unlocked, and as she stepped inside, she heard Neville clear his throat right behind her. Lavinia spun around to see him catch the door before it could close.

"Lavinia, I should probably go," he said.

He took a step forward, holding the door. Now his shoes were on the worn out motel carpet. He was in the room. She felt her eyelids stretch wide enough to hold ping pong balls, and she could picture her mother's dried up old bones doing a three-sixty, six feet under.

She forced herself to look relaxed. It would be rude to make Neville ill at ease, too.

"I'll go and let you eat your dinner," he said.

"Oh…well, okay. Thank you again for coming over, and for bringing my food." Her wish for him to stay was only said in her mind.

Lavinia stepped forward, her hand extended in a gracious pose, and he met her halfway, letting the door close behind him. The sound of the latch rattled her, but only for a moment. As he took her offered hand, he reached around her with the other and pulled her gently toward him. She caught the look in his eye just before Neville leaned in too close for her to focus on his face anymore.

If ever there was a kiss to rival the most romantic of Hollywood kisses, this wasn't it. It was awkward and unexpected, slightly off-center, with lips pursed too tightly. And it was altogether wonderful. In three seconds, everything Lavinia thought she knew about her life was altered. For those three seconds, she was no longer an old woman. She wasn't *Nana*. She was every woman in the world in the arms of every good man.

.

Chapter Twenty-two

The straps of Lavinia's heavy bag rested in their normal spot on her left shoulder, in the indention made over time by the weight of it. She considered tossing out a couple of the gags that she seldom used, to lighten the load. The kaleidoscope was only good for Dylan and Lucas's friends anyway. Adults were too persnickety about that sort of gag. Same with the whoopie cushion. No, she couldn't. As soon as she got rid of them, she'd have the perfect opportunity to use them and would be mad at herself.

She checked her makeup again in the mirror mounted over the dresser. *A little more rouge wouldn't hurt.* Then more rouge led to more powder. A few swipes over her nose and across the puffy pockets under her eyes with the soft, cottony disc cut the shine.

"Look at you!" she said to the mirror. "With a twinkle in your eye like a teenager."

She winked at herself, fixed the collar of her thin, blue blazer, and adjusted her pearls. She was ready to go do her civic duty.

The polls had been open for a couple hours already. Maybe she'd get there between the morning and lunchtime rushes. First, she'd swing by the bakery and grab a bagel. She'd probably eat half of it plain in the car on the way to vote and the other half with a packet of apple butter when she got back to the room. She could already taste the sweetness. Then maybe she'd watch some television or see if Sylvia wanted to meet for a late lunch or go shopping. Her feet barely touched the ground as she bustled about, preparing to leave and thinking about the day ahead. The world seemed newer today, and all its goodness was hers for the taking.

She picked up the car key from the table then stopped in the middle of the room to check her phone. She responded to another text message from Lucas, assuring him that she was okay and that she would see him soon, then she cleared the red notification dot with a white seven inside it. There were three missed calls from Amy Lynn, two from Lee, and one voice mail from each of them, all just since last night. She'd listen to the voice mails later. Doing it now might spoil her good mood.

Lavinia was two feet away from the door, reaching out for the knob, when someone on the other side of it knocked loudly. She instinctively took two steps backward, nearly tripping over her own feet. Then she froze.

"Heavens to Betsy! Who could it be?" she whispered. Housekeeping shouldn't come until at least ten.

She choked back excitement. It could be another surprise visit from Neville. Her stomach tightened and she held her breath. He'd left so quickly after their kiss.

Her mind whirled in a state of happy delirium. What did the kiss mean for their relationship, for her case, for her future? She'd even dreamed about Neville. They were sitting on the same bench at Waterfront Park where she had gone to pray, holding hands and feeding the birds. A sailboat in the distance caught her eye, and from far away she was able to make out the features of the vessel's captain. It was Edgar. He smiled at her and waved. She waved back, then the boat was suddenly at the horizon line, and it sailed out of sight. She had the sweetest peace when she awoke.

Lavinia dropped her bag on the table in front of the curtained window and pressed her torso into the door as she squinted one eye to see through the peephole with the other. She identified the visitor, closed both eyes, and touched her forehead to the cool wooden door for a count of ten as she gripped the doorknob with a trembling hand. She steadied herself then opened the door.

"You again," she said. "You have got to be kiddin' me."

The same officer stood there—the one who had shown up at Cypress Shores two days after the potluck—and he wore the same all-business expression he'd worn on that memorable day.

"Lavinia Louise Lebowitz Lewis, you're under arrest for simple assault, regarding the ingestion of a harmful substance by one Wendy Wisengood. You have the right to remain..."

Would Scarlett stay silent at a time like this? Would she hang her head? While he finished mirandizing, Lavinia fought the urge to yell and moan, and instead, she began to sing. It was a quiet song, not a statement of protest but one for her ears only, and it made each step to the officer's car easier than the one before it.

I have found His grace is all complete. He supplieth every need. While I sit and learn at Jesus' feet, I am free, yes, free indeed.

Thankfully, he didn't cuff her. At least he had that much compassion. But this time, she didn't give two figs if anyone saw her being put into a police car. She didn't know anyone around, and they didn't know her. Other motel guests didn't know she had two grandsons who adored her, or that her own son-in-law was an officer, or how much money she had. Passersby wouldn't have a clue that her late husband was a bank executive. They were all out-of-towners. Nobody would ponder her guilt or innocence. They'd be curious, but it didn't really matter. None of it mattered at all.

It is joy unspeakable and full of glory, full of glory, full of glory. It is joy unspeakable and full of glory, oh, the half has never yet been told.

"I need to call my attorney," she said as she slid into the backseat of the cruiser. Oh, how she wished Neville could be there now.

"Just as soon as we get to the station, Mrs. Lewis," the officer said.

She nodded, assuring herself everything would be okay. She maintained a relative measure of calm until a new thought crossed her mind.

"Wait!" she said in a panic. "Will I still be able to go vote?"

***

"You said we had until the end of the month!" Neville yelled into the phone.

He'd known the District Attorney for ten years, and he'd managed to avoid raising his voice to the pipsqueak until now.

"Neville, what difference does a few weeks make?" His volume competed with Neville's. "She posted bail. And there probably won't be a court date until after Christmas. If you think there's evidence in your favor, you still have plenty of time to find it before we go to court."

Neville would have rather been slapped in the face than condescended to.

"Have you forgotten that I don't have to prove anything? The burden of proof is on the state. And you have nothing but circumstantial evidence and you know it."

"Enough circumstantial evidence will carry weight with a jury."

"How much did Mrs. Wisengood pay you?" Neville spat. He didn't care that it was below the belt.

"I don't like what you're implying, Neville. I'm just doing my job. That woman spent over two weeks in the hospital. Your client knew she had an allergy. I have witnesses that saw and heard them arguing just a couple of months ago. She's played that same prank before. And the brand of toothpaste used in the cookies was found in her apartment. That's more than enough to charge her."

"Come on, Robert. My client is almost eighty years old, and because of this investigation, she's been kicked out of her home." Neville cringed that he'd brought up age. It was a card he never played, a discredit to himself.

"Cry me a river. It's not like she's on the street. Your client has more money than I do."

"It doesn't matter. This isn't fair!"

"*Fair?* What planet are you living on, Neville?"

When he hung up the phone, Neville wiped beads of perspiration from his forehead with his suit coat sleeve. His heart pounded in his ears. That arrogant jerk had about pushed him to his limit.

He reached into the cubby below the drawer on the right side of his desk, pulled out a small bottle of brown liquid and a glass, then placed them on the desk with a clanking sound. He poured the drink, just an inch-full in the glass, but he only stared at it. Somehow, having it at the ready was enough.

He leaned back in his chair, rested his intertwined fingers on his stomach, and switched his gaze to the ceiling. For the first time, it occurred to Neville that maybe he was too old for this kind of work. He was assuredly the only graduate of the University of Iowa College of Law class of 1964 who hadn't already taken down their shingle. Most had probably done it many years ago.

As much as he was respected, he wasn't blind to the looks some gave him when they found out he still practiced. And there'd been more than one comment about his age at the last bar association meeting for the region.

No, they weren't right. The stress of this case had nothing to do with his age.

Neville picked up the end of his necktie and held it to his

nose. It was the one he'd worn the day before, and it still held her perfume, a bold, yet feminine fragrance. Bold, yet feminine—like her. He needed to get to her, to tell her he would make it right. He just hoped it was a promise he could keep.

If Neville had been a praying man, it would have been the perfect time to close his eyes reverently and clasp his hands together. If his knees would allow, maybe even get down on the floor and plead to a Higher Power on her behalf. But he wasn't. And he did none of those things. All he could do was fume and worry and feel completely helpless.

.

Chapter Twenty-three

"It's just for a few days, Shirley," Neville said. "You could use a vacation, too, you know."

"But it seems so…so sudden." Shirley's normally pleasant face had a furrowed brow and a mouth turned downward at both corners.

"Not really," he reasoned. His hands went in the air and back down. "I've been mulling it over for a long time. And let's face it, I'm not getting any younger. I need to make a decision."

Neville sat in a chair in front of Shirley's desk, in the reception area of his office, like one of his clients giving a statement. "Donald is getting ready to sell his dream house, Shirley. He's my closest living relative, and he's a genuinely good guy. If he wants me to move in with him and keep him company, the least I can do is go up there and check it out, see how I might like it. See if it's somewhere I'd want to live."

"Sounds like a closing argument," she said.

The new, snarky side of Shirley didn't sit well.

"Just do your magic on that computer and find me an airplane ticket, *okay?*"

He stood and walked to the corner of the room, to the coffee maker on the credenza. Neville poured himself a cup, though it was the middle of the day. The mug he used was a bingo prize from the Moose Lodge. The blue-hair on his right had won it on a four-corner card but insisted he take it.

He took a sip too soon and burned his tongue, then he blew on the surface of the hot liquid and tried to block out the infernal pecking on the keyboard. He read the name of the insurance agency printed on the mug and remembered how happy the lady had been when he accepted the simple gift. She was one of the more tolerable ones at bingo, and not bad looking either. Maybe he'd sit next to her again sometime. Maybe offer to take her out to dinner.

He sipped the coffee again as soon as it was bearable. He needed the caffeine. Last night, all his crazy dreams of the last few months became a conglomeration of disturbing subconscious imagery and mixed-up imaginations. It involved him at all stages of life, from infancy to his current aged state. There were coffins, motorcycles, fish with legs, and at some point, at least a few characters from *The Wizard of Oz.* He tossed and turned so much that Alibi had gotten fed up and relocated from the bed to her chair in the living room.

"I thought about driving to Maine," Neville told Shirley as he stirred the coffee. "Making it a two- or three-day road trip. But I don't think my hips and knees, or my truck, would hold up that distance. It's already a toss-up as to which of us gives out first." He chuckled, but she didn't respond.

"I'm checking on a flight out of Raleigh, Neville," she said. "When do you want it?"

Neville scowled. Shirley's lack of enthusiasm was frustrating. She'd promised to support him no matter what, but now her tone proved otherwise.

"As soon as possible," he said. "It's a shame I've already missed peak foliage season. But I bet there's some pretty leaves still hanging on. And, hey, I'll bring you some maple syrup when I come back. Donald sent me some when he first moved there. It's terrific, and I bet it would be even better on your homemade pancakes than my toasted waffles."

Shirley kept her focus on the screen and pecked away at the keyboard then clicked the do-hicky under her right hand. He could barely stand the sound of it. *Clack, clack, clack, click, click.* He missed the days of calling a travel agent or the ticket counter. Things were so much more personal then. Human interaction had been derogated in favor of mechanical convenience.

"It looks like I can get a flight that leaves tomorrow morning," she said.

"Okay. And see about a return flight a week from tomorrow. Will you be able to check in on my cat while I'm gone?"

"Sure, Neville, but what about your clients?"

"Well, I've only got one. You know that. I'm sure you can handle anything that comes up with Mrs. Lewis. Just call me if we get a trial date."

Shirley looked away from the computer screen. She drew a big breath in through her nose and back out again for twice as long.

"Neville, I'm glad you are so excited to visit Donald. But something isn't right."

He sat back down in front of her desk and took a long chug from the now cool-enough coffee, wishing he had something different in the mug. From the look on her face, she expected a response, but he had none to give her.

Shirley, in her long, denim skirt with dark tights, clog shoes, and a long sleeved, button-up blouse, stood and marched around the desk. She leaned against it and gave him a cold stare, peering into his soul. He wasn't about to break. She stared even harder, with her reddish-brown eyebrows crinkled. His face began to get warm. He repositioned himself in the chair. She didn't speak until he could hold the stare no longer and looked away from her convicting eyes.

"Neville, I'm your friend. You can tell me what's really going on."

He leaned forward and set the empty coffee cup on the desk with a clank, then leaned back again in a slump, trying to formulate the right words as Shirley waited.

"I think I'm in over my head here," he said after a few moments.

"*With the case?* But this is nothing compared to some you've defended, Neville. I don't get it."

"I'm not talking about the case." He rubbed at his wrinkly forehead.

She sat down in the chair next to him and reached out a freckled arm, placing her hand gently on his sleeve. Such a simple gesture, but it helped pull the hard words out of him.

"I let myself get too close," he said. "To her. And I don't know what to do now." He turned toward Shirley. The compassion in her eyes encouraged him to keep talking, to not shut down like he wanted. "When she called me from the police station, when she got arrested, I was so upset, and so mad. I actually hurt for her, right in here." He put his fist to his sternum. "It's strange. I haven't even known her that long, but this is worse than if it were happening to me."

"Oh, Neville." Shirley patted him on the back then relaxed in her chair.

"I feel like a big dope telling you all this," Neville said.

"Well, you shouldn't. Who else are you gonna talk to?"

"How do you do it, Shirley?" he said. "How do you live with your own hurts, plus care about somebody so much that you carry theirs on top of yours? Isn't it too much?"

"It would be too much, if you didn't get to also share their joy. You get double of that, too." Her voice was so full of conviction. It wasn't cheesy, sentimental drivel that she touted. "Love bears all things, believes all things, hopes all things, endures all things."

Neville pretended to be annoyed. "That's from the Bible, isn't it?"

She answered him with a grin and a wink. He reset his brain with a deep, cleansing breath.

"You know, some people say," Neville said, feeling calmer, "that if you're having a hard time deciding between two choices, you should have someone else choose for you. Then your reaction to their choice will help you know which one you really want."

"Okay, then." She faced him and grabbed his arm with both hands. Without a hint of irony she said, "I think you should move to Maine. Go live with Donald and never come back to Southport."

Neville pictured the cabin in the woods and the beautiful lake. He imagined sitting on the deck of the cabin in the quiet of the twilight, having a drink with his nephew, then reading the newspaper by a roaring fire. Such lovely images, and they made his stomach twist into at least a half dozen knots. He could feel the desperation and the longing to smell the salt air, to drive the quaint, familiar streets again. He felt the anxiety of being away from Coastal Carolina, which had adopted him as her own sometime within the last twenty years. But most of all, he felt the pain of not being with Lavinia.

"Did that help?" Shirley said.

"I feel like a fool," he said, "but, yes, I think it does."

The office phone rang, and Shirley stood to answer it, switching to her sophisticated, professional voice.

"Neville McGrath, Attorney's Office. Shirley speaking. How may I help you?" A brief silence. "Yes, Mr. Proctor. Let me see if Mr. McGrath is available." She muted the phone. "Neville, it's Gordon Proctor. Do you want to take it, or are you too busy planning your New England getaway?"

He rolled his eyes, and Shirley flashed a toothy grin.

"I'll take it in my office."

***

Neville gripped the phone receiver in one hand, and an ink pen in the other. With any luck, the call would give him something worth writing down on the yellow legal pad in front of him.

"Mr. Proctor, I have to say I'm a little surprised that you called. I was beginning to give up on you," Neville said. The voice on the other end of the line was as gruff as it had been in person the day Neville stood on Proctor's doorstep at Cypress Shores.

"Lavinia Lewis thinks I framed her for that toothpaste prank, but I had nothing to do with it."

His directness was surprising, and it left Neville with nowhere to go.

"Um…okay, well do you—"

"I remembered where I know you from, Mr. McGrath. Or, at least, how I knew your name. My son, Jeffrey, paid you a visit four years ago. Asked you to represent him."

"Oh, is that right?"

"He was in a bind, and he heard you were the best around. You turned him down." He cleared his throat. "He wound up with some state-appointed bozo and he's been in prison since the trial."

Neville didn't know what to say. *I'm sorry* didn't seem necessary or appropriate. Most likely justice had been served. Mr. Proctor was obviously just bitter.

"Well, I can't take every case with which I'm presented. I'm sure you understand."

"Wouldn't have mattered anyway," Proctor said. "He confessed." The old man's bitterness revealed itself as brokenness in disguise.

"What was the charge?" Neville said.

"Attempted Murder."

"I...um...I'm sure that's been very difficult for you to deal with."

"Of course, it has. Especially because he's innocent. And I want you to prove it now."

"I don't understand." Neville gestured though no one was there to see him. "You said he confessed and that he's already been convicted. *Correct?*"

"Situation's changed. The case needs to be reopened." His gruff voice held a new tone, a pleading one, all mushed together with his cranky, crochety persona.

"I'm sorry, but I'm not taking any new cases right now," Neville said. "You see, I had been contemplating a move out-of-state, and then I—"

"I've got some information I believe you'll want, Mr. McGrath. It's something that might help Lavinia Lewis's case."

"*What?* What are you talking about? What do you know about Lavinia's case?" Whether a bombshell discovery or a nugget of truth, Neville did want it, more than Mr. Proctor could know.

"You agree to help my son, and I'll tell you," Proctor said.

***

Neville grabbed his keys from the hook on the office wall and his cane from the umbrella stand beside the door, then he rushed out to meet Gordon Proctor.

"Neville, is everything okay?" Shirley called after him. "Where are you going in such a hurry?"

He turned, holding the storm door open as the wind swept into the office. "Everything's fine," he said. "But definitely don't book any flights to Maine. I've got work to do here."

Chapter Twenty-four

Neville planned to meet Mr. Proctor at Local's Family Diner, only a block away from his office. Despite the name, the greasy spoon was loved by tourists and locals alike and welcoming of both.

He'd left the office so quickly, not thinking, that he had to sit in the truck waiting for twenty minutes. A lady in the car parked next to his stared at her phone screen, occasionally swiping across it with her index finger. She looked hypnotized, entranced by the electronic device. It probably made her dumber by the minute. Neville, free from the burden of such horrid indulgences, passed the time watching clouds roll by and making out shapes in them. One bunch in particular reminded him of a flounder—a flat, eye-shaped cumulus with a fan sticking out behind and wisps of cirrus fins all on top and bottom. He focused on it, trying to remind his anxious heart not to get its hopes up.

Neville got out of his truck as soon as he spotted Proctor arrive in a dark blue hatchback. The two old men greeted one another with only a nod, then Neville relied on his cane to follow him quickly inside the restaurant.

According to the dry erase board that greeted them, the specials were country fried steak, fried chicken, and meatloaf. The smells of all three mingled together in the air. Glasses and dishes clanged as busy busboys cleaned up from the lunch rush.

Neville tried to make small talk as they found a booth. When the waitress came, he ordered pie and coffee for both of them.

Neville studied the man across from him. He suspected Proctor was younger than him, though not based on appearance. *If I quit work, I might start to look like that,* Neville thought. He wondered what Mr. Proctor had done for a living. Maybe his occupation had contributed to a faster aging process. Or maybe it was genetics. Neville's father had always appeared much younger than he really was. Maybe he had a youthful gene. Or maybe he was fooling himself.

"My son fell in with a messed-up crowd in his mid-twenties," Gordon started out. "And he did some bad things. But he never hurt anybody."

Neville wanted so badly to jump ahead, to find out what he knew about Lavinia's case. But this was part of the deal.

"He thought he wasn't really doing anything too bad, because he didn't sell the stuff. He only drove it around. He was the…what do you call it?"

"The mule," Neville said, inferring that Mr. Proctor's son was involved with drugs.

"That's a good name for it," Mr. Proctor said. "My boy is a stubborn one. But I love him."

He got quiet while the waitress with a burgundy lipstick smile delivered two steaming mugs and two slices of apple pie.

"My wife died when Jeff was only seven," Mr. Proctor said. "For years it was just me and him. I did my best by him, but I guess it wasn't good enough." Warranted or not, the parental guilt poured out of his simple statement. The ones that tried the hardest were always the quickest to blame themselves.

"Anyway, to make a long story short…one of the top guys in this drug ring that Jeffrey got mixed up in, he beat some poor kid up real bad. As in, broken limbs and brain damage. But they made Jeffrey the fall guy."

"Why'd he confess to it?" Neville said.

"To protect me. They told him if he didn't take the blame, they would hunt all his family down and hurt them. As far as I know, I'm the only person who knows the truth. He confessed to protect me. And because they would have killed him if he hadn't done it."

"But what has changed? Won't he still be in danger if he tells the truth? Maybe we can discuss witness protection." Neville was already planning out a defense.

"Some of the guys involved have moved away from here, and the one that did it finally got busted for other crimes. He's serving a long sentence. So, Jeffrey doesn't have to be afraid anymore. He can tell the truth now, if we can get someone to listen."

The pies sat untouched, but Gordon took a gulp of coffee while Neville cradled his warm cup. He couldn't help but think that, if he'd taken the case four years ago, maybe he could have helped the young man.

"Do you have a picture of Jeffrey?" Neville asked. As much as he wanted to know what Proctor knew about Lavinia's case, he felt compelled to help, regardless of the trade.

The man reached into his back pocket and pulled out his wallet.

"It's pretty old," he said. He opened the wallet and held it out to Neville.

Neville squinted, looking down over his nose at Jeffrey's photograph in the dingy protective sleeve. It was from high school— a senior picture taken in one of those faux tuxedo fronts. The boy in the picture had kind eyes, with a hint of mischief in them. His mouse-brown hair was spiked, and a sliver of mustache rested on his top lip.

Neville wanted to remember him, but he couldn't. He wanted to recall why he'd turned down Jeffrey's case. There were generally only two reasons, though. Either his case load was too full, or it wasn't an easy win. Neville's conscience could only be clear with the first one.

"Mr. Proctor, I can't promise that I can get him released, but I can tell you…I'll see what I can do."

"Fair enough. I guess I'll just have to trust you." He turned his face toward the window beside the booth. Sunlight that was filtered through a blanket of clouds cast a yellow glow on his solemn profile. He spoke without looking at Neville. "I can't keep what I know a secret anyway. It wouldn't be right. Lavinia Lewis drives me up the wall most of the time with her stupid tricks and jokes, but I don't want her falsely accused."

"I promise, I'll do what I can for your son. Now,"—Neville took a bite of pie and swallowed quickly, trying to cut the tension at the table—"what can you tell me about this whole toothpaste-in-the-Oreos fiasco?"

Proctor had taken Neville's lead and was chewing his first bite of apple pie, too. Neville tried to remain patient while he finished.

"It may not be anything," he said.

"Just tell me what you know." He forced an encouraging smile.

"The day after the potluck at Senior Central, that Saturday, there was a car in Lavinia's driveway that I didn't recognize. Through my living room window, I noticed it as soon as it pulled up. It had dark windows, so I couldn't see inside. And it sat there for a long time. So, I watched to see what they were up to."

Neville put down his fork and took the notepad and pen from his breast pocket.

"About how long would you say the car was there?"

"Maybe ten minutes. I thought they could be waiting on Lavinia to get back."

"And you're sure Lavinia wasn't home?"

"I'd seen her leave about an hour before."

Neville fought the urge to interrogate. Some witnesses shut down under pressure. He needed Mr. Proctor to tell him everything, at his own pace.

"After about ten minutes," Proctor finally said, "this old woman got out of the passenger side. A little woman. She walked around to the driver side, near the front of the car, and just stood there until the driver rolled down her window. It was a younger woman, and she was yelling at the old lady, though I couldn't hear what she said."

"What did the driver look like?"

"Pretty. Blonde. Probably late twenties. She motioned for the old woman to go inside."

The waitress came back to refill their coffees. Neville smiled graciously at her, though he was about to burst. Proctor's story couldn't be told fast enough.

"That's when I stepped out onto my porch," he said. "I watched the lady go inside Lavinia's house, and after a couple of minutes, she came out and got back in the car."

Neville's heart raced. Finally, a path of clues to follow.

"I don't know if it means anything, but it seemed really strange," Proctor said. "I should have told you a lot sooner."

"I appreciate you telling me now, Mr. Proctor. Can you describe the woman that went inside Lavinia's house?"

"Oh, I didn't tell you that part." He brought a forkful of pie near his mouth. "I know who she is. It was the woman that Lavinia brought with her to the potluck."

***

"I have good news, Lavinia," Neville said.

She was hesitant to believe it. The roller coaster of emotions she'd ridden over the last week was much worse than a constant low.

The ups and downs were cruel and made her sick. All day she'd sat in her motel room with the curtains drawn, watching episode after episode of old black and white television shows, wishing for the kinds of problems that could be resolved in thirty minutes, in between commercials.

"I think we just got a break in your case, and it came from the last place you would have ever expected."

She whispered a prayer of thanks as Neville explained the meeting with Gordon and about the deal to help Gordon's son. It didn't seem real.

"I'm sitting in my truck now," he said. "I just finished talking with him."

"That poor man," Lavinia said when the story was done. "I had no idea his son was in prison." She put her feet on the floor and sat on the edge of the bed. "And he saw Rosie go inside my house while I was away?" Her head felt foggy. So much to take in at once.

"That's what he said. And I don't have any reason to doubt him, Lavinia. Her former nurse, was she a pretty blonde?"

"Yes, she was. I bet it was Jenny."

Lavinia wished they could talk about other things. He'd been so distant at the police station. He had to be professional, of course, but it was as if she was nothing more than another client, and she didn't know what to make of it.

"She must have put Rosie up to it, for some reason. She made her plant the toothpaste in your bathroom. That's what Rosie was trying to tell us with those songs. She was telling us that Nurse Jenny is a bad apple. I'm going over to Cypress Shores now to talk to her."

"Oh, I wish I could see Rosie, too. But I've had this horrible headache all day."

"Don't worry about it, Lavinia. I'll call you back as soon as I can."

Excitement and disappointment filled her heart like oil and

water, fighting for space and leaving her dizzy.

"I hope you feel better. And Lavinia?"

"Yes?"

"I miss you."

Three words even better to hear than the good news about her case. Joy washed over her like being baptized.

"I miss you, too, Neville," she said.

***

Lavinia paced in her motel room. She thought about Jenny and Rosie, and about Gordon and his son, and about Neville. Her heart pounded. Her blood raced. She sat down on the edge of the motel room bed, trying to catch her breath. What wonderful news she'd received. Neville had a clue, and he missed her like she missed him.

Lavinia became suddenly aware that her headache had gotten worse—as if her head was clamped down upon by an invisible vice. And her Buick might as well have been parked on top of her chest instead of outside. Dizziness overwhelmed her, and she struggled to maintain her composure. She'd experienced this before. She needed help.

She picked up the phone again and searched contacts for Lee's number. She used to know it by heart, but it wouldn't come to her, lost in the haze. *No.* There wasn't time. She grabbed her bag and sat down on the edge of the bed. She pulled out all the gags, with tunnel vision on her hands that moved in slow motion. One by one, she tossed them onto the bed, desperate to reach the bottom of the bag. In a fleeting moment of clarity, she chuckled. How funny it would be if they found her dead holding a rubber chicken. Finally, she pulled out the medical alert necklace. Her thumb found the bright red button just before the muscles in her hands became useless, then she became vaguely aware of the comforter on the motel bed against her right cheek.

Chapter Twenty-five

Thursday, November 8

Lavinia fought to open her eyelids. Something heavy held them down, kept them glued to her eyeballs. Or they'd been closed for so long her brain resisted waking. Maybe her eyes were broken, the muscles somehow damaged.

The left lid succeeded first, then the right, both sore from the strain of lifting the veil. An expanse of white loomed above her. Ceiling. She couldn't move anything except her eyes. A shift to the right. All gray. Gray walls. Light gray, like a storm cloud. Just like the walls in Rosie's room.

"She's awake," a familiar voice called. "Mama?"

Her eyelids filled with sand and closed before she meant them to. A familiar *beep beep* met her ears. It was the same electronic tone she'd heard in ICU with Edgar those last few days. *Someone must be sick.*

Then the world went black again.

***

"Hey, old-timer," a stranger called out. "Don't you know those things will kill you?"

Neville sat in his truck with the window down, parked outside the hospital, disregarding the *No Smoking* sign posted a few feet away. He turned to see two teenagers headed toward the entrance. The one that had commented on Neville's smoking was scrawny, even in a baggy sweatshirt. He slapped his friend on the back, laughing.

Neville stuck his head out of the window and yelled. "Like I've got much time left anyway!"

They didn't turn around but began to walk faster toward the building. Neville huffed in satisfaction.

The wind blew in his face and he retreated inside the cab of the pickup. He coughed before he brought the burning cigarette to his lips again. It had been so long since he'd smoked, he'd lost his taste for them, but it still felt good. Comforting between his fingers, natural between his lips. An old, long-lost friend come for a visit, to tell him, at least for two minutes, that everything was okay. He smoked it down to the filter, then pressed it into the clean ashtray. The last wisps of smoke floated across his face and drifted out the open window, then disappeared into the night air.

He stared at the hospital building, lit up against the dark sky. People came and went, with varying levels of urgency. Some walked quickly and their faces were contorted with worry. Others strolled, unfazed by the hurt of others so nearby.

Neville had visited Lavinia only briefly the night before. It pained him to leave, but Amy Lynn and Lee were there, and he felt out of place. He wasn't family. He wasn't sure what he was. But he knew he was more than her attorney. He'd gone home after the visit and cried into Alibi's fur, then crashed into bed where he dreamed about fishing on City Pier with Donald, dressed as the Tin Man. He was back at the hospital at nine the next morning and had sat by her side all day while family and friends came and went. As soon as he pulled into the parking space in front of his apartment that evening, he put the truck in reverse, turned around, and drove right back to the hospital. Now he wasn't sure what to do. Amy Lynn was spending the night. It would be hard to explain why he'd come back, and awkward. Maybe he'd just sleep in the truck. At least he was near her. It was some small solace to be outside the building where she lay, in a battle for her life, though she probably didn't know it.

He gripped the steering wheel until his hands hurt, then he let go and lit another cigarette. He'd give anything for her to wake up, to see her eyes, to hear her talk about playing pranks, to hear her laughter. For her to be herself again. He'd known her for such a very short time, yet he would do anything humanly possible to make her well if he could. It was the same desperation and helplessness as when his mother had a stroke. But this hurt was different.

Not knowing where he was going, Neville opened the truck door and stepped out onto the wet pavement. Black puddles all around him glimmered under streetlights. He reached back into the rusty old truck and mashed the second cigarette into the tray, then grabbed his cane. He closed the door with a loud creak, then headed for the hospital entrance slowly, ignoring the drizzle that landed on his thinning hair and tired face.

Neville was on autopilot. Maybe the cafeteria was open and he would get something to eat. Maybe, by chance, if he went back to her room now, she'd be awake. The tap of the cane against the hospital floor echoed through the hall with a larghissimo cadence. *Clack, clack, clack, clack.*

Before he reached the elevator that could take him to Lavinia's room on the third floor, his attention was drawn to ornate, wooden doors to his right. Majestic, important-looking, they seemed out of place in the sterile, uniform hallway. He ran his fingers down the dark wood, thinking how out of place he'd be if he went inside. But he did it anyway.

The hospital chapel was empty, and he was glad. It was embarrassing enough just being there by himself. The lights were dim, and a brightly back-lit wooden cross drew his focus to the front of the room. He sighed. *So, it's come to this.*

He slipped into a pew in the middle, on the left side of the chapel, sat down and stared at the cross. He leaned forward and drummed his fingers on the back of the pew in front of him. Other than the drumming, the room was silent, but the voices in his mind overwhelmed him.

Just over a week ago, Chuck prayed for Lavinia. Neville was there when he made his petition, so trusting and confident. Chuck had come right out and asked for God's will to be done for Lavinia. Now they were here, and it didn't make sense. How could this be the will of a loving God? Still, he had nothing to lose.

"I've never been a praying man," he whispered. His eyes were open, and his face pointed to the floor. "But I obviously don't have to tell you that, do I?" He sighed. "She thinks you're there. She believes in you. And if I don't, I've lost my mind, sitting here talking to myself." He slumped back against the pew and looked toward the cross again. "I've made it eighty years…eighty whole years without a woman. Only one other ever really caught my eye before now." As if the light from the cross illuminated his innermost thoughts, Neville told God, Whom he wasn't fully convinced could hear him, something he'd never even admitted to himself.

"It was nothing more than puppy love anyway, but I let it change me. Claudia joining the convent, it made me push all the others away. And I guess I pushed You away even harder, because she chose You over me."

He hadn't thought about her in years, his first and only teenage crush. It had seemed like the end of the world when she rejected him, but it was only a paper cut compared to the wound Lavinia's illness had caused.

"Now this crazy lady has walked into my life, and I actually want her to be there. I've only known her a little while, but I want to get to know her better."

He heard the door open behind him, and he got quiet. In his

peripheral, a petite, dark-haired woman approached and sat on the opposite side of the chapel. He stayed silent and still, frozen with awkwardness and barely breathing, until the woman, after bowing her head for a few minutes, got up and left quietly.

"Hey," Neville said, "I hope you give her whatever she was asking for." He leaned back against the pew, trying to figure out his purpose. Then he asked aloud, "What am I doing here?" Once more, but louder. "What am I doing here?" No one was around to offer a reason, but Shirley's words suddenly came to mind.

Love bears all things, believes all things, hopes all things, endures all things.

The answer wasn't crystal clear, but shrouded in Neville's doubts was singularity of purpose that suddenly and completely consumed his soul. "I have to believe for her. If there's a chance God can make her better, then I have to try and believe it. She's not awake to believe, so I have to do it for her. I'll be her faith right now, whatever that means. I just have to do it." His trip back to the hospital hadn't been in vain.

Neville left the chapel and headed back down the hall toward the exit on a mission. He believed now that Lavinia would get well, because he *chose* to believe it. And since she was going to get better, he still had a case to solve. He had to clear her name.

He stepped out of the hospital and back into the dark night, only it was less dreary now. On the way to his truck, Neville saw the same two punks who had ribbed him about smoking. They walked across the parking lot with another boy and two girls. Each of the gang had their heads down, staring at the phones in their hands like mindless robots. Neville watched them, hoping one of them would trip over a speed bump and fall on their face. They were probably texting each other; that's how silly the world had gotten.

Neville got into his truck still lamenting the evils of electronics. The ability to think for ones' self was slowly but steadily diminishing, being replaced by artificial intelligence for the sake of convenience.

"Nobody even talks to each other anymore," he huffed as he fired up the old truck engine. "Can't carry on a conversation yet they know everything about everybody."

Everything about everybody. An idea struck his brain and shocked his senses. It couldn't be that simple, could it? *Surely, the police in Florida have already thought of it. Or the police here.* Even if it were a one-in-a-million chance, he had to try. Yes, the thing that was a thorn in his side might be the very thing to prove Lavinia's innocence.

Chapter Twenty-six

Friday, November 9

"Shirley, I need your help."

Neville came into the office like a whirlwind. His excitement was spelled out by the allegro pounding of his cane on the floor with each step, as he hung up his coat then went to the coffee maker.

"Here. I can get that for you," Shirley said. She started to stand from her desk.

"No, no. I can get my coffee. But I need your help with something else."

"What is it, Neville? What's going on? I didn't think you'd be in. I was planning to forward the office calls to my cell phone and go home for the day."

"That's fine, Shirley, that's fine. As soon you help me with a few things."

"Whatever you need. How's Lavinia?"

"No change…yet. But this is about her. That app that she has on her phone, where you can see everybody and their entire life story—do you have that on your phone, too? Or any other like it?"

"Well, yeah. I have most of them, I guess. But you don't have to have a phone. It's all on the computer."

"Good. I want to find Jennifer Turner. Can you bring it up for me?"

"Well, sure." She looked as if she doubted it was really Neville, as if maybe a doppelganger had stolen Neville's suit and voice.

He came around her desk with his coffee as she pulled up the website.

"While we're waiting on the detective in Florida to find and question her, I have a good feeling there's something we can dig up right here," he said. "A clue about why she sent Rosie into Lavinia's house to plant that toothpaste."

"Neville, I've never seen you so optimistic, or so excited."

"I'm just feeling hopeful today," he said. "I have to have faith…for Lavinia."

She logged into her account and typed into the search bar, her fingers tapping out the fourteen characters of the name in two seconds. She scanned the pages of results while Neville stood over her shoulder.

"Hmmmm…" Shirley said.

"What is it?"

"Neville, there are forty Jennifer Turner's here. What else do you know about her?"

He gave the description, and she scanned profile pictures and searched for Florida locations. Neville paced behind her.

"Rosie seemed so relieved that I knew the truth, or at least part of it," he said. "It's a shame she can't testify."

Shirley stopped searching and spun her chair around.

"What do you mean? I've been studying a case with a mute witness. Shouldn't it be permissible?"

"But the District Attorney can contest it, and no doubt he would. He'd say she isn't a competent witness, and the judge would agree."

"But you said she seemed to understand everything you asked her."

"She was all there. Every yes or no question I asked her, she nodded right away to answer. She seemed so happy to be able to tell her story. At one point, it seemed like she wanted to speak. She opened her mouth and froze there with it open, and I thought something would come out."

"Poor thing."

"But she told me, in her way, that Jenny made her swap the toothpaste in Lavinia's house."

"Isn't this just the strangest case you've ever had?" She slapped the desk. "A criminal charge over toothpaste, of all things! I can't get it over how crazy it is."

He stopped and pondered the years, the lifetime of cases, defending some of the most unseemly characters imaginable. Though he'd only taken those with a clear path to acquittal, he'd still seen his fair share of wild cases. Lavinia Lewis topped them all.

"Without a doubt, Shirley," he said. "Without a doubt."

She turned the chair around and got back to work.

"Houston, Rhode Island, Washington, Albuquerque. Red hair, black hair, pink hair. I can't seem to find anyone on Facebook that matches the description of Rosie's nurse. I can try Twitter or Instagram."

"Try Jenny Turner first, instead of Jennifer."

"Oh, good thinking." She entered a new search and clicked return. "Okay, let's see. There's still nineteen of them. This may take me a few minutes. Several of them are blonde, and their locations aren't all listed in the search result."

"What does that mean?"

"It means I have to click on each of them to see what information they have set to public on their profile, to see if we can find her."

"Oh, okay." Neville stopped hovering and went around the desk to sit in the chair. "So, people can set what they want to show to the world and what they want to hide?"

"Well, yeah. You choose what to show to anyone and what to

show to only people you are friends with."

"How does it know who you're friends with?"

"No. Friends on here." She tapped the screen. "People you've connected with online. See?" She turned the monitor where he could see it and clicked a couple of times on the screen. "This is my friend list." He scooted up closer to see. "These are all the people that I've sent a friend request to and they've accepted it, or they've sent me one and I've accepted it."

"Oh, okay. I get it, I think." Neville rubbed his tired eyes and squinted at the screen again. "Hey, that's Lavinia."

"Yes, we're friends on Facebook. She sent me a request the day after we met." Shirley clicked on Lavinia's name to continue the lesson.

"See, this is her profile page. Because we're friends, I can see everything. But a stranger might only see her name and town and profile picture. Or just her name and picture. Or she could have it set to public and everyone be allowed to see everything. I don't recommend that, though."

"Hey, what does that little triangle mean?"

"Oh, this? That means it's a video."

"It must be the video of me and her at the park with her grandsons."

"Oh, I've missed this one somehow. Wow, Neville. This video has a ton of likes and views."

"So much for a low profile during the investigation," he said, chuckling. "Can you play it?"

Shirley clicked the play button on the screen, and Neville froze as his office became a time machine and he was transported to the moment he fell in love with Lavinia so unexpectedly. They were there together side-by-side, both panicked until they realized they'd been pranked by Dylan and Lucas. Then he whispered his plan of revenge in her ear and she went along with it, no questions. They made a good team.

A lump grew in his throat at the sound of Lavinia's voice in the video. It seemed like a month since he'd last heard it, but he'd barely even known her that long. The video ended, and he wiped a tear from the corner of his eye, hoping Shirley didn't see.

"Okay, let's get back to searching," he said.

With effort, he steadied his breathing while he waited on Shirley to find something.

"This could be her," she said after a moment.

He went around the desk again to see.

"That's her! The picture matches the one in her employee file at Cypress Shores."

"Okay, let's dig around here and see what we can find out about Nurse Jenny Turner," Shirley said. "We're in luck. It looks like her profile is public. I can tell you that she had a spinach omelet for breakfast yesterday and that she likes to ride motorcycles."

"Look there," Neville said. "It says her relationship status is single."

"Yep, that's what it says."

"Look at that picture, though." He leaned up and touched the screen, on a picture near the bottom. "She doesn't look very single. Is there a way we can check out her friends, too?"

The picture was of Jenny on a motorcycle and a man standing beside her with his arms locked around her waist, planting a kiss on her cheek while she touched his face.

"It's easy to find out who that is. She tagged him in the picture.

"She did *what?*"

Shirley blushed. "He's tagged. See? There's his name. *Wait!*"

They gasped in realization at the same time. She pointed to the screen and the man's name in bold black letters.

"Tyler Wisengood," Neville said. Before he could ask,

Shirley clicked on the name and navigated to Tyler's profile page.

"It was that easy?"

"Yep!"

"Now, if we're really lucky, he'll have a section that lists his relatives." She clicked a few buttons, then said, "Aha! See here? Mother, Wendy Wisengood."

"Nurse Jenny is Wendy's son's girlfriend."

He sat on the edge of Shirley's desk, in shock.

"I bet they were in on it together. They wanted to make her sick," Shirley said.

"I bet so, too. Although she could have had it out for his mother and he didn't know it."

She scrolled down the page finding picture after picture of the two of them together. "But here they are on Valentine's Day." She scrolled back up. "She moved all the way up here to get a job at Cypress Shores, and then went back home, and now they're together again. This picture was taken only a few days ago. He had to have known where she was and what she was doing in North Carolina."

From dinners out to intimate moments inside their home, they saw, in stills, a glimpse at the young couple's life together—a handsome, dark-headed man and a pretty blonde, both in their late twenties, seemingly in love, always hugged up close to one another. Nothing on the page hinted of a criminal mindset, except maybe a taste for expensive things, baubles outside of their expected means, proven by pictures of jewelry and motorcycles and high-class meals.

Neville felt somehow wrong. Like a peeping tom. The computer screen was a window into their lives, and they'd left the curtains wide open.

"I think I have some calls to make," Neville said.

"Your idea worked, Neville. I think you've just saved Lavinia."

***

Neville sat in his office, his hand cramping from holding the receiver for so long. He'd gotten in touch with the District Attorney and the local police. He'd even called the police in Florida, although Southport police said they'd handle it. He couldn't afford to rely on someone else. He was more determined than ever to clear Lavinia's name.

Before he could leave the office and head to the hospital, there was one more call to make.

"Donald, I'm so grateful that you care enough about me to invite me to come live with you," he told his nephew. "You're a rare breed, and I'm lucky to have you as family."

"But you're not coming..." Donald's tone was dejected but not surprised.

"No, buddy. I'm sorry. I've got to stay here."

"Still married to your practice, huh?"

"It's not just that..."

"It's okay, Uncle. You don't have to explain. I already knew you weren't coming, and I understand. No hard feelings at all."

"I hope not. I love you, Donald."

"I love you, too, Uncle."

Not all was right with the world yet, but for the first time in many weeks, Neville's heart felt at peace.

Chapter Twenty-seven

Sunday, November 11

A piano and violin duet played softly. Such peaceful music. It sounded like heaven, and it made Lavinia's heart happy and warm. Maybe she was there. But her eyes were closed. *Do people sleep in heaven?* No, there was a dull pain in her head. That wouldn't be possible up there. She must still be on earth.

She blinked the sleep away, remembering her beautiful dream in which she was seventy-five years younger, at the old church, running barefooted down the center aisle. She could feel the cold wood against her feet and hear her father singing. At least, it was her father's figure standing behind the podium. But the baritone voice that came from him was Neville's, and he sang 'Victory in Jesus', the same hymn that had pulled her from unconsciousness and away from the dream. A new, equally pretty song now came from a tiny speaker near her bed.

She was in a hospital bed, but other than the headache, she felt fine. She wiggled her toes. They felt fine. She wiggled the fingers on her right hand without any problem. She tried to wiggle the fingers on the left, but they didn't work. It had happened again; she knew it. But she was grateful to be alive. She tested out her lungs with the slowest, longest, deepest breath she could manage. They seemed to be working fine, but the deepness of the breath increased the pressure and pain in her head.

"Lavinia, darlin'?" a gravelly voice called.

"Sylvia."

"Oh, I'm so happy to hear you say my name. I'm so happy! You jus' don't even know!"

Sylvia's face appeared above her, and her eyes were filled with tears.

"You gave us quite a scare," Sylvia said. "But you're back with us now. It's a miracle!"

Sylvia reached to turn off the music.

Lavinia managed a smile, proving that the muscles in her face were working fine. Her most important accessory was intact.

"Hey, friend," Henry said, just coming into view.

"Hey, you," Lavinia said in a whisper. Her voice wouldn't come out like she wanted it to.

She may not have been in heaven, but she saw the faces of two angels anyway. Sylvia squeezed her hand.

"We're going to go call Amy Lynn and the doctor, honey. It's the first time Amy Lynn has left your side in four days. We practically had to push her out of here."

"Okay," Lavinia said.

Her mouth was dry. She desperately needed water. She also wanted to sit up to see what was going on around her. They'd be back soon, but if she could just find the button on the bed, she could call for the nurse. Her good hand fumbled at the bedrail. She turned her head, happily, without any trouble, trying to see the button.

"What can I do for you, Lavinia?" a voice said.

She wanted to cry. He was here. But he was also seeing her without makeup and with flattened hair. Never mind that. Renewed strength rushed through her body. When his face was visible, her heart overflowed. He had tears in his eyes, too.

"What do you need, sweetheart? Can I get you something?"

"Sit me up to see you better," she said.

"Maybe we ought to wait for the doctor to come check you."

"Please sit me up."

Neville did as she asked, pressing the button on the automatic bed until she told him when to stop.

"I'm so glad you're here," she said. "I'm so glad I'm still here."

He sat down in the chair next to the bed, grabbed her hand with both of his, and buried his face on top of their hands.

What a comforting presence he was. In that moment, she didn't worry about her prognosis and what life would be like after the second stroke. She was alive in the now.

He lifted his head and kept his voice soft and calm. "Lavinia, I have some good news." He paused and searched her eyes. "The District Attorney dropped the charges."

"What? Why?" Her head came off the pillow, but he stood and gently pushed it back down. He leaned on the bed rail, close to her face.

"How did you do it?" she said, still whispering.

"I think we ought to wait until you're feeling better. I don't want you to get too excited."

She found some strength in her dry throat. "Neville…tell me now, or I'll figure out a way to swap your multivitamin with laxatives."

"Okay, okay," he said. He sat back down, laughing, still holding her hand. "The long and short of it is, the DA knows now who really put the toothpaste in those cookies."

"Was it Jenny?"

"Yes, it was." He told her about Jenny and Wendy's son being a couple. "They plotted together, for insurance money."

"They wanted to kill her?"

He nodded. "They're obviously not the sharpest bunch, but Wendy had exaggerated her allergy to her son all his life. He was convinced fluoride would kill her. Jenny got the job there working with Rosie so she could find the right opportunity to poison her boyfriend's mother."

Lavinia closed her eyes. It was all too much to believe.

"I should stop. The doctor will be in here soon. We can talk later. I'm just so happy you're awake."

"No, keep going. I'm fine. I want to know."

"Okay." Neville took a deep breath and stroked her forehead. His hand was soft and cool against her skin, and the weight of it was proof that they were both real and alive.

"Jenny had the cookies ready for the potluck. That's how she planned to make Wendy sick. But when she saw your tray already out there, she was able to slip the tainted ones on top."

"But how did they know Wendy would go for them?"

"Oreos are her weakness. If she was at the potluck, she was sure to be the first to get one. Then when Jenny found out everyone was blaming you for it, she forced Rosie to plant the toothpaste in your apartment. She thought Rosie would never be able to tell anyone. And if Proctor hadn't been such a nosy neighbor, Rosie probably wouldn't have had the chance to tell us her story."

"How..." She stopped and swallowed hard. "How did you prove all this?"

"I didn't have to. The police talked to Wendy's son, and he cracked. Confessed to it all, right away. Seems like it was Jenny's idea to begin with. And she was apparently very persuasive."

"I can't believe it." There were so many more questions, but there'd be plenty of time to cover the details later. The important thing was, the crazy mess was over.

Sylvia came back in, moving with an urgency that could only be prompted by threat of snakes or best friends just awakened from coma. Henry followed.

"Amy Lynn and Lee and the boys are on their way," Sylvia said. "She started cryin' so hard when I told her you were awake that

I could hardly understand what she was sayin'. Where on earth is that doctor? I told them you just woke up all of a sudden and were talkin' like a politician!"

Sylvia crossed the room and poured water from a foam pitcher into a little foam cup for Lavinia. She tucked one hand behind Lavinia's head and brought the cup to Lavinia's lips with the other. Cold and wet and worth more than gold, the drink washed away the four-day silence and ignited Lavinia's passion and gratitude for all good, simple things.

"Thank you, sweet friend," she said. "What are the doctors sayin' about me, Syl? How bad was the stroke? I think I'm in a lot better shape than last time."

Sylvia looked at Henry, then at Neville.

"What is it?" Lavinia said.

Sylvia hesitated. "Lavinia, they told us not to expect you to wake up."

A dark-haired nurse with a ponytail and purple scrubs came in and introduced herself to Lavinia. She looked at the monitors. Her pencil hovered over the paper in the folder she carried. She paused to read, then looked at Lavinia, then the monitor, then the paper again. "I think I've picked up the wrong file here, sweetheart. Are you Lavinia Lewis?" Her accent was as thick as Lavinia's and she spoke too loudly.

"Yes, I'm Mrs. Lewis," Lavinia said, still weak.

"Well, this file says you had a massive stroke just a few days ago."

"Yes," Lavinia said, still putting the pieces together herself.

"I'll be right back, honey." The nice nurse made a quick exit.

"What day is it?" Lavinia asked her friends when the nurse was gone.

"It's Sunday, sweetie," Sylvia said.

"No, the date."

"It's the eleventh," Neville said.

"It's Veterans Day," she said. Her heart sank. "I always arrange for flowers to be put on Daddy's grave on Veteran's Day. I missed it this year, I guess."

"Her mind is so sharp," Sylvia said to Neville and Henry. Henry nodded and Neville's mouth hung halfway open as if Lavinia had just elucidated the mysteries of the ages.

"The day is still young, Lavinia. I'll figure out a way to get those flowers placed. I can make some calls. Don't you worry," Neville said.

She reached for him, happy that he was on the right side of the bed and not the left.

"Thank you," she said. "Wait. What about Gordon's son? Are you going to be able to help him?"

"Isn't that just like Lavinia? Four days in a coma and she's worried about somebody else," Sylvia said.

"I meet with the judge next week to talk about reopening the case," Neville said. "I think he has a good shot."

"You did all that so quickly."

"I should have helped Jeffrey Proctor four years ago. But I told you when we first met, I like to strike while the iron is hot." There was a twinkle in his eye. "I have to tell you, though, I don't believe it was all my doing. It all happened too fast, and you were so sick. We've seen two miracles this weekend. There's no doubt in my mind."

"Oh, Neville."

Sylvia walked to the door and peeked into the hallway.

"I think they've all fainted in shock. I still don't see the doc," she said.

"I'm not in a hurry to be poked and prodded anyway. I'd rather just be with the three of you, and the rest of my family when they come."

"Neville," Lavinia said. "I wanna know somethin' else. How did they find out about Jenny being Wendy's son's girlfriend?"

"Actually, you helped me." The pronounced creases at the corners of his eyes deepened as a smile spread wide across his face. "When you told me about the video that Lucas posted online, and we talked about how everybody could know anything about anybody, it made me think. I looked Jenny up on Facebook, and there she was in a picture with somebody named Wisengood. Well, Shirley may have helped some."

"So, you used technology to break the case, huh?" Lavinia said. She mocked a glib expression.

"Yeah, you got me. Social media definitely has its place."

"And what about Rosie? Is she okay?"

"Yes. She knows it wasn't her fault. I made sure."

Rosie was okay, and Gordon's son would be, too. Wendy was well and Lavinia had a redeemed reputation. She also had air circulating through her lungs, a beating heart, and a solid mind. She had friends by her side, and a man that loved her, even if it hadn't yet been said. The only thing missing was her daughter.

Lavinia had let pride get the better of her, and she had left Amy Lynn and Lee's house for no good reason. Now she just wanted to make up and tell them all how much she loved them. That chance came when they arrived, right after the doctor—who was surprised to the point of babbling—left the room, and with her good arm, she hugged each of them until they had to come up for air.

Sylvia and Henry had gone, but Neville watched the happy reunion from the corner of the hospital room. And like teenagers with a secret crush, Lavinia blew him a kiss when no one was looking.

Chapter Twenty-eight

Tuesday, November 13

"Do you think I should touch up my makeup, darlin'? I bet I could use some powder," Lavinia said as Amy Lynn came back into the hospital room. "I think I'll check my face as soon as I finish my snack. Maybe you can help me."

She motioned toward her pink makeup bag beside the sink. On the other side of the sink was a tall, clear vase of flowers—pretty roses. In the windowsill was another vase, with yellow daisies and a multi-colored *Get Well Soon* balloon tied around it. On the rolling tray table over her bed, beside her afternoon snack, was a third vase, an assortment of chrysanthemums, lilies, sunflowers, and eucalyptus stems. Three vases of flowers—one for each day she'd been awake—all of them from Neville.

"No, Mama. You don't need any more makeup. You look great," Amy Lynn said. "Pretty as a picture. And it's a good thing, because…you have a guest."

"Well, who is it? Where are they?" she said. Her voice was strong, almost back to normal. She looked around the room.

In answer to Lavinia's question, a nest of dark, black hair poked from behind the partially opened door, followed by a timid face. A woman in her mid-seventies froze and looked down at the floor in awkward silence.

"Oh, Wendy," Lavinia said. She was one of the last people Lavinia expected to see. "Well, come in and have a seat." She

motioned for Amy Lynn to clear one of the two chairs near the bed, and Amy Lynn moved quickly to relocate the giant pocketbook to the windowsill for their guest.

"I hope I'm not interrupting your lunch," Wendy said in her Italian Rhode Island accent. She shuffled into the room wearing a dark purple sweat suit with white stripes around the cuffs.

"You're not interruptin'. I was just enjoyin' a little dessert. First time I've had a puddin' cup in years. Do you want some water or something? There's a pitcher right there." She motioned, with spoon in hand, to another cart near the end of the bed. Amy Lynn, who was standing near the cart, looked anxious, lips turned inward and pressed together. Lavinia gave her a wink that said *all is well.*

"No, thank you, Lavinia. I'm okay," Wendy said. "I wanted to see how you're doing."

Lavinia reached for the cup and, careful not to turn it over, scooped a small bite out of it. Her left arm never moved from her side. She brought her right hand back toward her mouth and enjoyed the last bite of chocolate pudding. Lavinia returned the spoon to the cup and locked eyes with Wendy. She spoke from deep within her soul. "Don't worry about me, Wendy," she said. "I'm going to be okay."

A hint of a relieved-looking smile, made more obvious by hot pink lipstick, showed on Wendy's face. She took the seat that Amy Lynn had cleared, and Lavinia and Wendy stared at one another until Lavinia finally broke the silence.

"I'm sorry I didn't come visit when *you* were here in the hospital, Wendy. I wanted to, but I was…advised against it."

"I understand."

"But I'm glad you're doing better," Lavinia said. "How are things at Cypress Shores?"

"Oh, they're fine. But truth be told, it's a little boring without you around. Marvin especially misses you. He told me so yesterday.

Are you really doing okay?"

"My legs are getting stronger. I've been up and down the hall with a little help. I can't use a walker, and I'm a little off-balance because of the arm." She pointed with her chin to the motionless limb. "It's the only thing that seems to really be a problem right now."

"Oh, Lavinia, I'm so sorry I accused you!"

The pain on Wendy's face was much more than remorse. She was a broken woman. Lavinia could see it. The truth about who had poisoned her, wanted to kill her, was much worse than the lie she had wanted to believe. But Lavinia wouldn't bring up Wendy's son, or Nurse Jenny, or Rosie. There was no need.

"I forgive you, Wendy," Lavinia said "As sure as the day is long, I forgive you. But can you tell me why you did it?"

"Well, I thought it *was* you that put the toothpaste in the cookies. And it's true that it makes me sick."

"But only a little bit sick, *right?*"

She looked down and twiddled her thumbs. Bright red thumbnails raced around one another. "I've always had a tendency to exaggerate my allergy, I suppose." She looked up at Lavinia. "It's something different, you know? *Interesting.* People make a big deal out of it. And I've always figured, if I must avoid something so common that most people never think about, I might as well get some sympathy out of it. Does that make sense?"

Lavinia's heart ached for Wendy. Something must have been missing from her life, to make her need attention so badly.

"The fluoride in that cookie did worsen my colitis. I practically swallowed it whole. I guess I also didn't want to admit that I'd caused another bout by not listening to the doctor and eating the wrong foods."

Lavinia nodded slowly to let Wendy know she was following.

"But telling people I knew about your allergy?" Lavinia said. She cocked her head to the side.

"But I *did* tell you about it. Don't you remember? When you mentioned taking your grandson to the dentist. I told you I had to be careful about that because of the fluoride."

"You did?"

"Yes, and you told me you'd never heard of a fluoride allergy."

Lavinia felt the familiar confusion invade her mind. One more thing she'd forgotten. Her brain hurt and her heart began to race. Tears formed as she searched Wendy's eyes. Amy Lynn came to stand close to the head of the bed, and her hand came down to rest on Lavinia's head, but Lavinia shook it away. Losing her mind *and* having messed up hair was just too much.

Wendy shifted in her chair. "Um...*you know*...actually, now that I think about it, Lavinia, I believe Sylvia jumped in and interrupted me, when I started to say that to you at bridge club. She's always doing that. So, you probably didn't even hear me. And I'm probably remembering another conversation with someone who told me they'd never heard of a fluoride allergy. *Gladys Smith.* That's who it was. I'm so sorry, Lavinia." Her northeastern accent suddenly had a touch of southern grace.

"It's okay, Wendy." Relief washed over Lavinia. "And I'm sorry for what you're going through now." She gave Wendy a nod that told her she knew everything. Wendy only sighed.

"Mama," Amy Lynn said quietly. "It looks like you have another visitor."

Lavinia broke gaze with Wendy to look toward the door. Even if she were completely able-bodied, had she been standing, and if someone happened to have a feather in the room, she could have been knocked over by it. Two-thirds of all her enemies in the world had shown up there on the same day, at the same time. If Deborah

O'Connor who broke the knob off Lavinia's prized Tinymite Radio in the fifth grade showed up, the trifecta would be complete.

"Hello, Mr. Proctor," Lavinia said.

"You can call me Gordy," he said. He approached slowly with his brown wool flat cap in his hands. He nodded in greeting to Wendy who smiled and stood from the chair. She leaned against the wall beside the door, giving Gordon room to visit by Lavinia's bedside.

"Thank you for coming, Gordon," Lavinia said. "I owe you an apology. I thought you planted that toothpaste in my apartment. But thank you for telling Neville what you saw."

"I should have said something sooner, Lavinia. And I'm glad you're doing okay. Mr. McGrath called me this morning to talk about Jeffrey's case, and he said you were making a lot of progress."

Lavinia smiled at him. Somehow, Gordon didn't look quite so much like the ventriloquist's dummy anymore.

"Listen," he said, "I haven't always been the best neighbor. Ever since my son went to prison, I've had a hard time...dealing with people," Gordon said.

Wendy jumped in. "If you want to talk about sons causing heartache, I can relate. At least your own flesh and blood didn't try to off you." Gordon turned to Wendy with a surprised look on his face that quickly relaxed into a smile—something Lavinia had never seen there before.

"It's okay, Gordon," Lavinia said. "Maybe we can start over?"

He nodded, then he stood and put the cap on his mostly bald head and headed for the door.

Wendy said goodbye, and Lavinia thanked them again for coming. As Gordon and Wendy walked out together, Gordon said to her, "Maybe you and I should get together and talk sometime. I promise not to feed you any tainted Oreos." And they were gone.

Lavinia wagged her head, smiling at Amy Lynn. "Who would have thought?"

Amy Lynn fluffed Lavinia's pillow. "Mama, Lee's bringing the boys by after school, if you're up for it. You've had a lot of company today already."

"I'm always up for a visit with my boys. But maybe I will get a nap in before they get here. Do you mind fluffing the pillow on the other side, too?" With her good hand she pointed to the left side of the bed.

"Sure, Mama." She went around the bed to adjust the pillow. "You know, Dylan's been cleaning his room for you to come back and stay when you get out of here. Just for a little while. Until we make sure you're strong enough to move back to your villa."

"Such a sweet boy. Say, I do hope my stayin' again is okay with you, sweetheart. Marvin told me they have a room at the assisted living facility if I want it. Full-time nursing staff." She tried not to choke on the words. Assisted living was one step closer to *the home,* and her spirit wasn't ready for either place. "It's not as nice as my villa," she said, "but it *is* a nice place."

"Nonsense, Mama. You'll stay with us, and at the rate you're gettin' better, it will only be a few weeks anyway."

"Even the doctor said it was a miracle, how good I'm doing."

"It certainly seems like one, Mama."

"There's no doubt about it, sweetheart. Look at me, Amy Lynn. The fact that I'm sittin' up talking to you right now is nothin' less than a bona fide miracle." She relaxed back on the pillow and pressed the button on the bed to make it recline. "But I know another miracle that happened. I saw it just now, and you did, too."

"What are you talking about, Mama?"

"With Wendy and Gordon. And I think it's even greater than me being healed."

Amy Lynn looked as if she were trying to graph a

trigonometric function in her head.

"I'm talking about forgiveness, Amy Lynn," Lavinia said. "Miraculous forgiveness."

Chapter Twenty-nine

Thursday, November 22

The heat had finally and completely relinquished its grip on Southport for the season, and the cool air had a proper feeling of fall. Things were slower after the tourists went home. The town was returned to the locals, who thrived on the salt air regardless of temperature. They went about their days as normal, but with a greater sense of ease, like the leaves that drifted gently down to the ground from the tops of tall oaks.

The only changes at Cypress Shores were the ones that came with the time of year. Ducks overhead called goodbye on their way out of town. The trees had been brushed with new color. Lavinia's neighbors spent more time indoors, but they were still there, and her villa was just as she'd left it.

"I've got one more suitcase to bring in, Vinny," Lee said. He walked back from her bedroom where he'd placed the first bags, flashed a smile and patted her on the back, then headed to the car for the last one.

"I see they kept the dust bunnies out while I was gone," Lavinia said to herself. She turned her body around to the fully functioning side and wiped a finger across the spotless entryway table. She sighed a happy, peaceful sigh. "I'm gonna have to give those girls a good Christmas gift." She flipped the switched that brought the lamps in the living room to life, again with her right hand. It was good to be home.

Lavinia's left arm was still weak from the stroke, and the muscles in her hand hadn't worked since, despite intense physical therapy, yet she was grateful. The lingering affect was a daily reminder of the miracle—she was alive.

"Hey, Mama!" Amy Lynn said coming out of the kitchen. "Welcome home! And I hope you're hungry."

"It smells so good," she said. "I know my place is small, but it's so nice being back, and being here with all of you."

"Oh, it's fine. Lee's bringing in the folding table in a bit, and we'll put it at the end of your table. Plenty of room for the six of us. It will be the best Thanksgiving lunch ever. Wait and see."

Since the stroke, her frazzled daughter who lacked in social skills, had been replaced with a warm, bubby, vibrant creature.

"Are you sure you're okay with it being the six of us?" Lavinia said.

Amy Lynn answered by wrapping her arms around Lavinia and squeezing her tightly.

"Are you happy?" Amy Lynn asked as she pulled back to look at her.

Lavinia was so overcome with emotion she could only nod.

"Then I'm happy it's the six of us."

"Well, it would have been seven," Lavinia said, regaining her composure. "I invited Rosie, but her family was coming down from Roanoke. That nurse of hers said they were taking her out to a big, fancy dinner."

"Oh, how nice!"

"Hey, before I forget, I've got to tell you what Lucas said on the way over here. It was just the sweetest thing."

"What was it?"

"We were talking about how I can't drive for a while, and he said, 'I know you're sad about not being able to drive, Nana. But in about four years, I'll be able to take you anywhere you want to go.'

Wasn't that just the sweetest?"

"That's my boy!" Amy Lynn said.

Standing there in the breakfast nook of Lavinia's villa, they were more than mother and daughter. They were also friends, and two mothers, both proud of their children.

Amy Lynn went back to the kitchen to put the finishing touches on the meal as Lee came in with the rest of Lavinia's things. Dylan and Lucas came in and flipped on the television.

Lavinia peeked outside to see if Neville's car was there. Not yet, but there was a cab in Gordon's driveway. A young man got out. She watched as he stopped to admire the pink flamingoes that Gordon still hadn't taken out of his yard, then he walked toward the door. Gordon opened it and stepped outside. He gave the young man a long embrace with his face buried in the man's shoulders. There was no doubting what Gordon was thankful for on the holiday— Jeffrey was home for Thanksgiving.

As she watched the heartwarming scene, Neville's old pickup truck came cruising down the road and turned in to Lavinia's driveway slowly. Her heart did a flip at the sight of him, and she hoped Neville was able to see what he'd helped accomplish, before Gordon and his son went inside.

She met outside, halfway to the door, and he kissed her on the cheek with a tenderness that begged her to linger near him.

"Happy Thanksgiving!" he said. He stepped back and handed her the bag of dinner rolls he carried.

"Happy Thanksgiving!" She touched his face, bag in hand, smiling.

When they were all inside, Lavinia and Neville sat in the living room with Dylan and Lucas, while Lee helped Amy Lynn in the kitchen, and Neville regaled them with stories of hunting for the Thanksgiving turkey as a boy in Iowa.

"It was my first year hunting with my dad. I was about your

age, Dylan. And I was so excited to help bring home the main course of our feast. We started hunting the day before, but I missed every shot I had. But my dad was patient. He wanted me to bring home the turkey because he knew it meant a lot to me. So, Thanksgiving morning we went out early, and he told me he'd let me try until one o'clock. If I didn't get one by then, he'd have to do it."

Dylan and Lucas were on the edge of their seats, hanging on every word.

"I had a pocket watch that I checked every ten minutes, making sure I hadn't run out of time. And I fired more shells than I cared to lose."

Even Lavinia wanted to know if he ever got the turkey.

"It got later and later, and I was about to let despair get the better of me. But my dad kept encouraging me. 'You can do it, son,' he said. It was ten 'til one when we found a new clearing. We hunkered down and got quiet, but my heart was beating so fast I was afraid the turkeys could hear it. Five minutes passed and I was fighting back tears, when all of the sudden—"

"Hey, guys." Amy Lynn stuck her head out of the kitchen, snapping everyone away from the Iowa forest. "The bird's not quite done," she said. "I had to put it back in, but I think another twenty should do it."

Everyone nodded and immediately gave their attention back to Neville.

"All of sudden, a tom walked out. I steadied myself. I squeezed the trigger, and…"

He paused and looked at Dylan then Lucas. Their eyes were big.

"And I missed."

"What?" Lavinia said. She was more into the story than she had realized.

"Yes, I missed again. So, you know what we did?"

"What did you do?" Lucas asked.

"We went home and had potato soup for dinner. And we postponed Thanksgiving until the next day. Dad and I went out the next morning, and I got a bird on the first try. We brought it home to my mother, and we had our Thanksgiving feast at noon on Friday."

It was a good story, but Neville's storytelling made it even better.

"That's when I learned how much my father wanted me to succeed and that persistence pays off."

"That was awesome," Dylan said. "I wish I could do that."

"It does sound cool, but I think we'll stick to fishing," Lee said, coming out of the kitchen. "Maybe next year you can catch us a mackerel for Thanksgiving."

Dylan chuckled.

"Hey, Mr. McGrath, why don't you come outside with us and play football while we're waiting on lunch?" Lucas said.

Neville sat up straighter.

"Yeah, come with us!" Dylan said.

"I haven't played football in almost sixty years," Neville said. "But I guess I can give it a shot."

He slapped his knees and stood up, looking eager and ready to run plays, cane and all.

"Mercy sakes, don't fall and break a hip," Lavinia said.

"Don't worry. We're not playing a real game, Nana," Lucas said. "We're jus' gonna pass it."

"Okay. You boys have fun," Lavinia said.

The three of them soon disappeared, and Lavinia turned to her son-in-law on the couch next to her.

"Lee, while it's just me and you, I want to say thank you. You've been my rock through all of this."

He shook his head sheepishly and waved away her compliment.

"I mean it," she said. "You had faith in me from the beginning. And you were a big part of me finding my faith again. You had faith that me and Amy Lynn would work things out. And you hired Neville to help me." She gasped. "I forgot to pay you back, all the attorney fees."

"Well, there's nothing to pay back," Lee said.

"No, I insist. I intended to all along, but I got so distracted by everything—"

"I mean there's nothing to pay back, because he never cashed the first check I gave him. I tried my best to get him to, but he never would."

Lavinia's thoughts went back to that first meeting, when she flat-out insulted him, doubted his ability based on his age. How had she merited such kindness? Regardless of how, it was one of the many things for which she was grateful.

"Thank you for all your help, Lee" she said.

"You're welcome, Vinny."

"You know, I never imagined Amy Lynn could marry someone so much like her daddy."

"I appreciate that. Edgar was a good man."

"Yes, he was. But I don't mean Edgar. I mean my Samuel. You're so much like him. You have his heart—the way he always put everybody else before himself. And you're a good son to me."

Lee leaned over and hugged her, and Lavinia thought she saw a tear in his eye when he stood to leave the room, saying he was going to see if Amy Lynn needed more help in the kitchen.

The boys came back in just as Amy Lynn was headed out to call them. Neville looked none the worse for wear. They washed up quickly and gathered around the table. Dishes, bowls, and plates of various shapes and sizes crowded the tabletops. Everyone chattered about how good the food looked and how they couldn't wait to dive in. The mashed potatoes closest to Lavinia's place setting were especially tempting to her senses.

Neville pulled out Lavinia's chair for her and everyone sat down. As they did, an unmistakable blast of intestinal exhaust was heard by all around the table, and everyone's eyes went wide, especially Lavinia's since it had come from her chair. The noise and big eyes were followed by uproarious laughter from all four of the boys. The girls were more reserved.

"Okay, who did this?" Lavinia said as she removed the whoopie cushion from beneath her posterior.

"It was Mr. McGrath!" Lucas said. He was laughing so hard he almost fell out of his chair.

"But he gave it to me!" Neville pointed to Lucas.

She couldn't slap Neville with her left arm, so she gave him the stink eye instead, then she looked at Amy Lynn, expecting a scowl of disapproval. Instead, there was amusement. Lavinia let her laughter flow, not because of the vulgar prank, which she loved, but from the joy of togetherness and of laughter itself.

"Lee, why don't you go ahead and say the blessing. I think we all need some prayer," Lavinia said between giggles.

Wiping tears, Lee looked at Neville. "Maybe our guest would like to do the honor?" he said.

Based on Neville's lack of surprise, it was obvious Lee had consulted him beforehand, so as not to put him on the spot.

Neville nodded and everyone, now composed, bowed their heads. Neville reached for Lavinia's lifeless hand perched on the edge of the chair under the table. She felt the weight of it. The nerves in her skin sent touch signals to her brain.

"Lord, we thank you for this food and for the blessing of being together," Neville said.

He paused, and Lavinia felt a twitch in the pointer finger of her left hand.

"Thank you for the hope that we have in you," Neville

prayed.

At the word *hope*, Lavinia's pointer finger curled around to rest on top of his.

She opened her eyes and looked down at the miracle, then she looked up to see Neville smiling at her.

He finished his prayer with eyes open and locked with hers.

"We thank you for strength, and healing, and for a good future. Amen."

"Amen," everyone repeated, but Lavinia was sure *hers* was the sincerest of all.

After already too much food, dessert was served. When Neville had finished his pie, Amy Lynn offered him another piece.

"No, thank you, Amy Lynn. I better not overdo it. Lavinia and I are having dinner with Chuck and Shirley tonight."

Everyone had enjoyed each other's company and the wonderful meal, and as they sat recovering from their indulgence, the electronics came out. Lee and Amy Lynn brought out their phones, and so did Lucas. Dylan had a handheld video game. Lavinia refrained from bringing hers out at the table until she happened to hear it ding in her pocket.

"Oh, it's Wilmer," she said. "He messaged me to say, 'Happy Thanksgiving'."

"I thought you said he lives in Sweden," Lee said.

"Oh, he does. But he knows we're celebrating here. He's just nice like that."

"Should I be worried about this Wilmer character?" Neville said.

Lavinia rolled her eyes.

"See, this is what I've been talking about," Neville said. "Smartphones and devices have led to the decline of civilization, I tell you." He wagged a finger around, pointing at each of them.

Lavinia shrugged and smiled then placed the tiles in her

game.

"Well, they say if you can't beat 'em, join 'em, I guess." Neville reached into his shirt pocket and took out a shiny phone that had a touchscreen and didn't flip closed.

"When did you get that?" Lavinia said.

"Yesterday." Neville grinned. He touched the screen then turned it toward Lavinia. "I sent you a friend request on Facebook. Didn't you get it? Or do you not want to be my friend?"

She was too shocked to acknowledge his humor. "Well, I haven't checked."

She looked at his phone over the top of her glasses. The app was opened to his profile.

"Is that a selfie?" Lavinia asked, her pitch rising an octave.

"You know it! Shirley taught me how to do it. See you have to hold it up high, so it doesn't show a double chin."

The boys didn't look up from their screens, but Amy Lynn and Lee chuckled.

"Will wonders never cease," Lavinia said. "Will wonders never cease."

Chapter Thirty

Wednesday, November 28

Neville wore blue jeans, a flannel shirt, and a denim jacket, though it was a weekday. Lavinia loved the relaxed look, even more so than the handsome business suits she was accustomed to seeing him wear. She was dressed equally as casual, with jeans and a puffy, fleece-lined, pink coat zipped up to her chin, to help block out the wind coming off the water. Their clothes matched the mood of the morning and mirrored the feeling they each had being together. Every moment felt completely natural, carefree, as if all along it had been written into the plan.

"I'm glad you're not going to the office until later," Lavinia said. "I'm not in any hurry to leave." She snuggled closer to him on the park bench to keep warm.

Waterfront Park had only a few other visitors, probably locals. But as they sat there together, laughing and talking, enjoying the simple beauty of the waves, the boats, and the birds, it seemed to Lavinia that she and Neville were the only two people in the world.

"The joy of being self-employed," he said. "I've finally figured it out after all these years. I can set my own hours. *Imagine that.* I don't have to give it up, and yet, I can still take time for other things."

"Like our painting class tomorrow," Lavinia said with a wide smile.

"Yes, like our painting class." He gave a single, eager nod.

"Look out Senior Central! Neville McGrath is trying his hand at arts and crafts."

Once a month an instructor from the community college came to lead the seniors in a step-by-step class. This month, the painting would be a scene with snow-covered sand dunes and shore birds, and after painting, they planned to visit Rosie. Maybe they'd take her to the cafeteria for an afternoon ice cream.

"And you're happy with the new schedule?" Lavinia said.

"I'm happy with you. That's what matters most." He looked at her affectionately. "But, yes, I think taking a case at a time, when I feel like it, is the way to go. I hope to work part-time all the way up until Shirley finishes school. Then I can hand things right over to her."

"Oh, Neville, that sounds perfect."

Neville reached into his jacket pocket and pulled out his smartphone. She turned and retrieved hers from the newer, smaller pocketbook that sat on the bench beside her. The bag was easier to carry, and it was the perfect size for just the necessities—her wallet, makeup, a comb, car keys, and a pack of gum.

"Oh, would you like some chewing gum?" she said.

"Sure." Neville reached out to take a piece from the pack. "Ow!" He shook the shock from his fingers and laughed.

With her good hand, Lavinia squeezed his fingers gently. She giggled. "Are you okay?" she said, though she knew the gag was more surprising than painful. He nodded, and the smile on his face was one of forgiveness.

"You got me!" he said. "Like last week with those snap pops at my feet. I thought somebody was throwing firecrackers at me! You keep me on my toes in more ways than one, Lavinia."

She didn't carry the explosive trick noisemakers with her anymore, but she had managed to make room in the small bag for a few fun things, like the gag gum. For situations in which a rubber chicken and the like might be needed, she'd simply have to plan ahead and swap out the bag for the bigger one.

Lavinia gave him a real piece of gum, though he pretended to be scared to take it at first. She opened the word game app on the phone to finish the game she was playing with Neville. She laid her left hand palm-up on her leg and placed the phone in it. There was enough strength in the hand to hold the phone steady. Another ounce of energy returned each day, and all the fingers could move now, but slowly.

Lavinia dragged the tiles across the screen one-by-one and dropped them onto the board with the pointer finger of her right hand while Neville was busy typing away at his screen with both thumbs. As she touched the button to play her word, the phone dinged and a Facebook notification popped up at the top of the screen. She hunched with her face directly over the screen, pushed her glasses higher on her nose, and opened the app to read the notification.

Neville McGrath tagged you in a post.

It was his favorite thing to do—posting pictures of them together or funny things she did or said. The post he'd made about her snap pops prank had gotten a ton of likes and comments.

She clicked to view the post.

Neville McGrath is in a relationship with Lavinia Lewis. Both their names were in bold type. She looked at him, and he smiled and winked. Looking into his amber eyes, the beauty of a thousand sunrises and the joy of ten thousand laughs bubbled up from her soul and pressed against her chest from the inside.

It was no surprise. They'd discussed it Thanksgiving night, the same night she decided to slip off the wedding band she'd worn for most of her life. Now the ring dangled close to her heart from a pretty chain worn around her neck in place of the trademark pearls.

Having their relationship published for all the world, or at least for all their Facebook friends to see, was momentous—the modern-day equivalent of carving your initials into the bark of a tree with a heart around it or wearing his letterman's jacket and high school ring.

Already, the post had a comment. It was from Shirley.

I'm so happy for you two lovebirds! it read.

Lavinia clicked the like button on the original post and on Shirley's comment, then slowly typed out a one-handed reply. *Thank you, friend.*

"You know, Christmas is less than a month away now," he said.

"And I can't wait to see you as a wise man in the play at church," Lavinia said. "You'll make a very handsome magus."

"A what?"

"*Magus.* It's the singular form of *magi.* You know, what some people call the wise men from the East?"

"How do you know that?"

"Because Wilmer played it once, and I looked it up."

"Well, whatever I'm going to be, I look forward to being it."

"And you know what else we have to look forward to?" There were a thousand things she could have said. "Donald coming to visit. I can hardly wait to meet him."

"It will be nice to see him again, for sure. You know, he says he might bring his new girlfriend. Things are getting pretty serious already, and he's thinking he might not sell his lake house after all."

"Well, whaddaya know. That's wonderful."

"Did I tell you I FaceTimed him the other day?"

"No!"

"He showed me the whole house. Felt like I was there. And I got to meet Sheila—that's his girlfriend. The technology really is amazing. You were right, Lavinia, about how useful it can be. And not just for solving crimes."

Lavinia nodded, satisfied.

"So, what do you want for Christmas?" he said.

"I've been thinking about it."

"Oh, you have? I didn't expect you to answer so quickly."

"Then why'd you ask?"

The playful banter was one of the many things that made Lavinia love him so.

"There's only one thing I want," she said.

"Okay, what is it?"

"I want us to go to The Christmas House, up there on Moore Street, and pick out an ornament for my tree, together."

"That's all?"

"An *Our First Christmas* ornament. That's all I want."

"I think I can handle that," he said with a look of confidence.

Neville reached over and took her hand, helping her lock her fingers with his. The combined wrinkles on their merged hands resembled the waves.

She was completely caught up in the perfect moment, overwhelmed with bliss, but then a sneaky worry that she'd battled for weeks snuck back into her mind and sought to rob her of her joy. The only way to rid herself of the worry was to confront it.

"Neville, do you ever wonder what will happen to us, if it happens again?"

"If *what* happens again, darling?"

She nearly swooned at his new term of endearment.

"Another stroke. What if it happens again, as bad or worse than the first time?"

She hung her head, guilty for worrying.

"Then I'll be here to take care of you," Neville reassured her. "Remember, love bears all things, believes all things, hopes all things, endures all things."

"And what if it's something else. What if my mind goes, and it's not a stroke, and I don't even know who you are. What will we do then?"

"I'll still be here to help you, darling. Right by your side. Just like you'd do for me."

He was right. She would do anything she could to help him, no matter how old and feeble they both got.

Neville looked deep into her eyes. "And now I have the assurance that even after these bodies *do* give out, I'll see you again. It's incredible. I mean, who would have thought that a man could find the love of a woman and the love of Jesus at eighty years old?"

His young faith seemed as genuine as the feelings he professed to her. Only a few days ago they had stood side-by-side at Solid Rock Church, and he belted out "Victory in Jesus" in a strong baritone, with just the right amount of vibrato and with the passion of someone who truly understood what the song meant, even though it was brand new to him. The old hymns weren't yet part of his being like they were Lavinia's, but he had picked them up so easily, so naturally. It was as if the words and melody came from somewhere other than his ability to read lyrics and follow along with the piano.

"Thank you for the reassurance," she said, "and the reminder."

"Any time you need it." He brought his arm around her and gave her shoulder a gentle squeeze.

They leaned into one another's embrace and watched the moored boats bobbing with the ebb and flow of the water as the sun broke through the clouds and glinted off the waves. *Ebb and flow. That's how life is. Ebbs and flows. Always changing.*

A wave of frigid air came in off the water, and Neville hugged Lavinia even closer.

"Winter's comin' soon, I guess. Time to go into hibernation," she said.

"Not for me," Neville said. "I've been asleep too long already. I feel like I'm just waking up."

With his free hand, he scrolled through his Facebook newsfeed. He laughed at silly memes and clicked the like button on political posts and feel-good videos.

Lavinia started a new game with Wilmer on her phone. To her delight, all seven of her tiles on the first round formed a word. Double word score plus bonus for using all the letters equaled fifty-nine points. *Not a bad way to start a game.*

Neville leaned over and kissed her on the temple as she tapped the button to pass the play through cyberspace and off to her Swedish friend. She turned the phone to show Neville her high-scoring play, and he gave her a wink. It was the very best word to describe her current state. No matter what life brought her way, no matter the joys or pain, through laughter or tears, she intended to stay this way.

Content.

The End

Author's Notes

The idea for this book was born from a single word, which is the title. My family was in our minivan, on the way to my parents' house, I think, when my husband made a passing, harmless joke about my mother and her "shenanigans." I can't remember the context, but we laughed because the kids call her *Nana*, and it sounded like a play on words. After that one statement, I immediately began dreaming up a story about a prank-playing grandma.

Shenanigans is my third book. The first, *Grace & Lavender*, is set in the fictional town of Springville, North Carolina, in the Piedmont of my state, and is modeled largely after the place where I grew up. The second, *Where I Was Planted*, is set in the fictional town of Copper Creek, North Carolina, in the Mountain region. *Shenanigans*, of course, had to be set at the coast, and this was my first experience writing with a real town as the setting. (This is also the first book without an epilogue, but I hope you'll write one in your mind. What do you think happens to Lavinia and Neville? Do they get married? Do Neville and Alibi move into Cypress Shores with Lavinia?)

My husband and I have dreamed of retiring to Southport one day, just like Lavinia and Edgar (though it will be a toss-up since I do love my mountains, too.) It truly is one of my favorite places, along with neighboring Oak Island where my in-laws have a vacation house. I feel blessed to be able to share regular visits to this area with my husband, my children, and my husband's parents. (Sincere thanks to William and Carol for the many, many memories.) I aimed to capture the beauty and the feel of Southport in the story, though it's not an easy task.

Another interesting thing about the setting is that I wrote the story along the same timeframe as is used in the book. Though I started it in earnest around June 2018, much of the book was written in October and November 2018, when the story takes place. During this time period, the Carolinas were hit by Hurricane Florence, which devastated some of the real landmarks mentioned in the book. My heart ached to see pictures of the setting of my story, my home away from home, in such terrible shape. I feel confident, though, that by the time this book is published, the resilient towns of Southport and Oak Island, and hopefully even harder hit areas, will have been able to repair and rebuild.

A few more notes about timeline: Chapter Twenty-nine is set on Thanksgiving Day, 2018, which happened to be my husband, Alex, and my niece, Hollyann's, birthdays. They turned 41 and 11, respectively. (Hollyann was born on a Thanksgiving Day, Alex's thirtieth birthday.) Finally, the last chapter of the book is set on another family member's birthday, someone who is no longer here but holds a special place in my memory and heart—my maternal grandmother. I think she would have liked this story. *Chapter Thirty is for you, Grandma Grace. I love you.*

Other books by Heather Norman Smith:

Fiction

Grace & Lavender

Where I Was Planted

Nonfiction

Timeout for Jesus: Thirty Appointments with the Savior

To learn more, visit

www.heathernormansmith.com

and

www.facebook.com/heathernormansmith.

CPSIA information can be obtained
at www.ICGtesting.com
Printed in the USA
LVHW040805130820
663008LV00008B/1382